A Lesser Peace

A Lesser Peace

C.W. REED

ROBERT HALE · LONDON

ISBN 0 7090 7225 2

Robert Hale Limited
Clerkenwell House
Clerkenwell Green
London EC1R 0HT

2 4 6 8 10 9 7 5 3 1

Typeset in 11/15½pt Baskerville
by Derek Doyle & Associates, Liverpool.
Printed in Great Britain by
St Edmundsbury Press Ltd, Bury St Edmunds, Suffolk.
Bound by Woolnough Bookbinding Limited.

For Dave, Andy and Mike – the boys.

Now that ye have refused the Most Great Peace, hold ye fast unto this, the Lesser Peace, that haply ye may in some degree better your condition and that of your dependants.

Bahá'u'lláh – *Gleanings CXIX*

PART I
A DRESS OF GUILT

(Roger McGough)

CHAPTER ONE

'How are the boys? It must be a comfort for you, having them both so close to you again.'

May Wright stared at her mother-in-law, ashamed of her guilt, the flush of colour she could feel beneath the skin, the suspicion that the question was loaded with hidden meaning. 'They're fine. Though I don't see them that often. John's so busy with school, he hardly gets any time off during term. And Teddy.' She shrugged and laughed, disguising her discomfort. 'You know what he's like. Little Teddie's got the Scholarship coming up. Eleven this year, eh? I can't believe it.'

'I can!' The lines on Sophia Wright's face deepened, as the grey head moved on the high bank of pillows. All at once she looks every one of her seventy-six years, May thought, with compassion. She reviewed the changes she had seen in the older woman over the thirty-seven years she had known her; from the softly plump matron who had treated the frightened young girl with such blatant superiority, to the rigidly matriarchal figure who had gradually come to regard her with a genuine if some-what formal admiration. And now this sick old woman who, May thought, was wearily ready to relinquish her life. It would be yet another significant ending of an era in her own life, May reflected, when Jack's mother passed away.

With a display of her characteristic brusqueness, Sophia dismissed May's enquiries as to her condition, and steered the subject back to her grandsons – 'the boys', as she called them. John was thirty-two, and Teddy, only fifteen months behind him, had just a week ago celebrated his thirty-first birthday. Sophia was right, of course. It was a great comfort to May to have her two sons safely home again after the fearful things they had gone through; Teddy from his five-year sojourn in a German POW camp, and John from his service in the North African desert and Palestine. But her worries for them were far from over, even though they had been back in England and settled back into civilian life for over a year now. The euphoria of coming through triumphant after the world conflict had been short-lived, both on the public and private front. Britain was exhausted, and drained, in more ways than one. Hard economic and social realities had soon set in, as poor Mr Churchill had found. May had shed a few bitter tears and Iris had fumed impotently when, as a reward for saving the country and the Empire, Churchill had been tossed out of office, ironically by the men and women who had fought and worked so bravely for victory under his leadership.

'Things have got to be different now, mam,' John had said, against her protests.

'The toffs'll not have things all their own way from now on!' Teddy had declared, with typical vociferousness. More than ever, she could see and hear the echoes of her father's working class socialism in her younger son, and maybe the asperity she showed in her answer held just a hint of that illogical, instinctive sense of disloyalty she felt whenever she thought about her own humble roots. She could still hear the ringing tone of accusation in her dead da's voice. 'Getting too grand for the likes of us now, are ye, lass?' Partner in a highly successful café and bakery was a fair stride from the off-the-street terraced house in Gateshead where she had grown up.

But the differences the majority of the electorate had hoped for when they voted two years before gave little cause for cheer so far. Rationing was as stringent as ever; luxury goods, even for those who could afford them, were scarce. Great wastelands of weed-strewn levelled spaces marred the centres of most cities. The fabled National Health Service Bill was still being fought through Parliament and meeting fierce opposition. 'Fancy putting a rebel like Nye Bevan in charge!' Iris said scornfully, to Teddy's fury. 'What does *he* know about government? All he knows is how to oppose.' A doctor, a former Secretary of the British Medical Association, described him emotively as 'a medical führer', and the new scheme as 'the first step, and a big one, towards National Socialism as practised in Germany'. Suddenly the future seemed far less rosy, and fraught with uncertainty.

Just as it was on a personal level, May acknowledged. As though uncannily in tune with her thoughts, Sophia now asked about Jenny and Marian. Hitting the nail right on the head, May conceded, looking with increased sharpness at the tired, lined face on the pillow, and wondering if someone had been talking, and who.

At first, May had been concerned only for the state of her eldest son's marriage, with Jenny, his college sweetheart and first and only girlfriend. Theirs had been a chequered relationship, almost from the beginning. Engaged before they had even completed their studies, and then with Jenny teaching back in her native Cumberland and John over here in Northumberland. And then, suddenly, after three years Jenny had broken it off, and John was devastated.

May had not interfered or pried. She guessed it had something to do with the visit of the German boy, Horst Something-or-other. John and Jenny had first met him on a trip they had made to some summer camp in Germany. The follow-

11

ing year, he had come over to stay with Jenny and her folks. May had been secretly hurt at her son's insensitivity in asking if Horst could stay at Hexham. He had thought her attitude xenophobic, but she could not bring herself to feign friendship towards a member of the nation that had murdered his father.

After the outbreak of war, when he got his call-up papers, John had gone over to Keswick, partly at May's instigation, she could justly claim, and come back head in the clouds, despite the world crisis, his engagement restored. Not for long. The next bombshell had come a few months later, just after John had got his commission as a second lieutenant in the infantry. The pair of them returned from a trip to London as Mr and Mrs. Again, May had felt hurt and excluded, though she swiftly accepted Jenny's claim that it had been chiefly her idea for the ceremony to be kept secret, and was moved by the girl's plea for understanding, her desire, after their long and painfully unsatisfactory relationship, for things to be put on a permanent footing, without fuss and with minimal delay. In all, they had spent scarcely two weeks of married life together before John got his posting overseas. It was five years before they were together again; five years of loneliness, and danger. Jenny had joined the Wrens, been involved in some highly secret work, though she had not gone overseas.

It did not take long for May to see that all was not well with them – they were not as clever as they thought in hiding it, even in the joy of the family reunion in the cottage where John and Teddy had grown up. Over the year that had followed since then, things were little better, she suspected, though at least now they were living under the same roof once more. To May's great relief, and, she had to admit, considerable surprise, Jenny had at last agreed to give up her teaching post in the Lake District and join John at the boarding school in Corbridge, just down the road from May and Iris's home in Hexham, where he had worked before the war.

It was a doubly cruel blow to May to realize, perhaps somewhat tardily, that it was not just John's marriage that was making heavy weather. She had assumed that it would be a happy-ever-after scenario for Teddy and Marian when he came home, newly released from the prison camp, almost a year before his brother's demob. Marian had been ill – it had shown plainly in her face, her loss of weight, though even her physical ailments, brought on by the strains of bringing up little Teddie alone and her constant anxiety for her husband, would, May naïvely hoped, be eased by his safe return after so long. Marian had always been almost hopelessly besotted – May had frequently been privately angered by the girl's readiness to suffer and even condone Teddy's harsh treatment in the past. His desertion of her, only weeks after the wedding, while she was still pregnant with Teddie, had been an act of such cruelty that May still could not under-stand it, though she had tried hard to accept it as his blind panic at the forced marriage, his feeling of entrapment at the respon-sibilities of parenthood. Little Teddie was six months old before he set eyes on her, though, like Marian, May was too relieved at having him safely home from the war in Spain to hold on to her hurt and her anger.

Only a year later he was off again, rushing this time into the regular army as a volunteer, to embrace the conflict many people were still hoping could be avoided. The débâcle in France in the late spring of 1940 had been a nightmare time for Marian, and for May as she relived the horror of twenty-three years previously, when she had clung to the forlorn hope that Jack might some-how be found alive after the slaughter at Passchendaele. This time she had not been able to kindle that spark of hope, so that when she saw Marian, her face streaming with tears, waving the crumpled telegram, she had almost fainted, and, would have slumped to her knees had she not had Iris's arm clamped firmly about her. Until she realized that Marian was grinning hysterically through the storm of her weeping, and that Teddy *was* after all alive – a prisoner of war.

He wanted only to be home, to be with his wife and daughter. He had told her so, many times in his letters. And at last it had happened, and May had wept again, with such profound thankfulness. But here, too, so unexpectedly, shadow loomed. In February of the previous year, Marian had had a miscarriage – May, and apparently everyone else apart from Teddy and his wife, had not known she was pregnant. Disaster, right enough. Marian had been seriously ill again, taken months to recover. But even that did not explain the palpable tension May could feel whenever she saw the couple. And that would not have been very often, if she and Iris had not persisted in making regular Sunday visits over to Low Fell, to the neat little semi on the edge of town.

The wickedly severe weather that struck the whole country in January had curtailed those visits. Temperatures had fallen way below freezing, and fierce snow storms had added to the misery, precipitating a fuel crisis and power cuts. It was as though the elements had been waiting for the war to end to show that it wasn't only *human* nature which could inflict such pain, for March brought gales and terrible floods. And, lo and behold, just when we should at last have been looking forward to the relief of some spring weather, the snow had returned in full measure. 'April is the cruellest month,' Iris had quoted to her, from some modern poet or other, and how right it was. Outside, the snow was piled in high banks at the sides of every road, and May's feet, clad in woollen stockings with even thicker ankle socks over them, were just thawing out as she curled her toes in the luxury of the electric fire pulled as close as she could without actually catching alight. Downstairs, her heavy, fur-lined boots were dripping on newspapers in the icy front porch of the comfortable but over-large house Sophia shared with her youngest, Joe, still a bachelor as he approached his fiftieth year, and the only member

14

of the family still actively involved in the printing works his late father had established all those years ago.

'Iris dropped me off at the top of the bank,' May said now. 'We were too scared to bring the car down, the state the road's in. She'll be back later. She's got a few things to do.'

Sophia grunted. The lines on her brow deepened as she raised her eyebrows. Both sound and gesture seemed to the hypersensitive May to carry a suggestion of criticism or displeasure. Her words seemed to be at one with the conversation they had just had about the boys, and May's own sombre private reflections. 'You know, the wars – both of them – have played havoc with this family.'

'What—'

'She should never have married our Dan,' Sophia announced. 'I don't know what possessed the pair of them, after all those years. Neither of them were suited. Her least of all.'

May felt herself colouring up, felt the prickle of embarrassment, and reluctance, at the raising of this spectre. Iris, her closest and dearest friend since Jack's death, had married his older brother, Dan, in 1929, seventeen years after they had first met one another around the time of May and Jack's wedding. It came as quite a shock – a pleasant one, she always hastened to tell herself – when Iris came and, with an uncharacteristic shy tearfulness, asked May's advice about whether she should accept Dan's proposal. Almost asked her permission, in fact. The two women had been living together for ten years – had shared in everything; the bringing up of May's two boys, the building up of the café and the cake shop. Iris was genuinely unsure of what she should do, and May had urged her strongly to go ahead. 'I couldn't wish for anything nicer!' she had declared enthusiastically. And meant it, too. Dan, a crippled survivor of the war which had killed his brother, was drinking far too much. She knew how deeply his experiences had scarred him, mentally as well as phys-

15

ically. There was already some complex relationship connected with the war between Iris and Dan. They had met briefly out in France – it was the one episode in her life which Iris had never fully shared or explained to her. In the intervening years, May had been well aware of something – an intimacy, yet a kind of wariness also, between her brother-in-law and her friend. She was delighted that they had decided to spend their remaining years together.

The marriage had been a failure. True, there had been a companionship there, especially at the beginning, which both had claimed from the start was what they sought. But Dan's drinking had not decreased. Far from it. He began to spend nights away from home, and Iris seemed less and less concerned about it, content to go her separate way. She spent more and more time back with May.

Dan was killed in one of the first raids on Tyneside, in September of 1940. Ironic that, having lived through all four years of the violence of the Western Front, he should have been killed by a stray bomb from a hopelessly lost German plane. But that all paled into insignificance beside the fact that he met his explosive death in bed in a secret love nest, with a married woman who had been his mistress since before the time of his own marriage. The scandal was handled as discreetly as possible. Iris moved quickly back with May. Months later, she was able to admit tersely, 'I never did my wifely duties. Not properly – not enough.' Sex. The one subject which the two women could not share, even as a topic of conversation, even now, after twenty years of living together, of sharing a bed together on many, many occasions, and a relationship as close or closer than many married couples.

Sophia had never referred to the scandal of Dan's death. May had never discovered if she even knew of it. That was why she felt so disturbed at the older woman's reference to the marriage.

'You should have stopped her. Kept her with you. You're the only one she's ever been happy with.' May felt her skin prickle with embarrassment under her heavy winter clothing. She held her breath, lost for words. But Sophia ploughed calmly on. 'There's women like that. Who are no good with men. Especially a man like Dan. He never could settle after that terrible war. But she's been right for you, after you lost Jack. She's been the making of you, bringing you back to life. I didn't want you to go from here, with the boys. But anyone can see you did the right thing. And you've been right for her as well. The pair of you were made for each other.'

May's eyes were moist, she blinked rapidly. The older woman's shocking words stirred her deeply. Despite her embarrassment, she felt a great warmth for the wasted figure lying in the bed. She reflected on the truth of Sophia's words. War had indeed exacted a cruel sacrifice from the family. Taking May's one love, Jack, from her, leaving her a widow at twenty-three, with two infants. Crippling Dan, then destroying him twenty-two years later, to leave Sophia grieving for two sons. And now war was blighting the lives of both May's sons, too, for surely, if they had not been so cruelly separated from their partners for five long years, the difficulties both were facing in their marriages would not now exist? What those difficulties were she had little or no idea, but she prayed that they could be surmounted, and quickly. Otherwise, their future would be as bleak as the hard and unyielding weather which rattled the window on this bitter April evening.

CHAPTER TWO

Even in the fields the snow was taking on a soiled, tired look. The banks which had been shovelled and scraped to the edges of the drive had pitted, black, frozen peaks. 'Just shows how far out the muck from Tyneside gets,' Michael Fallon grumbled sourly. He sat in the tiny dugout euphemistically labelled 'Games Office', and picked at the laces of his sodden football boots. On the other side of the partition, the shrill raucousness of the group of second formers bounced off the clammy walls and rose with the billowing clouds of steam from the showers.

John Wright straightened up from removing his own boots and socks, noting how wrinkled and dead-white his feet looked. They were almost too numb to register the cold – but not quite, as throbbing life began to return. In spite of its discomfort, he glanced round the tiny, cluttered untidiness with familiar affection. The small, hinged lockers under the wooden bench, into which not one more item could be crammed; the shelves lined with sports apparatus – ropes, bundled nets, racquets, medicine balls, rugger and soccer balls. It always gave him a mean pleasure to imagine the horror on the faces of those members of the more traditional prep schools should they discover that hoofing the round ball up and down the pitch was a much favoured option in the games facilities offered at Beaconsfield. But then James

18

Challoner was an exceptional headmaster, and John thanked his lucky stars that he had found him – and just a few miles down the road from his own childhood home in Hexham. One of the most uncomplicated pleasures of John's return to civilian life after five years of warfare had been coming back to this modest haven of sanity and purpose, in this unpretentious country house pitched almost alongside the Roman Wall camp on the edge of Corbridge.

His eyes caught the bundles of venerable, frayed cricket pads, the bats with the black-bound handles protruding, which had been relegated to the top shelf. It was hard to believe that within a week or two they were due to be hauled down, along with the stumps and boxes of balls, inspected to see how much of the equipment they could get another season out of, and put to use against a background of fresh green, and dark foliaged trees, and the thick, chirruping hedgerow. Outside, although it was only a quarter past four, with plenty of daylight left, the sky was a uniform dead paleness, and a milky layer of thin mist was forming a foot above the expanses of frozen snow which had lain there for weeks.

'Oh to be in England, now that April's there,' Fallon quipped. He dragged his shorts down, pulled the jersey over his head. 'Bet you wish you were still out in sunny Palestine, eh? Even if the wogs are taking potshots at our lads!' Naked, he squeezed past John, beating him to the single shower stall. 'Bet the young blighters have run off all the hot water!' He raised his voice over the spattering water and the echoing cries from next door. 'And they're going ahead with this crazy idea of banning coal and gas fires. It's coming out in Parliament next week. Old Dalton's just raised all these bally taxes, and now he won't have anybody left to pay them. We'll all be dead of pneumonia!'

John picked up his boots, stuffed the soaking woollen stockings inside them, and stood. 'I'll get cleaned up upstairs. Can you

19

make sure this lot get out without wrecking the place? I'll see you for tea.'

The cold struck up through the damp stone floor, in spite of the clouds of steam drifting like thick fog about the slight, pale bodies. 'Come on, you lot! Get a move on!' John bellowed, as he passed through the crowded changing-room. 'I've told Mr Fallon to use a wet towel to shift anyone who isn't dressed in five minutes.'

'Yes, sir!'

'Sir, it's freezing!'

'Will Mrs Wright be opening Tuck Shop after tea, sir?'

'You'll be through your allowance before your first exeat, Heath! Come on, now. Hurry up, chaps.' At the sight of Heath's grinning face, John suddenly thought of Ron Maudsley, the private from Middlesborough in his platoon in the desert. The same cheeky-chappie cheerfulness, the same confident reliance in him. He left the hullabaloo behind and trotted barefoot along the draughty gloom of the corridor leading back into the main house. He kept up his swift pace across the hallway, and up the wide staircase. He and Jenny occupied the 'flat' on the second floor, just below the attics of the Edwardian house, and, like them, part of the servants' quarters when Beaconsfield was a private residence. 'Flat' seemed rather a grandiose description for the reasonably sized bedroom and much smaller, cramped sitting-room adjoining it. The narrow, cupboard-sized bathroom towards which John was heading was shared with Mike Fallon, whose room was next to theirs, and Roger Gibbon, another bachelor master from the floor below.

There was no sign of his wife as John dived into their quarters to grab his towel, dressing gown and soap bag. She was probably organizing the tea and toast which would presently be ready in the staff room, around the fire which, apparently, this Draconian labour government was about to ban until autumn. Or maybe she

20

was still beavering away with her art appreciation class, a voluntary activity which offered an alternative to running about after a ball on the playing field on a Saturday afternoon. Another indication of the unconventional educational principles instituted by James Challoner.

John got the geyser whooshingly away at the second match from the box of damp Swan Vestas kept on the high, narrow windowsill, and waited patiently for the dribble of water to deposit a reasonable amount into the tub. The black painted line at the five-inch level was still there, not that there was much fear of being profligate. You'd be here for hours if you wanted a hot bath of luxurious depth. But at least the tub was looking a lot cleaner these days, since Jenny's arrival after Christmas. He recalled its often unsavoury appearance when he lived up here as a bachelor before the war. Yes, Jenny had made a difference all right, in many ways. She had brought a gentle, much-welcomed feminine touch, as James had wanted. Both staff and pupils had fallen for her in a big way.

If only the same comfort could be found in their private relationship. Gratefully, John lowered himself into the biting heat of the water. He had run a minimal amount of cold into it. It would cool soon enough, and he cherished these rare moments of absolute privacy behind the locked door sufficiently to wish to prolong them. He had fondly hoped that when Jenny agreed to come to Beaconsfield after spending a whole term apart, she once more living with her folks and teaching in Keswick, he throwing himself gladly back into work here, they could begin to start healing the terrible wound that had seared their marriage, might still prove fatal to it. As always, he thrust that dire prognostication away from him, refused to examine it deeply. He still wanted Jenny, in spite of how much she had hurt him. He could not bring himself to countenance life without her.

She said when they were first together again that she expected

21

him to divorce her, that she had prepared herself for it. But she had also said she still loved him, always would. He was the one who had pleaded with her, pleaded for their marriage to be given another chance. Yet now, even the 'nobility' of his forgiveness of her infidelity seemed another obstacle in the path of their happiness.

'I was missing you so much – I couldn't stand it any more. Being alone—' That was part of the explanation she herself had given for her one act of unfaithfulness with Martin Castleton, while John was abroad. She had said those words that first night, with John fresh off the troop ship, his land legs still wobbly.

'I love you. I want us to give ourselves another chance,' he said. They had both wept, and clung to each other, and John had foolishly hoped that all would still be well. It would! he kept urging himself, and Jenny, in the tense weeks and months that followed. But there was little sign of it so far. In fact, in many ways it was worse now than in those first sensitive, bruised days, when they moved so tenderly and unsurely around each other's feelings. Now, it was not tenderness that kept them from speaking of their tortured feelings, but wariness, a fear of reopening old wounds that might not, this time, be patched up again. It was as well they had little chance nowadays to be alone with each other. Both of them seized the opportunity that being part of the busy school routine gave them to avoid such exclusive moments. John hated their weakness, vowed time and again he would break this uneasy, cowardly truce, and stayed for the main part silent. In the rare moments when they were open, and exposed their raw emotions, the atmosphere sparked with danger.

The last time had been less than two weeks ago, at his mother's place. They had come over from Keswick, where they had spent the Easter holiday with Jenny's folks, for a get-together for Teddy's thirty-first birthday, and had agreed to spend a couple of nights at 'Tea Cosy Cottage' before going back to the school. His brother and Marian, his wife, were staying overnight, too, and May and Iris were delighted at having them all together under one roof again.

There was a moment of awkwardness when Teddy declared that he was going to pop down to the Beehive 'for a pint' and to look up some of his old mates. 'Micky Ellerington and Louis Arksey,' he said, with a look directed at John as he mentioned boyhood friends. 'I'd ask you along, but I guess it's not your scene any more.'

'Why not?' May cut in quickly. 'You can always drink soda water or something. Take the girls with you. Keep you in line.' She smiled at Marian and Jenny, to show that she was joking, though everyone knew she was half in earnest.

John sensed the tension, and Teddy's hint of disapproval. It was always like this whenever his 'new religion' came up. Even his mother was far from being at ease with it. The very name, Baha'i, sounded mystically Eastern, and totally un-English. He had discovered the Faith, or, rather, it had discovered him, while he was serving in Haifa, where its focal point, its modest world headquarters, was situated. It was just after the time when his world had been shattered by Jenny's letter, with its bald announcement of her adultery. Indeed, he himself had worried that this new belief may have caught him on the rebound. But the more he learnt about it, the more time he spent with Baha'is, the more it took hold of him, the more sense it made of life, despite his personal sadness. Even so, he had not declared formally for the Faith until several months after his return to England and civilian life. He had met up with the few Baha'is scattered across the north of England and spent time with them at 'firesides', the frank examinations and discussion of the tenets and the scriptures which were coming to mean so much to him.

He could tell his mother was uncomfortable when he came back after one such weekend and told her he had officially been accepted into the Baha'i community. Like many others, he guessed, she had been hoping that, once back and absorbed into life at home again, this aberration, caused by too much time spent in such traumatic circumstances in far distant places, would fade, and he would be restored to 'normality'.

'What about Jenny?' she asked, her troubled expression reflecting her state of mind.

He laughed. 'What about her? She's still good old C of E, don't worry. I won't be trying to convert her, or taking another wife. She's happy for me.'

Those were her very words when he gave her the news over the telephone. But subsequently she had told him, more than once and in a dismissive tone, 'Look. You do what you feel you have to – it's your life. Just don't ask me to change my beliefs, because I can't. And let's agree now not to discuss it, ever.'

'What, man?' Teddy had adopted an air of incredulity. 'You cannot have a drink? What? Not even a half shandy?' As always, as an added way of needling, he broadened his Tyneside accent way beyond his normal speech. 'I'll tell you now, it'll not catch on round here, kidder!'

Now, to combat the atmosphere of hostility he could sense at his suggestion of an outing to the pub, Teddy shrugged and said offhandedly, 'Please yourself.'

Marian had already interpreted his quick glance and, her fair complexion colouring up, made noises of demurral. 'Oh, I don't think I'll bother, if you don't mind, pet. It'll be packed out. And that smokiness—'

Teddy nodded in relief. He looked mischievously at Jenny. 'What about you, Jen? Has our kid made you give up the booze and all? I see he hasn't got you off the fags yet.' He feigned an expression of sudden horror. 'Hey! What else have you had to give up, John? Not *all* worldly pleasures, I hope?' He winked lasciviously at Jenny, who returned his look coolly.

'I'm sure I don't know what you're talking about!'

It was John who felt his face grow hot, for Teddy had touched a raw nerve. 'We can go for a drink if you want to,' he said to his wife, aware that he sounded stiff, and unable to prevent it.

'Heaven forbid! Your religion has enough martyrs as it is. I'm sure your pals wouldn't appreciate our sobriety,' she went on, turning to Teddy. 'Wet blankets aren't conducive to a good party atmosphere.'

John felt that surge of anger and frustration swell up like sudden bile. 'Why don't you go on your own with Teddy? Far from giving up the booze, you'll probably find she can drink the lot of you under the table!'

'Well, well! That sounds like a challenge! What do you say, Teddy? Dare you be seen out in public with your brother's wife?'

'Don't be so daft!' May snapped, then everyone began talking at once as Teddy rose and so did Jenny. 'There's plenty of drink here—'

'We won't be long,' Teddy said appeasingly, glancing over at Marian, whose face was even redder.

'Don't speak too soon!' John could see the glint of challenge in Jenny's face. 'I'll try not to make you have to carry me home, but you know what Wrens are like!'

They were all still up, sitting round the fire, in the living-room that had once been the original café when May and Iris had started their business venture twenty-seven years ago. May tried to stop herself from glancing at the clock, but she was well aware that it was 10.30 before Teddy and Jenny came back, ruddy-faced and bringing in the smell of the unseasonable cold, as well as the whiff of alcohol and sparkling-eyed gaiety it induced. Like giggling adolescents who know how annoying the grown-ups are finding their behaviour.

John felt that stabbing love, and sadness, as he saw the

animated look on his wife's face, and encountered the quickly flashed glance, half guilt and half defiance, that she flung at him. 'Managed to stay till closing time then?' May said, with acid lightness.

'And resisted the temptation to stay for the lock-in, mam!' Teddy beamed back at her. 'I reckon we could have been there till all hours.' They had hung their heavy outer coats in the hall, and Teddy came and stood in front of the hearth, his back to the fire, grinning at the half circle of seated figures facing him. 'You want to watch this lass of yours, kidder! Talk about the life and soul! The lads were all over her!'

John felt the rush of blood, the rapid thumping of his heart, as the anger surged up within him. His fingers curled into fists. He could feel his wife's steady gaze on him. 'Howay, lass! Bunk up, man!' Teddy slapped at Marian's thigh, and she moved at once out of the deep armchair, while Teddy slid into the vacated space and pulled her boisterously onto his knee. His arm held her, and she tugged decorously at the hem of her dress, to cover the exposed nylon clad limbs.

'Ooh! You smell like a brewery!' She giggled, to cover her embarrassment as he nuzzled his face blatantly into hers.

'And don't you just love it!'

Afterwards, when they had retired to their bedroom, John, already under the covers, watched Jenny swiftly undress. They were both aware of the awkward tensions inherent in these intimate acts, and there was a self-consciousness about her haste. She bent, half turned away from him, and pulled the thick winter nightgown over her head to conceal her before she slipped off stockings and step-ins. She was careful not to touch him when she climbed in beside him. 'God! It's still like mid-winter!'

'Here! Aunt I put a bottle in earlier. It's still hot.' He pushed it across. His foot touched her leg, which he sensed rather than felt withdraw a little.

'I don't think the lovebirds were suited at us going out together, were they?'

The anger flashed again in him, at her cruelly mocking reference to his mother and Iris. He knew it was a term that came from Aunt Julia, mam's younger sister and implacable opponent. It added to his rage and, before he could stop himself, he answered, 'Well, that must have made the trip even more enjoyable for you!'

'Still, as long as *you* weren't jealous. It's comforting to know that you can trust me with your brother. Not to mention all his lecherous chums!'

John's rage died as swiftly as it had arisen, and he felt the old familiar weariness, the longing to change this aridity between them. He reached out tentatively, touched her cotton-clad shoulder, softening his voice with appeal. 'Jenny . . .'

'No soul-searching tonight, Johnny, please! I'm not used to boozing any more. I've already got a thick head, and my guts are rumbling ominously. Night night.'

John felt the movement as she turned her back fully. He lay in the dark and let the misery wash over him. He had a sudden urge to violence, to pull her round to him, to force himself on her. He felt his body stir with lustful excitement, and he lay still, full of self-loathing, doing nothing, letting his desire drain away, until presently he heard the heavy, regular breathing of her deep sleep.

Sex. The old monster. Rearing its ugly head yet again. How appropriate, John acknowledged, lying back in the water, observing his thickened, stirring penis, evidence of his resurgent lust. He gave in to it, letting himself drift in its sweetly wicked abandonment, until he sat up all at once and guiltily began to wash his upper torso vigorously. That was the bedrock of their trouble, their sexual relationship. Had been from the beginning. Their enforced celibacy during the years of their engagement, when he had felt so ashamed of his carnality, with absolutely no idea that Jenny, his beloved, virginal Jenny, was suffering the same, or similar, tortures of frustrated desire as he was.

He discovered, with something of a shock, that he still found that very hard to comprehend. Even though, poor girl, she had struggled so hard to confess it. True, long after the event itself, when they had been reconciled after the long break-up of their engagement, but still he could understand something of the enormous courage it took her to tell him. She had given her virginity to their German friend, Horst Zettel, without love, without anything except that basic instinct of sex she had been unable to withstand. But surely, John reasoned bewilderedly, Horst must have seduced her, been the guilty party in bringing about those circumstances which had led to them . . . savagely he mocked at himself for his fastidious horror at forming any detailed visualization of the act itself, the mechanics of it.

She had been distraught, genuinely tormented, at her confession to him. And desperately, lovingly, he had pushed it as far from his consciousness as he could, claimed that it didn't matter, that they were together again, and wholly believed her when she said she had never, never stopped loving him.

And then it had happened again. After their reunion, after their marriage. While he was away, his very life in danger. With this bastard, Martin Castleton. Again, once only, and after months of pressure, months of intimate time spent working together. Just one moment – no, several hours, he torturedly reminded himself – of weakness, when through her very loneliness and missing of their love, she had given in. John kept on telling himself he could understand it, could comprehend the desperation that, all at once, had shattered her resolve like a bursting dam. But secretly he wasn't sure of his own magnanimity, couldn't be sure that he *did* understand, after all, how she

28

could have let another man make love to her, when she still had *him,* their love was still intact, no matter how lonely she was, no matter how many miles apart they were. There were ways of at least assuaging that sexual hunger, as he well knew, however shameful, however uncountenanced by religion or morality. He thought of all the colourful, crude metaphors for self-abuse he had learned in the service. And, vaguely, he knew that females were capable of finding solitary relief, too. Why then had she taken that desperate step of breaking their marriage vows, of betraying their love for a second time?

Somehow, stumblingly, he had asked her if their sexual love was inadequate for her. With utter conviction she had assured him that this was not so. He pinned his hope and faith that their relationship would survive on this. And yet it was sex which was the greatest danger threatening them, he was sure, in the eleven months they had been living together again. It was a shadow they were both afraid of. Their first attempts to make love, in the first days of their reunion, had been all that he had feared. He had been impotent, the nightmare coming true as he lay in sweating panic on her. 'It's been so long,' he murmured, racked by shame, hating himself, and her, too, for not miraculously curing him.

'Of course. It'll take time. Never mind. It will be all right.' She had reassured him, and he had heard her muffled weeping in the early hours.

The rare attempts at sex since then had been hurried. They had achieved congress. He had penetrated her, and come quickly, and failed to satisfy her, he knew, despite her almost urgent denials. And worse, she rejected his efforts to bring her that physical satisfaction, wanting him now only to 'be quick' in achieving his own climax inside her – and making sure he did not impregnate her when he did so. Most nights, they lay side by side in the same bed, with long lonely miles between them.

Downstairs, in the comfort of the elegant drawing-room which was now the staff sanctum, with its long double bay windows look-ing out on to the terraced rose garden, and the lawn which stretched to the tall row of trees that hid the distant playing field, Jenny was sitting beside the blazing fire, on a low stool. She was wearing her dark brown slacks and a rusty coloured, high-necked sweater. Her dark honey hair swung free, in the simple waved style cut short to the lobes of her ears, as she leaned forward, holding the long toasting fork to the flames. She was the focus of the small group of males sprawled in the worn depths of the chintz furniture, and was enjoying their adulation. Even crusty old Nichols, James's chain-smoking deputy, was not immune to her charms.

John felt the depth of his love for her as he saw how desirable she was, and how his colleagues responded to her. I love you! he bellowed in his mind, but he noticed how her complexion pinked a little deeper at his entrance, and how her gaze flickered swiftly away from his. 'We were beginning to wonder if you'd drowned in the bath! I hope there's still some tea in the pot. You'll have to get some more hot water from the kitchen if there isn't. And this is the last crumpet, I'm afraid. You've got to get in quick with this greedy lot!'

CHAPTER THREE

The rain was slanting down in solid grey lines when Teddy came out of the pub. Across the road, the high iron gates of the shipyard were still closed. He belched softly, felt the dull weight of the five pints of Scotch ale bloating his gut, the slight disorientation in his brain. He shivered, and turned the collar of his mackintosh high on his neck, wishing that he had brought his hat. The holiday mood swiftly evaporated, and he hesitated for a second, wanting to turn back to the smoky warmth inside. Maybe he could persuade Ellen, the barmaid, to give him one more drink. But she had already called Time for the last time and was bad temperedly sending the last of the regulars on their way. They jostled him as they passed, swearing volubly at the onslaught of rain.

It was always the same, Teddy reflected sourly, setting off reluctantly towards the trolley bus stop by the grass covered bomb site. The pungent unpleasantness of the smell from the nearby glue factory was wafted strongly at him on the wind, and he belched again, almost gagging. He heard his mother's voice clearly in his head. 'After the feast comes the washing-up.' Right, as usual. He recalled the anticipation, the warm comradeship engendered by the sudden closing of the drawing office because of the power cut. It was localized enough to keep the hundreds of men in the yard at their reverberating work, so the draughtsmen had slipped away with the half guilty delight of schoolboys playing hooky. The dinner break was over, so the bar was quiet again, the welter of empty glasses still littering every table, proof of the busy trade plied for an hour every day, when hundreds of grimy workers shoved and jostled and stood, shoulders rubbing, round the slopping counter, or huddled on stools at the small, round tables. The office lads usually sneaked out five minutes early, and Teddy was often among the first of them. He had seen the frantic efforts of the bar staff to pull the foaming pints and line them up ready on the counter for the noisy tide of drinkers that would presently spill in through the double doors.

More and more, he was looking on the time spent in such places as precious respite. The pub was a cosy haven from the increasingly unpalatable world outside. His mouth was often dry, his throat aching for the sweet sensation of that first creamy slide of ale. He valued these blue-starred oases in the industrial desert he was caught in. But it wasn't only in the harsh landscape of the yards and the coaly river banks he felt trapped. That desolate feeling did not diminish during the lengthy, crowded bus rides out of city and town, increased the further he got from city grime towards the clean country air and the pin-neat orderliness of his suburban home.

'Come on, man. Let's have another.' He had clutched at sleeves, urging his work colleagues to have one more drink, to stay in that cosy sanctuary, where everything was so uncomplicated, where relationships were so solidly simple. A man's man, that's what he was. He appreciated male company, knew where he was with them. Most men felt that way, he was sure.

He flinched away from the memories of the POW camp, of Tony Ellis's pretty young face. He had befriended the boy – and that's all he was, a youngster, a slim eighteen-year-old, who had no business being locked up with all those hairy-arsed pongoes and fly boys. 'Young-un', they all called him. No wonder the kid had turned queer, the way they had all treated him, subjecting him to a constant barrage of sexual innuendo, and worse. Though he had been inclined that way from the start, Teddy guessed, with those effeminate features, that cute, short tongued, soft speech.

Teddy couldn't deny his own sexual attraction towards Tony. But he had sternly suppressed and banished it. It was, after all, the enforced celibacy, the lack of any female contact – they went months without even seeing a woman – and the smothering physical confinement, which brought such unnatural tendencies to the level of consciousness. And he had remained a true friend, unlike some of his fellow prisoners. They had beaten and then raped Tony one night, because of his association with a German guard. And then with the camp commandant himself. Tony had disappeared, transferred to another camp, they all thought. Teddy had believed he had gone from his life altogether. It was not until the end of the war, after his own return to civvy street, that he suddenly found himself summoned to a military inquiry and questioned closely about Young-un, and his liaisons with the enemy during his time at the camp. It appeared that Tony had thrown in his lot with the Germans, had worked for their propaganda unit in Hamburg, run by the notorious Lord Haw-Haw, William Joyce. His boss had been hanged last year, and Tony had faced the death penalty himself, though it had been quickly commuted to 'detention at His Majesty's pleasure'.

Teddy had finally been permitted to visit him, in the legendary 'glasshouse' at Aldershot, shortly before his transfer to a civilian prison. Teddy had been appalled at its effect on the youngster. His months there had left him traumatized, to the point where he had tried to take his own life. Since his transfer to a civilian prison, he had fared slightly better, and was apparently coping. Teddy had seen him twice in the intervening year, unable to break the promise the desperate youth had extracted from him at their first post-war meeting.

'I've got no family – nobody!' His young life had been spent in children's homes, and with a series of foster parents. Pathetically, he had attached himself by proxy to Teddy's family while in the prison camp, almost as eager to hear news of them as Teddy, and avidly staring at the few photographs Teddy was able to show him. He wrote long, rambling letters to Teddy from 'the Scrubs', detailing all the trivia of prison life, and all his rambling thoughts about anything and everything. Dutifully, Teddy struggled to reply, in the monthly letter Tony was allowed to receive.

Teddy guessed that Marian was shocked at this strange relationship, though she had never said so. Not that she said much about anything that mattered these days. Tony was undoubtedly the least of her worries, would remain the least of anybody's worries for a lot more years, Teddy surmised, except perhaps to those who would keep him all those years under lock and key. And probably not much of a problem for them, either, for Young-un was learning to adapt, to make the best of his bleak existence, which was only what he had been trying to do for all his twenty-one years so far.

Teddy had tried to explain his close link with the youngster, and Marian had dutifully listened and tried to show sympathy. But that was in the early days, two years ago now, when he was still drifting in his fluffy state of euphoria at being back in the world he had dreamed of and imagined so intensely during the five lonely years of his captivity. He had told her, in the letters she had kept like sacred relics, how much he wanted to be back with her and little Teddie, how much he wanted to make up for all his failures, his desertion of her, in that former life 'before the war'.

And at first she had clung with him to the realized dream, with a desperation that made his heart ache literally with love, a painful knocking and tenderness under the ribs. But gradually

34

he became aware that her desperation was not decreasing. There was a tension about her, an inner tautness, that showed in the set expression of her face, and most of all in her troubled eyes. When they made love, he began to see that her passion was not wholly genuine, that the ferocity with which she matched his was assumed. She was locked in to some private fear which she could not share with him, and that locked-in anxiety began to show itself more and more, in her tightened muscles, her rigid body. And, worst of all, the violent fits of weeping that would seize her when the act was done, the sobbing that became more extreme. 'Take no notice, pet!' she would gasp, while he held her, appalled. 'It's just me.'

She could, or would, give no explanation, and instinctively he did not press her for one. Instead, he tried to supply it himself. She was still afraid that one day he would up and off again, desert her the way he had, unforgivably, as soon as the honeymoon had ended, and she was still pregnant with Teddie. But, after weeks, then months, then a year and more of proof that this time he intended to keep his word to her, the situation did not ease. His guilt became tinged with resentment, then baffled exasperation. What more proof did she need, for God's sake? He was here with her, came home to her every day, from a job that was becoming as irksome as he had found it in the early days. He was trying his level best to be what she wanted. What she said she had always wanted. Breadwinner, husband, father.

But even with 'little' Teddie, the relationship was not as he had so rosily fantasized. She was a skinny-legged stranger in so many ways. Shy, reserved, staring at him with those great dark eyes, in a way he could not fathom. Speculating, brooding, almost. Certainly unchildlike. Until, as they became more familiar with each other, he realized that she saw him more as a rival, someone who had come with unfair, sinister advantage to supplant her mother's love for her. Of course, he made excuses for her. She

35

had never known what it was like to have a dad about the place. She and Marian had been an exclusive unit. The bairn was bound to resent his intrusion into such a close attachment. Nevertheless, it rankled. Especially when she played them off, one against the other. If he denied her something, or chided her, she would run straight to Marian, often weeping dramatically, her reaction outrageously excessive.

Before her tenth birthday last November, Teddie had been going on about arrangements for her party, expressing her discontent with the arrangements they had made. Teddy's anger at her ingratitude had grown, until he snapped at her, accused her of being a selfish little cat. She had flared up, until he lost his temper and he struck her, a resounding slap across her white thigh, on which his handprint formed a flaming brand. She yelped, as much with shock as pain. 'I hate you!' she screeched, the tears splashing hotly on cheeks as red as the spot where he had smacked her. 'I wish Uncle Jim was still here. He wasn't mean like you!'

Teddy was more angry with himself for striking her, but he could not back down. 'Get on up to your bedroom!' he yelled back at her. 'And stay there till you learn to behave, you spoilt little madam!'

Marian came hurrying in, the alarm plain on her face. Teddie swept past her, wailing loudly, and clomped upstairs. Her door slammed to. 'What on earth's going on?' Marian's voice was shrill, too, with accusation.

'That lass is ruined! She needs a firm hand. She's far too cheeky!'

'I'll go up. Calm her down. She'll make herself ill.'

'Who the hell is Uncle Jim?'

Marian swung round. Teddy was startled at the look of fleeting horror on her face. 'What? Who – what you on about?' She was still. Her eyes, glittering with tears, stared at him fixedly.

36

All at once, he felt bewildered, out of his depth at the incomprehensible degree of tension he could sense all about them.

Marian was struggling for words. 'He was – Jim Moody. He was one of Dora's fellers. From the works at Birtley. She used – he used to come here, sometimes.'

'Huh! She brought her fancy men here, did she? Very handy! No wonder she was so matey—' He stared in surprise at the abrupt way Marian rushed out, leaving him in mid-sentence.

He soon lost heart when he found that he could do nothing to ease his wife's private doubts or ghosts. Even the sex he had revelled in lost much of its appeal, except as a necessary means of assuaging his own imperious appetite. He no longer sought to bring her physical satisfaction, too. He gave no thought to the possible consequences of these essentially selfish acts. He was shocked when she told him one day that she was pregnant, more so because of the grave manner in which she broke the news. 'Everything's going to be all right,' he said, but he sounded uncertain. He was filled with compassion at the anxiety he saw reflected in her gaze.

'I think so. I told you. I had some bother with my insides. A couple of years ago. Woman's troubles.'

He recoiled from the ludicrous mystery of the phrase, his own ignorance, and lack of courage to break it. 'It'll be all right,' he repeated, more heartily.

Inevitably, he was wrong. She miscarried two months later, was ill for weeks. With his Aunt Julia and cousin Dora practically living with them, to look after her, Teddy felt even more like an intruder in his own home. They seemed so familiar with the place, and with Marian. He felt excluded, as though they shared secrets he was not privy to. They were like a constant irritating itch to his peace of mind when they were around. Both mother and daughter had a kind of cool, mocking way in his presence. A half-hidden sneering smile whenever they spoke to him, which privately infuriated him more and more, as though they were laughing at him. Ironically, Marian seemed more tense and uneasy than ever in their presence.

He felt helpless to stop the erosion of hope that had overtaken him. More often than not, he huddled beneath the blanket of self-pity he drew around him. He saw as naive that illusory promise of peace and contentment he had clung to in the aridity of imprisonment, that vision of hearth and home and all encompassing love with Marian and little Teddie. Marian's miscarriage was the physical embodiment of the death of his foolish optimism.

He so much wanted another child. A boy. He was deeply ashamed of his secretly cherished wish. He loved Teddie fiercely, of course he did. But their relationship was uneasy. He caught her glancing at him warily, with that dark-eyed look of uncertainty. And why not? he reflected guiltily. He had been away for most of the nearly eleven years of her life.

It was little wonder that Marian was even more demoralized than he was. He had left it far too late to be a proper husband, to play the pipe-and-slippers role. He had been foolish to believe she could accept his transformation, given the unsteady course of their eleven years of marriage. He guessed that she had been pinning her hopes almost as desperately as he on having another baby. He wondered if she shared his unexpressed belief that the new child would be a sign of their new, more mature love, in a way that his daughter could never be. To him, Teddie would always be the product of those golden, selfish days of lustful romance, his initiation into the glories of sexual love, when his golden haired girl had welcomed him into her bed with an unthinking eagerness and ignorance that matched his own.

It was wrong, he had always known, to think of himself as entrapped. Or at least to think of himself as the sole victim. Marian was caught just as much as he was. Except that she could face up to the consequences of their passion. Embraced it, the roses-round-the-door completeness of their love, signified and sanctified by their baby. He had tried to embrace it, endured, numb with the horror of it all, the build-up to the wedding, the preparations for setting up the new home, until his nerve broke and he had run to Spain, to other dangers, even to other arms, another exciting body. He could see how deeply Marian must have loved him, to welcome him back with open arms.

But this time, since his return from Germany two years ago, there was a smart of injustice he could not dismiss, however shabby it was. She had not given their happiness a real chance; there was an edginess, almost a fear on her part, something that held her back from him. Even the sex that had bound them together so fiercely in the first place was no longer the abandoned bliss it had been. She had been ill, she told him, though she was vague about the details, and claimed to be well again. He was ashamed of the thought that she was using this as an excuse to help explain the barrier of reserve which lay between them.

In the sixteen months since the miscarriage, the downhill pace had quickened. The sexual side of the relationship had deteriorated to virtual non-existence. For months, she had been too ill for any activity at all to take place. The doctor had insisted on seeing Teddy – Marian had got herself all worked up about that, too – and had told him plainly that he considered it unwise for Marian to have any more children. Teddy experienced a shaming, ambivalent sense of relief when Marian refused to consider the possibility of an operation to sterilize her, though he was careful not to put any pressure on her. 'It's up to you, love,' he told her.

In his more bitter moments since then, he had thought that a surgical operation, however risky, might have been better, after all. The infrequency of sex, with the long days of abstinence between Marian's periods to avoid the times of highest danger of conception, and then the awkwardness and forethought required for her to 'kit up' with the vaginal sponge and spermicidal jelly, took away any of the reckless rapture they had known in their courtship. And all for a few hasty minutes of penetration, while she lay passively enduring and he quickly sought relief. In spite of her tears, and her apologies, she told him plainly that she wanted it thus, that she no longer wanted anything other than his physical self-gratification within her. He took her at her word, soon gave up any attempts to prolong their lovemaking, to arouse her. Over and out.

He had always liked a drink, he would be the first to admit. He used it as a shield now, between him and those problems always waiting there at home. He joined the Thomas Wilson's Working Men's Club, a five-minute walk along Durham Road, by the tram terminus and next door to the 'George IV'. He became a regular in both establishments. 'Just nipping out for a pint, love.' She would not object. Perhaps, he consoled his conscience, she was as glad to see the back of him for a while as he was to escape to the smoky fellowship and the tang of the beer. The 'while' grew longer, with each passing week, each month.

The rain had stopped by the time he made his way downhill, through the neat, grass-verged avenues of red-roofed houses to his own home. He had thought about carrying on along the main road, towards the school at Harlow Green, where Teddie would soon be coming out with the others, but he decided against it. She might be more embarrassed than pleased at having a parent come to meet her. Especially her dad. And especially now that she was one of the élite, a member of the top class, Standard V, the Scholarship class. Besides, his bladder was uncomfortably reminding him of the volume of beer he had consumed.

He didn't bother getting out his key, for he knew Marian would be in, with Teddie expected home so soon. At least Marian would be pleased at this rare treat of having him home three hours earlier than usual. As though in mockery of this last thought, when she appeared in the kitchen doorway, her expression was one of ludicrous, open-mouthed dismay. He realized why at once, even before she called out in surprise. He could see the fug of blue smoke behind her, smell the aroma of Park Drive, and hear the rasping, raucous tones of his Aunt Julia.

'Hey! Ye've not got your fancy man calling, have ye?'

All the bitterness and rage and frustration welled up inside him once more, along with the sour taste of the ale and the ache of his bladder. 'I might have guessed it was you. I could see the smoke pouring out from down the street. You'd think the house was on fire.'

'Nice to see you an' all, pet!'

Her cackle rattled vindictively at him. He saw that look, the flicker of alarm in Marian's eyes. Once more, his fury surged, and he wondered yet again why his wife insisted on being so thick with this woman. Their intimate relationship struck and irritated him, without his knowing what exactly it was that disturbed him so. But he felt excluded whenever Aunt Julia and his cousin, Dora, were around. Both mother and daughter had this superior, knowing air about them, a veiled mockery, in all their conversations with him. He had made his feelings clear, with increasing plainness, and eventually their almost daily visits had tapered off. Or so he had thought. Now, he wondered just how regular these daytime meetings were, how long they had continued without his knowledge.

The gravelly, mocking tones went on. 'Phew! Easy to tell what *you've* been doing.' She wafted her hand in front of her face. 'You smell like a brewery! And *I* should know. You'll have to get together with your Uncle Alf. You've got a lot in common. What's up? Not got the sack, have you?'

The reference to her pit man husband angered him even more. What right had she to compare him with that pathetic, pot-bellied drunkard? Mind you, with a bitch like Aunt Julia for a wife, who wouldn't want to spend as much time as he could swilling ale? For all Alf's size, this sharp-faced, razor-tongued harridan had her man well and truly under her thumb. Pointedly, Teddy looked away from her, directing his explanation to Marian. 'They shut the office early. Blasted power cuts again! I had a couple of gills at dinner time, with the lads,' he added, grudgingly, and heard his aunt's derisive snort of triumph.

He turned his back on them and clumped upstairs. In the lavatory at the head of the staircase, he urinated with savage force and considerable relief. As he came out, he heard the low tones of his wife, the rasping voice of Julia. He couldn't hear what they were saying. They sounded conspiratorial. He went along the narrow landing to the bedroom, sat on the edge of the bed and dragged off his tie and the starched collar. He bent and unlaced his shoes, eased them off, and lay back on the cold eiderdown. He heard the voices grow louder, as the two women stood in the hall, saying their farewells. 'Tara, Teddy, pet!' Julia's voice, that mocking note still evident, came up piercingly. He made no answer.

Marian appeared in the bedroom doorway, that sick, worried expression on her face. 'All right?'

'How long has this been going on, eh?' His voice was harsh with accusation. 'Sneaking round here behind my back! You'd never have told me, would you? I've told you! I don't want her coming round here. Or young madam Dora! Treating the place as if it was their own. I'll not have it! Right?'

The colour flooded her face. 'I can't just tell them to stop coming round, can I?'

'Why the hell not? I'll do it, if you want me to. I'll send them both packing, don't you worry! You're too soft with them, that's *your* trouble! You act like you're scared stiff of them. They just think—'

'What do you mean, scared stiff?' He was startled by her shrill cry, the wild look. 'Why should I be scared? Maybe I *want* to see them! Maybe I need them! Maybe I needed them all the time – when you were away. When I – was alone—' Suddenly, her breath caught and she gave a violent sob, began to weep abandonedly, her hands pressed flat against her face, her whole torso shaking.

Appalled, he rose quickly, went to her. 'Hey! Hey! Come on!' He gathered her in his arms, cradled the heaving shoulders. She cried like a child, huge, desolate gouts of grief. The blonde head rested on his shoulder, his hand came up, caressed it gently. 'Don't get upset, love,' he whispered, against her hair. 'Don't let's fall out. Not over bloody Aunt Julia!' He tried to move her head, still gentle, so that he could look into her eyes. He smiled, trying to calm the tension. 'My fault for coming home early, eh?'

She clung tighter to him, pressed her wet face against him, let the weight of her body lean into him. He felt her encased breasts, her belly and thighs, their receptive concavity. His hand moved, to the swell of her girdled behind, its constrained smoothness. He thrust her hard into him, pushed back against her loins, his desire hard and throbbing. His lips nuzzled below her curls, to her earlobe, the sweetness of her warm neck. His mouth moved, demandingly, and she raised hers to meet it, with the full softness of her lips. The passion moulded them; for a long second she surrendered to it.

Again, he was startled at the force with which she struggled free, pushing away from him. Her head down, breathing heavily, she turned, as though in panic. 'Teddie – she'll be in any minute. I mustn't – I don't want her to see me like this.'

She hurried out, across the few feet of landing, to the bath-room, whose door banged noisily shut behind her. For an instant, he had a powerful urge to rush after her, drag her back to his embrace, then the feeling died, and he stood there, diminished and pathetic, in his collarless shirt, and his stockinged feet, and his despair.

CHAPTER FOUR

Sophia Wright died on the day the wedding of Princess Elizabeth to Lt. Philip Mountbatten was announced. The July weather was sultry and overcast, with distant grumbles of thunder. The feeling in the family at her death was tinged with relief that her suffering was over. From the mainly exploratory surgery in the spring, her decline had been swift. For a while, when she was first admitted to the private nursing home, standing in its well-kept grounds off Durham Road, and overlooking the same view of wooded valley and hillside that Sophia had enjoyed for so many years from her own upper storey windows, she had appeared almost to bloom in response to the increased dosage of drugs they gave her. She was sprightly, business-like, with all her old imperiousness. If she was afraid, she hid it well. Later, they found that she had planned her own funeral meticulously, with Joe, her youngest son, who had never left the family home, except for his brief spell of military service as a young man, at the end of the Great War.

But the cancer spread with remorseless swiftness, and the suffering became etched in deep lines across her face. Soon she was unable even to leave her bed to sit in the chair by the window. She drifted in and out of spells of drug-induced sleep, or half-conscious sighs and moans. 'Why don't my boys come to see me?' she asked May plaintively, and May was not sure whether she was referring to her grandchildren, May's own two boys, or to the dead Dan and Jack. Other times she could be disconcertingly sharp-eyed and attentive. 'Why did you marry our Dan?' she asked a discomfited Iris, who was paying a duty visit to keep May company.

'He *did* ask me.' Iris just stopped herself from adding 'Mrs Wright'. Unlike May, she could never bring herself to address her as 'mother', nor, she was sure, would the older woman have wished her to. They had met infrequently over the thirty-six years of their acquaintance, and never comfortably since Iris's marriage to Dan, eighteen years ago.

'You needn't have said yes!' Sophia's jaw snapped shut. The flesh had fallen away from the pallid face, leaving only grimness.

She was right, of course. She would have taken great satisfaction if she could have known how many times Iris had castigated herself for her acceptance. Iris shifted her bulk in the uncomfortable restriction of the hard chair and attempted an embarrassed heartiness. 'True enough! Still. Water under the bridge now, eh?' She glanced appealingly across at May, who leapt gallantly to her aid.

'Has Cissy been in to see you, mam? She was on the phone at the weekend. She said she was popping in.'

Sophia nodded. 'All the way from Gosforth!' she said sarcastically. 'I don't know how she manages!'

Grateful to be off the hook, Iris only half listened to the laboured conversation. Sophia's bluntness had disturbed her. Her mind strove to shy away from her tempestuous relationship with Dan Wright. Her single foray into the realms of love. Or at least heterosexual love. She looked across at her darling May, felt the assuaging tide of real tenderness as she gazed at the still slim, trim figure, leaning forward now, one thin hand laid on Sophia's wrist, on the counterpane. Her darling would be deeply shocked at the tenor of her thoughts now, in spite of their closeness. But Iris was forced to acknowledge, at least to herself, the all-embracing nature of her love for this still lovely woman. It included that now long familiar ache of unfulfilment at the impossibility of expressing that love in any physical terms. The very notion would be abhorrent to May, and Iris was well schooled in suppressing her own desire, perverse as it undoubtedly was. She could even assign to herself, somewhat self-mockingly, a certain nobility of sacrifice in conquering such primitive emotions. In any case, it did nothing to lessen the love, the real love, that she felt for, and shared with, her one true partner.

She could not be closer to any other single person. They had been together since the end of the war. Not the war that had just finished. She had been shocked, not long ago, to see the conflict that had stamped itself so permanently on their young lives referred to in print as 'World War I.' It made it seem like a piece of history. Which it was, she supposed. They themselves were now a part of that history. Wars had scarred all the generations of this half-century. It had opened with the South African War. She could vividly remember the flag waving, the decorated streets and the cheering crowds during the first May of the new century, when the news of the relief of Mafeking reached England. She had been seven; she remembered being woken by the noise downstairs, then her father had come up to the nursery, where she slept with her little sister, Helena. Nicholas was dressed for dinner, and he was smoking a cigar, and he smelt of cologne and a strange aroma she didn't know at the time was whisky. Next day, he had taken them out in the carriage, riding all the way down to the River Tyne, to let them see all those narrow, cobbled streets festooned with banners and flags, and people dancing, and sitting at long tables right there in the roadways.

That was a distant war, and a mere sideshow for the conflict that had cast its shadow over whole nations. The First World War.

47

They gave it capital letters now, classified thus for the history books. The war which had scarred so many lives dear to her. The dearest of all, May, had lost the man she loved so deeply, robbed of a whole lifetime together, of John and Teddy's father, when they were only infants. And it had scarred her own life, too, Iris had painfully to acknowledge. That sad young man, Lionel Strang, whom, out of misguided compassion, she had allowed to harbour false hopes that one day they might become life partners. And to whom, out of an even more misguided sympathy, she had been prepared, so she thought, to accord the gift of her virginity. It shamed her still to admit that that was only a half-truth, or less. What she had tried to solve, that gloomy afternoon, in the dusty attics of Ferncliffe, the Strangs' impressive residence near Morpeth, was the enigma of her own sexuality. She had convinced herself that what she was about to do was in the nature of 'noble sacrifice'. Lionel, home on brief leave from the Front, was transformed from the brash young man he had been before active service. Quiet and abstracted, there was a haunted quality about him and a desperate need for her tenderness that made her feel closer to him than she had ever thought possible. Surely she could overcome that perversity which made her shrink in repugnance from the idea of sexual love?

But the reality had been very different. Her noble ideals had vanished with the desperate, brute violence of his assault on her. The fierce, bruising kisses, making her lips bleed, the rutting thrust, the clutch of his hand, tearing, clawing, ripping under her skirt, searching out the most intimate part of her body. She had fought him off, run weeping from him. He had wept, too, later, when they said goodbye. He was humble, beaten, so that she remained confused once more, after he had left her again. Weeks later, he was dead.

In France herself, with the Ambulance Corps, she saw at first hand the awful mutilations, the suffering, and the paradoxical bravery. She was disgusted by her own former callous patriotism, the tub-thumping war effort meetings she had attended so enthusiastically, with her delighted, and surprised, father. So there she was, in the midst of all that carnage, bewildered, unsure of her whole life, afraid; racked with guilt over Lionel's death and the fact that she had sent him to that death without the consolation and comfort of having loved her.

It was that guilt which drove her into Dan Wright's arms, and the shared bed for that one strange night in Amiens. She was grateful for his unsentimentality, for his refusal to gloss over the grotesque circumstances of this sick, weird girl asking for sex. It wasn't quite a nightmare, but a shockingly painful experience. When she scrambled ashamedly from the narrow, creaking bed in the cold dawn, she knew that her lifelong doubts about the nature of her sexuality had been resolved. The 'noble sacrifice' had come thirteen years later, when she had once more climbed into a bed with Dan, on their wedding night. It was a sacrifice she had made as infrequently as she could, and never with anything other than secret revulsion.

As if the sufferings of 1914–18 had not been enough, war had come again. It had claimed Dan's life. Poor Dan, who had survived all the horror of that first war, crippled and scarred though he was, had not escaped the second. And still it spread its shadow over their lives, in spite of the peace that had come at last, two years ago.

The deep thankfulness which both May and Iris had felt at the safe return of John and Teddy was marred now by a new anxiety, for both boys, at the unhappiness becoming increasingly apparent in their private lives. 'Oh God, Iris! What's going wrong? They've gone through so much, both of them. Why can't they enjoy some peace? Jenny – I don't know what happened, but there's something – they're not happy, are they? And poor Marian! I'm sick with worry. She's making herself ill all over again, poor girl!' Helplessly, she had glanced across at Iris, those large brown eyes luminous with her fears.

'Come here!' And Iris gave all that she could, her wide open arms, comforting bosom, and her steadfast love for the woman who moved needfully into her embrace.

Jenny peeped into the sick bay, exaggeratedly miming a cautious glance before entering the room. Five of the beds, separated by the metal lockers, were empty. In the sixth, in the corner furthest from the door, a boy was sitting up in his blue striped pyjamas, his black hair standing up untidily. 'Matron not around?' Jenny whispered.

Michael Porter's thin face lit up. He grinned widely. 'It's all right. She's just gone, miss.'

'Here. For goodness' sake keep them out of sight, or you'll get me shot.' Jenny's heels clicked on the worn linoleum as she came across to the bed and perched on its edge. Michael's eyes widened as he took in the unusual outfit; the smart, full dress with the black three-quarter coat open over it, the dark nylon stockings and high heels, and, most exotic of all, the little black hat, with its wispy veil lifted over its tiny peak. 'Hope I didn't give you a fright, done up like this. We're off in a minute. How are you feeling?'

'Gosh! Thanks, miss. Bullets! My favourite!' He pushed the twist of paper under his pillow. They weren't his absolute favourite, but he wanted desperately to please her. She must have used some of the precious 'points' from the ration book to buy them, and he gazed at her devotedly. 'I'm loads better, now. Matron's going to let me get up after lunch. I could be out of here by Sunday.'

'Then it'll be time for you to pack. Where are you going first?'

'To my gran's. In Harrogate.'

Jenny saw that brief flicker of pain flash across the sensitive

50

face. Porter's parents were out in India. One of her first jobs at Beaconsfield had been to comfort the ten-year-old one freezing night, when one of the prefects had come to John and told him, 'Porter's blubbing, sir. He's in the upper corridor.' At John's instigation, Jenny had taken over, and led the shivering, woebegone figure along to the candlelit flat and the comfort of two thick rugs on the lumpy sofa. That January was the severest on record. In fact, the Head had been on the point of closing the school at one stage, for the misery of the biting cold was made worse by the plague of power cuts. 'Remind me. We *did* win, didn't we?' James asked sourly. Most people felt that way. A year and a half of peace, and we staggered from one crisis to the next. Shortage of fuel, people out of work because of it, and rationing more extreme than it had been during the conflict.

Jenny, feeling lost and lonely herself, could identify all too well with the slight, trembling body she held close. She pulled his head into her breast, felt the slim frame quiver, stiffen in fleeting resistance, then collapse with limp gratefulness against her. He cried out his fear, in great gulping words punctuated by sobs, as he clung to her. He was worried sick for his parents, and his infant sister, with news of riots and wholesale slaughter in India, as the vast country moved towards troubled independence. One of the older boys – of course, to Jenny's fury, he wouldn't say who – had callously taunted him. 'Shame about your old man, Porter! They'll be slitting all the white throats they can lay their hands on now!'

'There, Michael, come on now. They'll be all right. They'll be home soon, I expect.' She held him protectively, her eyes stinging with tears. She kissed the top of the tousled head.

'You – you're not supposed to call us by our Christian names!' gasped the boy, snuggling into her fragrant warmth, and already feeling better.

'Well, I'm just a newcomer, aren't I?' Jenny smiled, her lips

51

moving against the dark hair. 'I won't tell anyone if you don't. All right?'

'Yes, miss.' From then on, he had respectfully worshipped her.

She knew he was deeply disappointed that, with independence only a month away, his parents would not be returning to England. He had hoped that at least his mother and sister would be home. 'Maybe,' Jenny said diffidently, 'you could spend a few days with us. I mean at my home. In the Lake District.' She saw his face light up again, and she felt a prick of guilt and uncertainty. She hadn't mentioned it yet to John, and wished she had not said anything. Then she felt the warmth of the boy's devotion as he gazed at her.

She stood, shook out the skirts of her dress. 'Do I look like a crow? Or more like a witch?' She grimaced. He knew she and John were attending Sophia's funeral.

'You look – smashing, miss!' He flushed, as he remembered Lloyd's crude adjective assessing Mrs Wright. 'She's dead sexy.' Michael had been livid, but Lloyd was a year senior, and a lot heftier. He had kept silent. Now, as he watched her passing out of sight, shameful though it was, he had to agree that Lloyd was right.

The sun had disappeared by the time the large group of mourners filed out of the chapel at Saltwell Cemetery and followed the coffin to the graveside. The grey clouds billowed, grew darker still, bruised with their rain, and the thunder rolled an accompaniment to the vicar's penetrating voice. 'Very dramatic,' Iris whispered. Beside her, veiled and black-clad, like most of the women, May gave a fleeting smile, and sniffled quietly.

The end of an era. The phrase kept echoing in May's head as she watched the coffin lowered, heard the rattle of ritual earth flung by Joe, before she took her place in the procession, to stand for the last time at Sophia's feet in silent respect. It was genuine on her part, though it had come slowly, almost grudg-ingly, when she thought how superior Sophia's attitude towards her had been when Jack first brought May to the family home. Relations had not really begun to thaw until John's birth. May could not ignore the genuineness of his grandparents' love for the baby, and for Teddy, when he had come along fifteen months later.

Jack's death had been a cruel blow for them, too – they had stood by May, made sure that her two boys should want for noth-ing. At first, May's mother-in-law had seemed almost resentful of May's partnership with Iris, her independence as their business prospered. Gradually, though, the success of the two young women, and May's equal dedication to the upbringing of her two boys, had brought Sophia's admiration. The death of Jack's father had revealed surprising strengths in Sophia's character which, perhaps, she herself had not known, never having been required to call upon them. But the last blow – the death of her eldest, Dan, under such ignominious circumstances – had been the bitterest of all. No one knew for certain whether Sophia was aware of the details of those circumstances, or, if anyone did, they did not let on, and Sophia herself never made reference to them. But old age seemed suddenly to catch up with her then, in her seventy-first year. She became almost reclusive, scarcely left the house and did not encourage visitors. When her illness took hold, Joe reported that she had declared herself 'ready to go'.

There was a substantial, buffet lunch back at the family home, given the exigencies of the times. Cissy, as elegant as ever in her mourning clothes, said to May, 'I told Joe he should have had it at the Springfield or somewhere, but he insisted Ma wanted it to be at home.'

'What's Joe going to do now?'

Cissy raised her eyebrows eloquently. 'Well, he says he's going to stay on here. Looked quite miffed when we suggested he should find something smaller.' She laughed dismissively. 'It's not as though he's going to go mad and start kicking over the traces, is it? And it's not likely he'll find himself a wife at this stage of the game. He'll be fifty next year, for God's sake! He'll rattle around in this place like a pea on a drum. He has someone in to clean and cook a bit, but I mean! Just look at the place! You can see it's not being looked after, even now. You know what domestic staff are like nowadays.'

May thought of her own Ruby and offered a silent prayer of thankfulness. David, Cissy's husband, joined them. His long face was furrowed with deep lines. His gold-rimmed spectacles added to the impression of advanced age, and his shock of hair, though luxuriant in its waves flowing back from the prominent temples, was already a silvery grey. Though only three years older, he might well be mistaken for the father of the smart figure beside him.

'How's business?' he asked May. Their relationship had been cool, even strained, since the time he had involved John in that business with the Jewish girl in Berlin, the summer before the war. It wasn't until months later that May discovered John had been thrown into a German gaol, kept there all night before they released him. And all because David Golding had asked him to take some papers for one of his Jewish friends, to help get their daughter out of Germany. There had been a hell of a family row when the truth had come out. Cissy had been as angry with him as May. Not that that surprised her. The marriage had never been love's young dream. With typical impetuosity, the thirty-year-old Cissy had returned home from an excitingly fast life down south with an expensive engagement ring on her finger, and the studious but astute business man on her arm.

David had never made much of his Jewish background, until this business with Sara Arad had come up. May recalled her name because John had mentioned he had met her when he was in the army, in Palestine. She had eventually succeeded in getting away from Germany – unlike her poor parents – and had settled in Palestine, again thanks largely to David's assistance. Jenny had once teasingly referred to her as 'John's little Yiddish piece', and said he had written that he had spent a weekend with the girl in Haifa. But Jenny had laughed, and seemed perfectly at ease with it. May was the only one who had felt privately uncomfortable. 'Doesn't seem right, somehow, does it?' she confided to Iris.

Even Iris had fondly teased her for her attitude. 'You old puritan!'

Now, May answered David's query in a friendly fashion. 'Well, it's like everything these days. We started off quite well.' There was no need for her to explain that she was referring to the coming of peace two years ago, even though the café and the shop had never closed. 'But now, with the rationing the way it is. And when they brought in bread . . .' Even during the war, bread had not been rationed. It had begun only last year, and now so much flour was being extracted from the wheat that the infamous 'British Loaf' resembled nothing more than a dirty grey sponge. 'What with that *and* the sugar being cut again, the shop and the bakery aren't doing much at all. The café's still ticking over, though. Iris is on at me to sell out.' She shrugged. 'But finding a buyer and getting anywhere near a decent price would be difficult.' She smiled almost apologetically. 'In any case, I don't spend that much time on it. Not like in the old days. I'm pretty much a lady of leisure, as it is. My manageress, Ann Swainsby, runs the place practically by herself.'

'About time, too,' Cissy said forcefully. 'Time for you to do a little living, eh? Show them we're not quite over the hill yet!' She lightly punched May's arm to emphasize her point. In exactly a month's time, May would be fifty-three. Cissy was only two months younger. You've already done enough living to last a lifetime, May thought, without real malice. But, for the first time, she felt a stirring of sympathy for the silver-haired David, standing unsmilingly between them.

'If you're serious about selling up, I could put out some feelers.'

May politely waved aside his offer. She wanted to put off making a decision, though her practical reasons for delaying were not her real motives. Again, that portentous phrase loomed in her thoughts. The end of an era. The Tea Cosy had been such a vital part of her life, a regeneration of it, after Jack's death. She was reluctant to let it go. Instinctively, she glanced about the crowded room for Iris, who was so inextricably linked with these reflections. Iris was urging her with relentless patience to give up the business. She herself had withdrawn from taking any active part in it years ago, from around the time of her marriage to Dan. She was still, however, the principal partner, as she had been from the very beginning, when it had been her capital which had made the venture possible. Iris always pooh-poohed such niceties. 'Look! It was *your* capability and your capacity for sheer hard work that got the thing going. Without you the whole thing would have petered out. Just another one of my bees under the bonnet, which I'd have got sick of. But you, you wicked little slave driver! You kept us at it – and for the last twenty years nearly you've got along fine without me. Surely you can relax at last. Let's spend our autumn years in decadent leisure, my love.'

Whenever financial matters cropped up, Iris tried to bluster and browbeat, out of the best possible motives, as May well realized. 'Look, my love, we're not going to descend to such pettiness as to squabble over whose is what – splitting the electric and arguing over who pays for the loo paper!' Switching from bludgeoning humour to a pleading seriousness, her fleshy face coloured up even more vividly, her grey eyes sought for acceptance. 'Look! We've been together long enough now. You know whatever I've got is yours, and vice versa.' She went on quickly, over May's protest. 'Daddy's money's left me well enough off. If I pop my clogs tomorrow, it's yours anyway. And some for John and Teddy and so on. There's no one in my family who needs anything, or would expect it.' She paused, ploughed on, embarrassed but determined. '*You're* my family, for God's sake! I've no one else.'

May was silenced. She opened her arms, and they sat and hugged on the sofa. They sniffled, blew noses, and Iris heaved herself upright, her hand heavy on May's knee. 'Coffee!' she said decisively, and headed for the kitchen.

May caught sight of her friend, tall and imposing in the formal black in spite of her bulk. She was talking to John and Jenny, part of a larger group. She extricated herself from Cissy and David, and edged through the crowd. Iris's face lit up with that special, loving smile. 'Ah! There you are. Everything all right?'

May nodded. Jenny was sipping at a stemmed glass with some dark liquid in it. 'Mustn't get too tipsy. I'm on duty tonight. Wouldn't do to breathe fumes all over the little monsters!' She raised her glass in a swift toasting motion, towards May and Iris. 'Well, here's to us Mrs Wrights. Four of us left now. Shame Marian couldn't make it. It's ages since we've seen her. We must try and arrange something.'

May's fleeting irritation at her inappropriate flippancy was forgotten in her new anxiety. 'Yes, you should. I'm worried about her. She's not at all well, still. And Teddy – ' She looked around for him, the frown deepening. 'Where's he got to? He should get himself off home—'

'He'll be in the kitchen, I expect.' Jenny grinned. 'They've set up a keg of ale in there. That's where all the men keep disappearing. Except my good-living husband.' She smiled brightly at John, and grabbed his arm. 'Lips that touch liquor shall never touch mine!' she quoted, laughing.

John looked uncomfortable, despite his returning smile. May

wondered distractedly, not for the first time, how much of a bone of contention between the young couple John's new religion was. 'Well, I wish you would convert that brother of yours,' she muttered worriedly. 'If anyone needs to sign the pledge he does!' May felt Iris's knuckles brush against hers, as her hand hung by her side, and, unseen, their fingers intertwined in a tight hand-clasp. They were so close, thank God, and May's eyes pricked and moistened with love.

CHAPTER FIVE

Teddy let himself into the silent house. The hall was in deep gloom because of the summer storm. He caught sight of his dim reflection in the small oval mirror in the centre of the coat-stand. Drops were beaded on the brim of his hat, which was darkened and heavy with the rain that had soaked into the felt. He removed it, eased off the sodden raincoat and shook it before hanging it up. He could feel the sharp throbbing at his temples, and the fierce heartburn deep in his chest. Too much Exhibition Ale – he never trusted those firkins for home use. Uncle Joe had had it set up on a cradle in the kitchen, but draught beer belonged in a pub cellar. It was too tricky for amateurs to be messing about with. Teddy had thought it looked a bit cloudy right from the beginning. He had switched to the spirits after only three or four pints. Now he conceded that that might not have been such a wise move, either, though he attributed his present discomfort more to the sandwiches and other insubstantial pastry things provided at the luncheon.

The living-room was in semi-darkness, despite the fact that it was not yet four o' clock, and he shivered with damp chilliness. The neatly empty grate, with the guard in place and the brass-handled fire instruments gleaming from the tiled hearth, added to the chilly atmosphere. The brooding silence disturbed him.

59

He felt impatience stirring again, a rising anger as he wondered where Marian had got to. She had claimed she wasn't up to facing everyone at the funeral. Got herself into one of her states about it, until he had given up trying to persuade her at the threat of more tears. But she clearly wasn't too unwell to go off out somewhere. Perhaps she'd walked up to meet Teddie from school. His rage flared, for all at once he was sure she must have walked the two miles along the top road, towards Birtley, and the pit where Uncle Alf worked, and Julia and her brood lived, in the terraced cottages beside it.

He went back out into the hall, intending to put the kettle on in the kitchen. Then he froze as he heard a noise from above. 'Marian?' There was another noise, heavier, and he went upstairs and along the passage to the closed door of their bedroom.

The first thing that held his gaze was the row of flickering candles on the windowsill, in front of the drawn curtains. There were others, on both wings of the dressing table, their lights reflecting in the mirrors to make their number seem double. He saw that they were small nightlights, balanced on saucers and small dishes. His heart raced in uncomprehending fear as Marian, huddled on her knees before the dressing table, turned her head towards him. She was shrouded in some dark cloth, a scarf or a shawl, which she had draped over her head, like some biblical figure, bizarrely in tune with the myriad pinpoints of light flickering all about her.

'What—'

She did not look startled at his entrance, though he guessed she had not been aware of his entering the house or his approach. Her eyes were luminous, sparkling with tears, and their trails glinted on her cheeks. 'She knows. Your grandma. She knows all about it.' Her voice was hoarse, the words caught up in her weeping. 'I've prayed and begged for forgiveness, over and over. But it's no good. I killed him! It was a boy, I know it was! Ask

Dora – she saw it. I was so wrong – and wicked! I shouldn't have done it—'

'No, no, love! Don't be daft! It wasn't your fault, any of it. It – just happened. Nobody's fault. You mustn't blame yourself.' He fell onto his knees beside her, snatched the covering from her head, grabbed her to him, hugging her tightly, rocking her gently. His throat, too, was choked with grief. His hold released any constraint within her, and she began to sob wildly, her whole body ravaged by her distress, while he cradled and rocked her back and forth, holding her to him. 'Shush, love, shush.'

'No,' she moaned, 'you don't understand. I've been so wicked, God's going to punish me. He already has – after you came back. But now – I was thinking – about your grandma, and—'

Again, he shushed her, and continued to hold her. His own mind was spinning with the shock of it all. Clearly, she'd had some kind of mental breakdown. But what on earth did she mean, with that talk about killing? And Dora? Why had she said. . . ? An awful suspicion began to form in his mind, which he tried to push away. 'I killed him', she'd said. 'Ask Dora.' Had the miscarriage been brought about deliberately? With Dora's help? Just the sort of help the young trollop would know about. But no! It couldn't be. Marian had wanted the baby as much as he did, surely? No, it was just the feeling of guilt because she had miscarried, through no fault of her own. Things hadn't been right in any case. She'd been ill while he'd been away, she'd told him. After the miscarriage, Dr Leeson had called him in, told him how dangerous it could be if Marian became pregnant again. In fact, he had been so insistent Teddy had begun to feel angry. It was as though the doctor were somehow blaming him for her getting pregnant in the first place. Which would have been fair enough if Teddy had been aware that there was any danger then. But nobody had said a dicky bird about it. Certainly not Marian, and not their officious GP.

He pushed his ignoble thoughts firmly out of his mind. She was certainly ill enough now, and it was all the more frightening because Teddy didn't understand it. 'Come on, love. Get up. It's all right now. I know—'

'You don't!' The heartfelt strength of her cry shook him. He had tried to lift her, but now, free from his embrace, she slumped, lying on the floor, in the narrow space between the bed and the dressing table, and gave way to hysterical grief. He saw her pale hands form into fists, pummel the floor in front of her. 'I'm wicked! Wicked! I need to be punished.'

In a panic himself, he became rough with her. 'Get up! Come on!' He clawed at her, dragged her up, heaving her onto the bed, dragging the shawl from her. Then he saw that she had another, white garment, wrapped around her, and he recognized the intricately laced pattern of Teddie's christening shawl, which he had not seen for years. Not even, he recalled painfully, on the occasion for which it had been intended, for he had been away in Spain when the ceremony had taken place. 'Let's get you into bed, love. You need to rest. I'll get you something.'

He was pulling down her stockings when he heard his daughter's shrill cry of fear from the doorway. 'What are you doing? Mam! What is it? Get off her!'

She screamed and ran forward, grappling with him ineffectually, and he raised an arm to thrust her off. 'Your mam's ill!' he shouted, over her cries. 'Calm down! We've got to help her.'

'Mam! What's he done to you?' Teddie was crying, too, but Marian lay there, and gave no acknowledgement of her presence.

'I'm trying to get her into bed. We'll need the doctor. Help me, Teddie, for God's sake!'

His words began to get through to her, and she stared, frightened, at the flickering lights in the darkened room. 'Get those ruddy lights out. Open the curtains a bit.' Teddy tugged and pulled. Marian lay unresisting, but unhelpful, so that he clumsily dragged off her dress, wrestled with the pink brassiere and the girdle. 'Go down and make a pot of strong tea. Bring up a cup. Lots of milk and sugar.' In an agony of embarrassment now, Teddie was glad to escape, to have something to do.

Marian's weeping had eased from the earlier hysterical violence to a steady desolation of moaning sobs. Her face was swollen, her eyes closed, and she made no response to anything Teddy said to her. He finally got her into a nightgown and under the covers. She turned her blonde head away from him, towards the window. He was sitting on the edge of the bed, one hand on the curve of her shoulder, when Teddie brought the cup of tea. He felt a quivering smile tugging at his mouth when he saw that she had used the best tea things, the rose pattern of the Royal Albert cup and saucer, on which lay an ornate teaspoon.

He had to repeat his murmured command to drink. 'Come on, love. Have a sip. You'll feel better.' Finally, she stirred and swivelled round on one elbow. She made no effort to take the proffered cup, but slurped in noisy obedience when Teddy held it to her lips.

'I want you to stay with your mam. I'm just going up to phone Dr Leeson. I won't be long.' He saw the fear and uncertainty in his daughter's dark eyes. 'You're a big girl now. She'll be all right. I'll only be a few minutes.'

She followed him out onto the landing. 'What happened?' Her face looked pinched, and very pale, but he could detect the suspicion, the tremulous defiance in both her tone and her look. 'What made her – like this?'

Teddy frowned. 'I don't know. I found her up here, with all those candles lit. It's something – I think she's been ill a long time. Since last year.' He was angry with himself for feeling defensive, and for the embarrassment which prevented him from talking about the miscarriage. 'I'll not be long.'

Dr Leeson came soon after seven. He was up in the bedroom

a long time, while Teddy hovered wretchedly at the foot of the stairs, and his daughter sat tensely in the living-room. The light was on, because of the heavy clouds, and although it wasn't quite dark, Teddie could see a dim reflection of herself in the window that looked out on to the back garden. At one point, Marian's wailing rose, and Teddy felt his nerves jangle, but the soothing rumble of the doctor's tones persisted, and the noise died down again. It was a long time before he came downstairs.

'I've given her something to calm her. But I think she needs to be taken into hospital. You don't have a telephone, I suppose? No? That's all right. I'll make arrangements. Transport? No? I'll organize an ambulance. I'd like her in right away. It will have to be the General for now, but possibly we might see about moving her in a day or two. Winyard House would be the best place. I'll see how they're fixed.' He paused, stared at Teddy as though he was debating what to say next. 'She's got a lot preying on her mind, Mr Wright. This is some sort of breakdown because she can't cope with it. You'll have to be very patient – and understanding. It won't be easy. There are things you and your wife need to get sorted out. Cleared up, as it were.'

'What? What sort of things? I mean – there was the miscarriage, I know. But that—'

'Yes, well, we'll have to give it time. Have some things ready. Wash things, clothes and so on. I hope you won't have to wait too long for the ambulance. I'll telephone as soon as I get home.'

He could see the anxiety on Teddie's face when he told her. He wanted to go to her, to hug her, but it seemed almost as if, aware of his wish, she was putting up some kind of invisible barrier. She stood, stared at him, again with that wariness and uncertainty that hurt him so. 'She'll be all right, won't she?' He knew she desperately needed reassurance, but he thought he could detect once more that hint of accusation in her voice.

John could see the tension between his mother and Teddy, and was relieved when his brother eventually decided to leave, as May had been urging him to do for some time. She even suggested that John could maybe run him along home, but Teddy had swiftly demurred. 'Good God, mam! It's less than a mile. The walk will do me good.'

'But it's raining. You'll be soaked through—'

'What's wrong? Don't you trust me? I promise I'll be a good boy and go straight home. No popping into the George for a quick one, honest!' His tone was lightly barbed with sarcasm. 'Anyway, they'll be shut by now. It's after three.'

'He's far too fond of his drink, that one,' May said, after he had finally departed. 'Maybe we should just call in on our way back afterwards. See how Marian is.'

'Best not,' Iris answered diplomatically. 'We can go over on Sunday, if you like. She might fancy a drive out somewhere.'

May flashed her a worried, grateful smile, and John was struck once more by how closely in tune the two women were, and how much they relied on one another for support. He felt a sudden stab of envy.

'Have you two got anything sorted for your holidays yet?' His mother had turned to Jenny. 'Not that you can do a lot with petrol being so short. Somebody was telling us they're talking of cutting the basic ration *again*! We won't be able to go anywhere soon.'

'John's going off to some convention or other. A summer school, or something. A Baha'i thing.'

'It's only for ten days. Across near Manchester.' His tone was uncomfortably apologetic. He hoped his mother wouldn't leap to defend him, for he knew how difficult she found it to accept his adherence to this, in her opinion, strange faith. He also knew how much May's rallying to his cause would put Jenny's back up.

Perhaps Jenny was sensitive to the atmosphere, too, for she went on brightly, 'I'll probably go and stay at home for a while, until they get sick of me. It would be nice if we could get away to the Continent for a bit. But all these restrictions – you can't even take any money with you now!' She laughed. 'Not that we've got any, on the pittance James pays us. Still, John will find himself with plenty to do, I dare say. You'll end up doing what you always do, helping James to stop the old place from falling about our ears. Paint and patch up, as usual, before the monsters return.'

'You need some time off, the two of you. On your own. You should try and find somewhere.'

John could sense a subtle hint of reproach towards him, and he felt it was unfair of her to put the onus on him. Yet he also acknowledged his own stirring of guilt. He had been far too ready to go along with Jenny's reluctance to face the problems that lay massively between them. Foolishly, he had hoped that just being together again, living as man and wife, would in itself heal the wounds of their broken relationship. Especially when Jenny had surprisingly agreed to take up the offer of the post at Beaconsfield. But in the half year and more since that had happened, the situation was no clearer, and both of them had tiptoed around it, taken every opportunity to avoid confrontation. He vowed to himself yet again that that would stop. 'We will, mam. I'll make sure of it.' He had perhaps spoken more firmly than he had meant to. For a second, his gaze met Jenny's. It pained him that he could not read what lay behind that steady regard, and he moved away almost gladly towards David Golding, who was standing momentarily on his own by the much depleted table of food.

The serious face lit up with genuine warmth. The crowd had thinned out a lot now, and they were able to have the chance to talk alone. It wasn't long before the conversation centred on the topic close to both their hearts – Palestine. 'I haven't heard from Sara for a while,' David told John. The lines on his face seemed to deepen as he shook his head. 'I don't see how the United Nations are going to be able to sort things out. In her last letter she was saying all the kibbutzim are being trained now by the Haganah. They seem to think war is inevitable, as soon as the British pull out.'

'We don't seem to be doing much good. The sooner we hand over the better. I hear they've kidnapped two more army blokes.' Two sergeants had been seized just last week by Irgun, the Jewish terrorist organization connected with the late leader of the notorious Stern Gang, and were being held hostage in an effort to prevent the execution of three Irgun members sentenced to death by the British authorities. 'I'm afraid the poor devils have had it,' John continued. 'We can't afford to make bargains.' He felt somehow disloyal at his unhappiness with the British government's role in this mess. Even now, the survivors of the horrors of the Nazi death camps were being turned away from the Holy Land, herded into more camps, on the island of Cyprus.

'Partition isn't going to work,' his Uncle David said. 'And we've made sure the Jews are greatly outnumbered. It seems to me they're in a hopeless situation.' He paused. 'I'm beginning to doubt I did young Sara a favour when I helped her to get out there.'

'She wouldn't be alive now if you hadn't.' Only last year, again largely through David's painstaking investigative efforts, Sara had received final confirmation of the deaths of both her parents. They had been deported to the Lodz ghetto in 1941, then 'resettled' in the camp at Chelmno a year later, where their lives had been ended in the gas chamber.

But David was too painfully honest to ease himself off the hook. 'I could have persuaded her to stay in England, perhaps.'

John shook his head. 'I don't think so.' He recalled the tanned face, the clear eyes of the young woman he had met in Haifa. 'It's really her home now. She belongs there. I suppose she's ready to lay down her life for it. Just as we were against Hitler.'

His mind went back to that dazzling sweep of bay, the high mountain as its dramatic background, on which nestled the simple shrine where he had discovered new meaning to his life. The words of Abdu'1-Baha's prayer came into his head, as they so often did whenever he thought of that blessed, troubled spot, and the upheavals it was going through:

O Thou kind Lord, unite all. Let the religions agree, and make the nations one, that they may see each other as one family, and the whole earth as one home. May they live together in perfect harmony.

CHAPTER SIX

Sara felt Bernard's sweat-drenched hand clasp hers even more tightly, as the first of the half bricks and jagged stones flew over their heads from the back of the crowd towards the khaki figures, who looked oddly impotent despite their steel helmets and the long rifles they held before them. They retreated before the barrage, towards the edge of the quay, and the rolls of barbed wire that ringed the area around the newly docked ship. The rusted hull of the *Exodus 1947* stood high out of the water. The chipped paint and splintered wood of the upperworks were evidence of the firing which had taken place before the vessel had been brought into Haifa harbour under Royal Navy escort. The three shrouded bodies had already been carried down the gangplanks, watched by the lines of silent passengers thronging the shoreward side of the ship. Sara wondered what conditions must have been like on board, for it was said that four and a half thousand refugees had embarked at Genoa. This was the sixth boat in the past four months to try to break the blockade, and by far the largest.

Word of her impending arrival, and her interception by the British navy had spread rapidly, and practically the entire younger population of the kibbutz had piled into the trucks and the venerable bus to make the journey up the coast. Sara's heart was thumping, with excitement as much as fear. This time a large crowd had gathered on the shore, determined that these new arrivals would not be turned away and hauled off to the camps on Cyprus. She clung even tighter to Bernard's hand, comforted by the strength of his grip, as they were swept even closer to the barriers by the pressure of those behind. She could see the soldiers flinching, turning away, holding out their rifles in front of them in a pathetic effort to ward off the rain of missiles. One or two went down, their weapons clattering on the hard, dusty ground, their hands clutched to their bloodied faces.

An NCO, his features a choleric red, began screaming at the wilting line, and they stood firmer. Sara saw the rifles raised menacingly now, pointing at the baying crowd, and her throat tightened in alarm, then she stiffened at the crash of the volley, the singing of the bullets passing closely overhead. There was a roar of straining engines, and shrill cries of alarm now from behind them. All at once, she and the people around her were buffeted violently, and she heard screams. People near her became entangled in the coils of wire, the crowd was parting, and suddenly she saw a terrifyingly inhuman figure bearing down on her. Khaki blouse and shorts, the three-quarter stockings, the hobnailed boots, but, towering above, the frightening black gargoyle of the goggled mask, with its corrugated trunk, and the arm raised, wielding a long cane.

Bernard pulled at her, and they tried to break away to the right. Someone cannoned into her, and her hand slipped from its hold, and she fell on hands and knees in the gritty earth. She saw Bernard turn, then an agonizing pain flared across her ribs, smashing the air from her lungs, cutting off her breath, so that she was incapable of movement, even of sound. She seemed to hang on the pain, before she folded, and as she did so, curling on her face in the dirt, another slashing burn of pain struck at the bottom of her spine, just above her buttocks, and burned

70

down her limbs at the second blow from the baton. She couldn't move, her legs tingled and burned, but then, despite her tortured ribs, she found enough air within her to scream as her dark hair was seized in a wrenching grip and she was pulled along, her scalp lifting, searing, her limbs and body scraped cruelly along the gravel. The soldier dragged her along like a ragdoll, for several yards and at great speed. She felt her clothes being torn, the skin on her arm, her knees, being scored by the tiny stones.

He let her go, and booted her viciously, aiming for her behind, but striking just in front of her left hip, at the top of her thigh. She lay stunned, semi-conscious for a moment, lost in the pain and fear, as shapes swept by, trod on her, stumbled over her, in the thick fog of pale dust. The fog thickened, then suddenly everyone around her was doubling up, coughing, spitting, crying out in fresh horror. Dimly, she wondered what was happening. She lay gazing up, seeing the choking figures clutching at themselves, holding handkerchiefs to their faces, or tearing at their shirts to remove them for the same purpose. Because she was stretched on the ground, it took a few more seconds for the tear gas to reach her. Then she felt it burning into her, she was blinded, panic-stricken, spitting, eyes and nose streaming, and she flopped about, trying to force her limbs to move, her awareness of her pain fading in this new nightmare.

A figure dragged her up, she staggered against him. The arms tightened about her, hauling her along, and she realized it was Bernard, his blurred features dark with blood, his white shirt deeply stained with it. Somehow, they stumbled clear of the area of conflict, away from the docks, reaching the railway lines, stumbling on across the tracks, to collapse with scores of others on the narrow scrubland between the railway and the road that ran parallel to the docks. The sprawled figures all around them were gasping and coughing, some retching, nearly all sobbing.

Miraculously, buckets of water appeared, someone passed her a scrap of filthy cloth, blessedly soaked, and she held it over her burning eyes, her tear and mucus-coated face.

With vision restored somewhat, consciousness of her injuries returned. Her blouse hung open, exposing her brassière. A long, ugly, raised bar of flesh ran along her left side, under her breast and following the line of her lower ribs. Her arms and legs were gashed and scraped, with trickles of blood here and there, the raw wounds plastered thickly with dirt. But perhaps the worst agony of all was in her lower spine. Her buttocks and her legs still tingled, felt oddly numbed, and she had difficulty in controlling her lower limbs.

She was lying half on her front, propped on one elbow, scarcely able to sit up, when another ragged volley of shots rang out. They heard a chorus of fierce yells, and more figures came spilling over the tracks again, glancing back over their shoulders. 'Baton charge!' The billows of acrid, pale gas rose in their wake, and all around her weeping individuals began to haul themselves to their feet.

'Get across the road! Get up the hill. They won't come that far after us!'

Somehow she found herself on her feet, with Bernard's arms supporting her. Half-doubled, she loped along, dragging her feet, her hands clasping his shoulders. The busy lines of traffic were halted, blasting their horns to add to the din and confusion. Once across the highway, people scrambled over the low wire fence which was already sagging, and up through the old houses at the edge of the German Templar colony, into the scrub-covered rise at the foot of the mountain. As predicted, the soldiers halted on the far side of the rail tracks, forming a line against any assault.

The youthful crowd spread out over the rocky slopes, and sank down again. They could see the *Exodus*, small in the distance, over the low roofs of the sprawling buildings along the railway lines. They watched in almost total helpless silence as events unfolded. Two gangplanks had been raised, and the dark dots of the passengers came spilling thickly down, to be met by the lines of uniformed men, herded roughly into queues, then into squatting circles, penned in by their captors. Attempts were made to break out, and rifle butts and clubs were used. They could see the dark gowned female forms and the diminutive dots of children, who were not spared the brutal treatment. A more determined resistance, assisted by a group from on shore, was met with more rifle shots, the puffs of smoke looking oddly harmless from this distance. The blue clouds lifted, and thinned into the sun's still fierce haze. All at once, arcs of water rose, forming small rainbows, as fire hoses were turned on the protesters, and they fell back, turned, curling themselves into black balls against the ferocity of the jets.

Gradually, the knots of resistance gave way, were broken. Some figures were herded into the backs of military trucks, and some kind of order was restored, though all the time there hung in the air a muted buzzing, like a colony of roused bees. It became clear that the refugees from the ship were being marshalled once more and forced to board other, smaller vessels and immediately driven below decks. Another, larger ship made her way slowly inshore, as close as she could get. There was no room for her to come alongside, but presently the onlookers could see the smaller vessels ferrying their human cargoes out to her.

'They're turning them away again,' someone said bitterly. 'Off to the camps in Cyprus.' In fact, they were to suffer an even harsher and more ironic fate, for their final destination, on this new vessel, the *Empire Rival*, was the port of Hamburg, and a Displaced Persons camp on the hated soil they had so longed to escape from. The vivid shades of the sunset over the sea blazed across the sky before the scene quietened, the soldiers reformed into lines, climbed aboard their vehicles and roared off, head-lights stabbing into the quickening gloom. Sara wanted to cry, with pain and weariness. She could not walk without Bernard's help. His brown hair was a matted mess, the blood had crusted darkly on his brow and face and neck.

'It looks worse than it is,' he assured her. He lifted the edge of her blouse, and stared at the dark weal on her side. She was no longer embarrassed about his seeing her full breasts confined in the cotton cups of her brassière, but she held the tattered blouse together as they hobbled arm in arm down onto the roadway, and eventually met up with others from their kibbutz. The warm night was velvety black, with insects buzzing about the street lamps, before they found their bus. A jeep full of the European police pulled up beside them, and the officers dismounted. They were all armed, and stood in silence until everyone had boarded the bus, into which two of them then entered, checked papers, and ordered to drive off. Sara felt ashamed of her gasp of relief when the bus pulled away without incident.

She felt as though she had been away for days when, at last, showered and changed, her injuries treated at the sick bay, she sank exhausted on to her narrow bed in the room she shared with three other girls. The doctor had strapped up her ribs on her left side. He had carefully examined her lower spine, and declared himself satisfied that she had not sustained any serious damage. 'You'll find it hard to sit down – or stand up – for a while,' he smiled. There was a large, spectacularly coloured bruise in the join of her left thigh spreading up into her belly where the soldier had kicked her, and though it hurt abominably when touched, the doctor also assured her that it was nothing to worry about. 'A few more inches to the right and life really would have been miserable for you!' he joked.

He had given her some tablets for the pain, and though she began to feel drowsy, she was sure she was too uncomfortable to sleep. She heard one of her companions call out, and looked up to see Bernard standing in the doorway. Part of the front of his hairline had been shaved, and he had an impressive bandage covering his brow, over which his hair stood up in a comic coxcomb. He looked uncharacteristically shy and uncertain, even though there was a thoroughly relaxed attitude towards the sexes mixing. 'Just came to see how you were.'

'I feel like someone's been playing football with me.' There was an awkward pause.

One of the other girls gave a gurgling laugh. 'Why don't you two go over to Hut Three? There's no one in the duty room. It's free tonight.' Bernard crimsoned. 'Oh, you Brits!' she continued, teasingly. 'So damned formal. For God's sake, Sara, take him away, will you?'

It was true that he was from Britain. There was a strong link with British Jewry, which had been maintained since the founding of the kibbutz. Bernard had come out a few months after the war's end, one of the few lucky ones to squeeze in as a legal immigrant. He had served in the RAF for the last two years of the war, as ground crew, and had never left England. He was three years younger than Sara. She knew he liked her, was attracted to her. She had had only one serious relationship so far in her twenty-five years. Carl had been British, too, one of the first batch to come out when the kibbutz was still newly established. She had loved him, deeply. So she thought. But not deeply enough to give up her life here, her adopted home. When he was invalided out of the British army in 1944, he had changed. Life back on the kibbutz irked him, he found it impossible to settle down. He had lost all his enthusiasm for what they were trying to achieve here, was determined to get back to Britain. 'It's where I belong, after all. Why don't you come with me?' But she couldn't, and though she wept bitterly for several nights after he left, she soon realized that she could never regret her decision.

All at once, she remembered Bernard's hand gripping hers, his turning back for her, his arms around her. Groaning, she slowly rolled off the bed, came bent and barefoot towards him. 'Come on then,' she said briskly. 'Good night, girls. See you in the morning.' They left the hoots and catcalls behind them.

They lit candles in the privacy of the small room at one end of the one-storey hut. Sara was wearing only a loose shirt and a pair of white panties, which she did not remove as she eased herself down on the narrow, creaking metal bed. 'We can't get up to anything wicked tonight, I'm afraid.' But she quivered with plea-sure as he bent and tenderly kissed the dark bruise at the top of her thigh, and the loose shirt was no deterrent to his rapturously gentle exploration of her freely hanging, voluptuous breasts. Just as his shorts proved little protection against her skilfully deter-mined assault on his roused manhood and the climactic relief she swiftly brought him.

Sara dreamed she was standing naked in an office in the squat military court building perched on the crest of Carmel. She was surrounded by British soldiers, who were grinning, devouring her with their eyes. She kept her head down, staring at her flex-ing toes, hot with shame, yet aware, too, of an even more shameful beat of excitement within her. She could see the curve of her brown belly, the thick, springy growth of her dark pubis at its base.

'Here you are, sir. She's ready for you. Look at the arse on this one, eh? Made for it, these Jewish tarts!'

When she looked up at the approach of the officer, she found herself gazing into the gentle, reproachful face of John Wright. His light drill uniform was crisply spotless, sharply pressed, his buckles gleamed, the brown leather of the Sam Browne running diagonally across his chest, richly polished. Her face burned, she felt the tears spill from her eyelids, trickle down her cheeks. 'Sara.' The sad, rich deepness of his voice was as she remembered; she felt its quivering effect on her flesh, as though he had touched her. 'Why have you been so wicked? We have to punish you.'

He laid the slender swagger-stick on her breastbone, exactly between her heavy breasts. She felt the tiny hardness of its silver ferrule press coldly on her skin, thrust against the hardness of bone just beneath, in contrast to the rich, soft swell of the flesh at either side. The tears came thickly, she could not speak, yet still, in spite of her shame, the sick excitement surged, she felt her nipples hardening, proclaiming it to his mild, sad gaze, to all those other glittering, merciless eyes . . .

She started awake, and, for a few disorientating seconds, she was shocked at the intimate clasp of the naked body entangled with her in the darkness. She felt the cold clamminess of Bernard's sex on her thigh, their flesh, slippery with sweat, the acrid odour assailed her nostrils. She felt the clinging wetness of the cotton pants, the pulse of her arousal. Grunting with pain, she disengaged herself from the embrace and dragged the shirt off over her head. She rolled her hips, grunting again at the pain of her movement, and eased the panties down off her limbs, tossing them on the floor, where Bernard's crumpled shorts lay. Her movements woke him, he came snorting from his deep sleep. She hung over him, her body pressed to him, her hand wantonly seeking out his penis, manipulating it as it had before.

'I want you to do it properly,' she whispered, her lips searching for his.

He caught at her wrist. He was hard again. 'Are you sure? Is it – will it be all right?'

'Of course! Don't be too rough, though, will you?'

Her body was sure, at least. She moved onto her back, raised her knees, her feet planted firmly on the rumpled sheet, hauled him on top of her. When she lifted her belly, the pain in her lower back and her buttocks made her gasp with its severity, but, with fierce urgency, she guided him to her, smothered another cry at the stabbing thrust of his flesh into her tightness. Each time she tried to respond to his plunges, to meet his battering invasiveness, the pain in her spine, and her clasping thighs, flared anew, so she had to lie still, which caused more discomfort. But she embraced the pain as she embraced his rutting body, was fiercely glad of it, and felt close to him when he quickly came and his hardness died inside her, and he lay heavily on her, their sweat-slick bodies cooling in the first grey dimness of the dawn.

At the end of the month, the bodies of the two kidnapped British sergeants were found, hanged and booby-trapped. Feeling ran high, the volatile atmosphere on the kibbutz reflecting the rest of the country. Sara was one of the founding members. She had helped to establish the settlement four years ago, in the swampy land along the coast between Caesaria and Netanya. A large contingent of immigrants from Britain was mixed with pioneers from the Baltic states, financed by the American Zionist movement. The British influence was still strong. A number, like Bernard, had seen service with the British forces.

She was full of compassion for the private conflict Bernard and others were going through. Ben-Gurion summed up the emotive paradoxes of the situation when he spoke before the United Nations Special Committee on Palestine. 'It will be to the everlasting credit of the British people that it was the first in modern times to undertake the restoration of Palestine to the Jewish people.' Yet now both sides were fighting, as well as Arabs and Jews, and the British press was full of outraged demands to 'bring our boys back home'. At the beginning of September, UNSCOP announced its plans for the future of the territory. As expected, its solution was the creation of two separate states, with Jerusalem and its environs, plumb in the middle of the large central block of Arab land, to be an international zone.

'Well, at least we won't be in the Arab zone,' Sara said, as she leaned beside Bernard over the sandbagged parapet of the look-out post beside the main gate. She had used her big-eyed persuasion on the Youth Leader, to make sure she was on duty with her new lover. Bernard had been issued with the heavy British service rifle, which was propped upright beside him. Sara had not been given any weapon, only the unwieldy binoculars slung around her neck, and little use now that darkness had fallen and the moon was not visible. The defence committee was a lot cagier now since the British authorities had been carrying out much more extensive arms searches. The new location of the armoury was kept a secret even from the majority of the kibbutzniks, and Sara wondered just how quickly the settlement would be able to arm itself in the event of a surprise attack.

'It won't work, splitting up the country piecemeal like this,' Bernard observed. 'Nearly a quarter of our population will be outside the state, in Arab territory, and we'll have nearly as many Arabs as Jews in our land. It's a total mess.' He smiled wryly. 'Not that it will ever come about. Ben-Gurion needs to take charge now. We've got to reorganize ourselves into a proper national army. It doesn't matter a damn what the UN decide. We're going to have to fight for every inch of territory or be pushed into the sea.'

For a second, his words chilled her, until she pushed them aside. She grabbed his hand, put it to her breast, and let her hip rub against his. She was still astonished, and secretly shocked, at how sensual she had become, how fiercely she enjoyed the sexual love they shared. 'We'd better make the most of what we've got, then,' she murmured, in her siren's voice. She nodded off towards the dunes and the ruins of Caesarea. 'What was it the gladiators said? "Eat, drink, and be merry." Let's forget the food and drink, and get straight down to the merry!'

Her hand moved suggestively to his loins, and he jerked away, with a snigger of shocked delight. 'Fornicating on duty! I'll deal with you later, you hussy!'

'Yes, please, sir!' she giggled.

CHAPTER SEVEN

Julia's eyes widened in surprise when she saw Teddy standing at her front door, then a look of wariness came over her hardened features. 'Why ye bugger! What a fright you gave us. Only the tally man comes to the front door. Howay in. How's Marian? Not worse, is she?'

'No, she's all right. Settled in now, at Winyard House.' The front room seemed untidily cluttered compared with his own neat living-room. He felt almost claustrophobic as the heat enveloped him. In spite of the warm August day, the red fire in the high, old-fashioned grate glowed brightly; a large, soot-blackened kettle stood on the hob to one side, above the oven whose metal knob shone with silvery brilliance. The rail below the high mantelpiece was draped with Alf's thick pit shirt and dark trousers, and a pair of voluminous underpants. 'Alf working?'

His aunt gave that harsh, scornful bark which she gave almost every time her husband's name was mentioned. 'No, he's early shift. Home at two, guzzled his dinner, had his wash and off out again. Supposed to be helping his marra at the allotments. He'll be in the Welfare by now. We'll see nowt more of him till he rolls in with a bellyful after ten.'

There was a clatter down the thinly carpeted stairs and the dainty figure of Julia's youngest, Rose, appeared. She was wearing a dark, belted coat tied at the waist, and little else, as far as Teddy could tell. 'Hiya, Teddy!' She afforded him a generous view of her pale legs as she sat in the high-backed armchair near the fire, and drew her heels up on its sagging seat. Her feet were bare, and he could see the dark polish on her toenails. He acknowledged the elfin prettiness which was a family trait, at least among the younger members, and no doubt Julia herself when she was a girl. In this instance, it was largely spoilt by the arch worldliness of the smile Rose aimed at him. At sixteen, she looked as though she was all set to follow in her older sisters' footsteps. 'About bloody time an' all!' These words were directed at Alice, who appeared from the back kitchen, her yellow hair crimped in steel pincers. She was wearing a shining satin slip, though she had draped a towel shawl-like around her shoulders in a gesture towards modesty. Teddy saw the thin lace edging of the hem, above her bare knees.

'Get yourself upstairs and get some clothes on!' Julia snapped. She sounded genuinely embarrassed.

'Gerraway, mam! He's family, aren't you, Teddy? There's nowt here he hasn't seen before, eh?' She beamed that challenging grin at him, her hips rolling provocatively in the shimmering pink material as she came round the table in a cloud of fragrant perfume. He watched her slight bottom undulating as she passed him on the way out, with another bold trill of laughter.

'I hope you've left some hot water for me!' Rose yelled after her.

No wonder Alf escapes whenever he can! Teddy thought, imagining how helpless his weak willed, easy-going uncle must be in this household of women. 'Is Dora in?' he asked. He cleared his throat. 'It's her I really wanted to see.'

He could sense the sudden stillness, the wariness in his aunt's spare form. 'Oh aye?' Her face was alert, she stared at him. 'What about, like? What's the young madam been up to now?'

'It's nothing. Bit personal,' he muttered, colouring.

'Personal? I think you'd best explain yourself. I'm her mother, in case you'd forgotten. There's nothing you can't tell me.'

'It's all right, don't worry.' He was angry at being put on the defensive. 'It doesn't matter. Just tell her—'

'If it's help you're wanting, with the house, or little Teddie, you can ask *me*. These lasses!' She shook her head. 'Soon as they come in from work, they're off carrying on with lads, all three of them! Useless, the lot of them!'

He was wondering how he could extract himself from this awkward situation when he heard the back door open, and young Rose's squeal of mock alarm. 'Hey, man! Mind that door! I've got nowt on and we've got a visitor!'

Dora herself came in through the kitchen door, closing it hastily behind her. Teddy could detect the same cautious, guarded expression in her eyes when she saw him. 'Hallo there. This is an honour.' The cool, mocking expression stamped itself on her features.

'You're back early!' Julia cut in, speaking quickly, over her daughter's greeting. Teddy wondered if she was uneasy because she had not told him of her eldest girl's proximity.

'Aye, well. Peg's fella's coming round. I didn't want to play gooseberry. How's Marian? Have you seen her today?'

She sounded genuinely concerned, he acknowledged grudgingly. 'I called in on my way from work.' He shrugged. 'She doesn't seem much different.'

'We'll have to get down to see her,' Julia said. 'It's only just down the road. I'd like to visit her. When's the best time?'

He felt guilty again at his uncharitableness at not wanting them to go near Marian. But then he remembered why he had come, the ways in which his suspicions had been picking at his brain night after lonely night since Marian's breakdown. He answered Julia's question curtly, giving them the official visiting hours. 'They only allow two visitors. I'm there most nights. There's Wednesday afternoons, and Saturday and Sunday. Mam and Aunt I pop over quite a lot—'

He sensed the prickle of contempt at the mention of their names. 'I thought Winyard was a private place. It must cost a pretty penny, I dare say,' Julia went on.

For a second, he let her remark hang in the air, nearly refused to answer it. Then he said baldly, savouring the idea that the truth would annoy her all the more, 'Ma and Aunt I are helping out, otherwise I'd never be able to afford it. You're right. It's damned expensive.' He went on even more bluntly. 'Dora, can I have a word with you? In private? Maybe we could go for a stroll. I'll not keep you long.'

He saw her glance across at her mother, both exchange a look of complicity. Dora's face was red. She stood, patted her blonde hair, which was hidden beneath a green turban. 'Well, I'm not dressed for going out—'

'We'll just walk down the road,' he rejoined irritably. 'We're not going wining and dining!'

'Dora!' Julia's voice was hard with warning. 'You – mind your manners!' she said, after an awkward pause, as they left by the front door.

At the end of the row of miners' cottages, Teddy turned down, away from the main road, heading along the broad dirt pathway they called the 'back lane', with the hen runs, the tar-paper huts and bright wooden pigeon lofts made from oddly assorted old pieces of timber. 'What's on your mind?' Dora asked, her voice abrasive, and edgy, he was sure.

He gave a quick look around. Apart from a few distant figures working on the long strips of gardens, and a nearer bunch of youngsters playing round one of the gates leading to the rear of the houses, there was no one else in sight. He stopped and she faced him, her face screwed up quizzically, bold still, but underneath he could detect her nervousness. It spurred him on. No need to beat about the bush any longer. 'Marian's been saying some strange things, since – she's been taken ill. She mentioned your name. Something to do with the miscarriage. "Ask Dora," she said. "She knows." *What* do you know?'

'Eh? What you bloody on about? I don't know what she's talking about. I didn't even know she was carrying!'

He was disconcerted by the genuineness of her surprise. 'You and her were thick as thieves while I was away. You were more round ours than your own home. Why should she go on about killing the baby? Why should she say you know?'

'You're daft as your lass! I *don't* bloody know! Don't know what the hell she's on about. And I don't suppose she does, neither! She's doolally, isn't she?'

Dora's face was flushed. She turned to move rapidly away, and agitatedly Teddy grabbed her by the arm, pulling her forcibly back. 'Who the bloody hell's this Jim feller, eh? Jim – Moody, I think she said.'

Dora stopped, and he was startled at the look of undisguised fear that flashed across her face at the name. He saw the hesitation, the frantic searching for an answer. 'He – was just one of the blokes. He was at the works. He used to come round – he came to a few of the parties – the get-togethers we used to have. New Year's and that.'

'Aye!' The bitterness and frustration overtook him. 'I can guess! One of your fancy men. Marian told me—'

'*My* fancy man?' He could not miss the scornful incredulity of the inflexion. She snatched her arm violently away from his restraining hand. 'Get off me! It's your wife you should talk to, not me! Except you can't, can you? She's never been able to talk to you. You were never around, were you?'

'You watch your mouth, you cheeky young bugger!'

'Not too young to remember your carry-on, though! Have you

forgotten? I was there the day you came back from Spain, wasn't I? The first time you saw your Teddie. When she was six months!' She turned back the way they had come, and he had to stride along to keep pace with her. 'I don't know what you're getting at, but I know nowt about her losing the baby. She didn't try to get rid of it, if that's what you're getting at. Not with *my* help, at any road!'

'Whose, then? Your mam's?'

Again, that strange, wild expression on her face. 'You *are* bloody mad! You should be shut up with your wife! Now bugger off and leave us alone! I'm not staying to talk to you!'

She stormed off, and he stood gazing after her, taking in the violence of her emotion, the way her voice shook with threatened tears.

'I need to talk to you. Can you come back to the house?'

The pleading look on Teddy's face was close to desperation. Jenny felt herself colouring under her make-up. Frantically, she searched for some way to avoid having to agree. 'Well, I've got to catch the six o'clock back to Hexham. I told John I'd be back—'

'Please, Jenny! It's important.'

·She felt her stomach churning as she nodded, giving in to his urgency. For a brief instant, she cursed her decision to spend the Saturday afternoon visiting Marian in the nursing home. Though that was a euphemism, at least for the wing of Winyard House in which Marian was a patient. Asylum was nearer the mark, though both the inmates and their families would shy away from such an unpleasant epithet. Jenny felt she had enough problems to hold in at the moment without the heart-to-heart Teddy seemed to crave.

She felt worn out, her nerves stretched, after the long, and mostly painful, two hours she had spent with Marian in the uncomfortably hot sun lounge, in the heavily cushioned furniture, which seemed to imprison you in its grip. The late August sun beat mercilessly through the long windows and the glass of the roof until her light summer dress clung damply to her, and the backs of her bare legs were wet on the upholstery. She was glad to escape at last into the neat gardens, after the ritual of the post-lunch cups of tea had been got through.

It was only the second time she had seen Marian since her breakdown, and the first time they had been alone. She had put on a lot of weight, was almost plump. There was a docility about her, a placid expression on her open face, which was, at first, misleadingly reassuring, until Jenny recalled that it probably owed more to sedation than nature. It was strongly rumoured that such places relied heavily on medication to keep their patients tranquil. No one seemed able to give any estimation of when Marian would be fit to return home. Teddy had been vague when she and John had last seen him, two weeks ago, at Hexham. Little Teddie had been staying with May and Aunt I, and Jenny had suggested she spend some time at Keswick, with her folks. She would be company for Michael Porter, whose grandparents had been happy for him to stay a large part of the summer with John and Jenny.

'Up and down, you know,' Teddy had volunteered laconically.

Her mother-in-law told Jenny privately, with deep concern, 'Sometimes she seems perfectly fine. You know, normal. But then she still has these fits of depression. Weeping all the time.' Instinctively, she lowered her voice a little. 'Teddy admitted she doesn't seem to *want* to come home. It's like she feels safe in there. Away from – you know. The real world.'

That was the clear impression Jenny had received herself. Marian greeted her cheerfully, her face alight with pleasure at seeing her. But then, breathlessly, her speech quickening, her face turning pink, she swiftly steered the conversation away from

87

any meaningful reference to her condition, or to the family. 'We thought we might take Teddie over to Keswick for a while,' Jenny began. 'We've got—'

'We have to do basket work in here,' Marian interrupted, almost at a gabble. 'Weaving and all that. I'm getting quite good. I'll show you some I've done, if you like.'

Jenny soon saw that she was shying away from anything but the lightest of small talk. It became a strain to keep the conversation going, and she began to snatch surreptitious glances at her watch, whose hands were moving with painful slowness towards four o'clock.

Jenny became convinced that it was cowardly, and certainly not helpful, to allow Marian to remain in this escapist condition. When they were safely isolated on one of the paths, screened from the house by the carefully trimmed bushes, she made a last determined effort. 'When do you think you're going to be able to get back home? Teddy misses you so much. And Little Teddie. They so much want you—'

Marian gave a muted little whimper of distress. 'No, I can't. I'm not allowed.' Jenny was alarmed at the immediate transformation from that sunny calm. 'You don't know! Nobody does!' Her hands were knotted, twisting in her lap. She began to take aimless little steps, back and forth, turning away, then back to Jenny, in hasty repetition. 'Listen! You haven't told her, have you?' From the tone of her question, it was clear she was seeking reassurance. 'You're not going to say anything to Teddy's mam? About you and that bloke. That soldier. You mustn't! Promise me! She mustn't get to know! None of them. Teddy – and John.'

She was sobbing. Sickened, Jenny remembered the afternoon four years ago, in the meadow by the river at Hexham, she in her uniform, as they both confessed their guilt of infidelity. The look of fear on Marian's face, the tears streaming down her cheeks, were every bit as tortured as they had been then, and Jenny was horribly afraid that, for her sister-in-law, the time between no longer existed.

Marian had wept all the way back to the building, though she allowed herself to be led along by Jenny's guiding arm, in fact, seemed pitifully relieved to get back to the building's shelter and the soothing care of the uniformed nurse who took charge of her. Jenny was still in a state of anxiety when Teddy made his unexpected appearance. 'I just thought I'd look in. See how she is. Hang on. I'll come with you.'

They walked slowly along the wide pavement, Jenny's arm linked through his, like any married couple out for a stroll. It was still hot. One foot was rubbing painfully against the strap of her sandal, but she soon forgot her discomfort and her irritation that he had not suggested taking the bus for the mile and a half walk back to his home.

'Maybe *you* can tell me what's going on, 'cos it looks like no other bugger can!'

She was taken aback at the blunt directness of his tone, as well as the rudeness of his language. It caught her on the raw. She was well aware that he used it deliberately, with the intention of shocking her sensibility. She knew he saw her as rather effete, an over-delicate product of her background. He had adopted the same attitude the night she had taken up his challenge and gone with him for a drink back in April, on the occasion of his birthday. Now it angered her. Why did he have to be so aggressive? His own background had been as privileged as hers, but he harked back endlessly to the working-class origins his mother had long left behind, when he was still a toddler. John was far more tolerant than his wife, more amused than anything at Teddy's intransigence. It needled her. She guessed that Teddy knew it, and enjoyed using it against her. She strove now to keep her temper, even to heighten her pose of cool detachment.

89

'What on earth do you mean?' She kept her hand lightly in the crook of his arm.

'I mean with Marian. There's something – I realize now, she's never been right since I came home. Something before I came home.' He told her of Marian's behaviour, her strange ramblings the day she became ill. 'I'm sure ma doesn't know anything about it. But Aunt Julia – and Dora. There's something they're not letting on.'

All the while he was talking, Jenny was reliving the scene of an hour or two ago, Marian's tortured expression, the guilt that was tearing her apart. Jenny felt the convoluted links with her own situation, the secret of her unfaithfulness that she and John shared, that still held them in its binding chains, in spite of her agonizing confession. But at least she had tried. It was the guilt, the terrible strain of keeping it from her husband, that had so damaged Marian. Perhaps there was still a chance for her, if only the truth could be released. And then there was Teddy's baffled helplessness. She owed it to both of them to speak. Someone had to. 'Listen. We have to talk. Let's wait till we get back to the house.'

When Teddy had let them in to the heavy warmth of the silent house, the late afternoon sun was slanting strongly in through the wide front window of the living-room. She sank gratefully on to the sofa and eased off her sandals, rubbing at her bare feet. She drew them up, at her side, tucked the skirts of her thin dress decorously round her calves. 'Could I have a cold drink?'

She realized how tensely Teddy was holding himself in check. He brought her a glass of squash. 'Well?'

Suddenly, she was frightened, felt literally sick, her stomach turning. She cleared her throat. 'Sit down. Nobody else knows about this. Not your mother, or Aunt I. Not even John.'

'For Christ's sake! What is it?'

The violence of his speech helped her. She gave a bitter laugh, stared at her folded feet. 'What is it your mum always says? "We Wrights stick together." Well, she's right. Even the wives. Both of us. Marian and me. We both have our secrets. In the war – I met a chap. An army officer I worked with. I slept with him, while John was overseas. I told him later. John.'

'He knew?' Teddy sounded disbelieving.

She gave another bitter laugh. 'Yes. He forgave me.'

Shocked as he was, Teddy's mind was racing ahead. 'You said Marian—'

'You ought to know. Keeping it to herself is destroying her. While you were in Germany – Marian got pregnant. She had an abortion. It—'

'Jim Moody!' he whispered.

'Eh?' She gestured dismissively. 'I don't know. It doesn't matter. She sent him packing. He didn't even know—'

'What? All this time – and bloody Julia and that little tart – they knew all right! Laughing at me, all this time.'

'It's over and done with. What matters—'

'You and her – the pair of you. Making cuckolds of John and me!' He gave a harsh, painful bark of laughter. 'What a bloody laugh, eh? You wouldn't believe it! Like some dirty bloody joke! And our John knows, you say? You told him?' He shook his head, laughed aloud again. He was moving around the room, shaking his head. 'Well, there's a turn-up!'

Suddenly, he came and stood towering over her. She kept still, her feet folded primly to the side. She did not glance up at him. He seized her bare arms, pulled her viciously upright. 'What a chump! What a pair of chumps! My God! I need to make up for lost time. Pretty Jenny! You're a dark horse, aren't you? Our kid not man enough for you? Mebbes that's what's wrong with Marian and all! What do you reckon? Let's find out, shall we? Anything goes, eh, lass?'

He grabbed her tightly, pressing her body to his. When she

instinctively turned her head aside, he seized her hair, dragged her face round to his, kissed her hard, with brute sexuality, his lips, his gnawing teeth, on her mouth. She kept her own lips closed, did not struggle, the breath whistling through her nose. She was panting when he let her go. She slapped him hard with her open palm, on the right side of his face. His eyes blazed into hers. 'Feel better?' With equal brutality he pushed her back down onto the settee. 'Pull the door to when you leave. It's a Yale.'

She heard it crash shut, his ringing steps down the path, the click of the wooden gate. She was taking in great gulps of air, her heart pounding. She realized she was trembling violently, she could not have stood even if she tried. She didn't weep, sat there, staring at the lengthening bars of the sunlight on the patterns of the carpet.

CHAPTER EIGHT

Michael Porter watched Teddie bend and select a stone from the pebbled shoreline of the lake. She straightened, leaned back, kept her right arm low, her elbow jutting backwards, her forearm moving horizontally, to send the flat stone skimming low, then bouncing on the placid surface of the water. 'One! Two! Three! Four!' she crowed triumphantly.

Michael smothered his flash of embarrassment and irritation. 'Very good!' He nodded gallantly and was rewarded by the dazzling beam of the smile she flashed at him. He studied her lithe, thin figure in the pale blue sleeveless blouse, the long brown legs in the khaki shorts innocent of any cover. He noted the blacked-over scab on her knobbly left knee, where she had grazed herself on the gnarled bole of the tree they had climbed last week, their second day here at the Lakes. He remembered with pleasure how she had sat there in the grass, wincing and hissing with the stinging pain, but trustingly allowing him to dab at it with his handkerchief. He had felt protective and tender, aware of his year's seniority over her.

They had already got over that initial shyness of their first meeting, at Teddie's grandmother's at Hexham. He had to admit she was much more self-possessed about it. He had had very little to do with girls, apart from his sister, who had been an infant of five when he had last seen her, almost two years ago now. He was beginning to feel dismayed at the presence of this stranger, as tall as he was for all that she was a full year younger; disappointed after he had so looked forward to spending the coming weeks with Mr and Mrs Wright. Teddie – it was weird that she should have a boy's name, and that everyone should use it; even weirder that she should prefer it to her real name, Edwina, which he thought was very nice. He was afraid she was going to turn out to be a 'bossy-boots', but he soon realized that her chattiness and her readiness to take the initiative were only because she was making up for his own clumsy shyness. Also, to his private amazement, she wasn't concerned with 'girlie' things, like dressing-up, and hair, and keeping clean. In fact, she seemed more than glad to get out of her frocks and white ankle socks and buttoned-over shiny shoes, and get into shorts and blouses that were no fancier than his own school games kit. By the time they made the trip by train to Keswick, with Mr and Mrs Wright – 'Uncle John' and 'Aunty Jenny' to Teddie – they were firm friends.

Now, as they stood by the foreshore of Derwent Water, Michael was shocked at the extent of his feeling for her, and wondered if he could be 'falling' for her, whatever that might mean. He pushed away the crude definitions which that slimebag Lloyd and his ilk would use for it.

'I wish I didn't have to go back to Gran's,' he said, with sad and simple honesty. 'I wish I could stay with you – your uncle and aunt, till term starts.' He saw Teddie's face fill with compassion and her own genuine regret. Suddenly, his face was hot, he felt his eyes itching. Oh God! It felt just like it did when he was going to blub. He turned and bent hastily, searching for a flat stone again.

'So do I. I'll miss you. You *will* write, won't you? You won't forget when you get back with all your friends?'

94

He thought of Lloyd again, and some of the other seniors, if they found out he was writing to a girl. On the other hand, he would be proud for people to know. He'd want to show off a bit, it would increase his standing with lots of his chums. He assured her that he would. 'Every week. Maybe you could visit one Saturday? Or maybe I could come to Hexham on exeat.'

The exotic novelty of the Latin word struck her. 'Mind, you're dead lucky going to Beaconsfield.' Then she remembered Aunt Jenny telling her about Michael's parents, how they were out in India, and how worried for them he was. She knew there was some kind of war going on there, that India had ceased to be a part of the Empire a few weeks ago. Just last week there had been some news about killings, thousands, two different religions fighting over something. Maybe he wasn't so lucky after all. But she went on hastily, 'I mean, being at boarding school and every-thing. Learning so much.' She grinned at him, pulled her monkey face to make him laugh. 'Hey! Do you think they could teach me to talk posh like you do? Dead swanky! I'd love it!'

'You sound fine to me.'

She grimaced again. 'Get away! I don't suppose I could ever get rid of this Geordie twang. They'd just laugh at us if I did!' She thought of her own imminent return to school. Or, rather, her new school, for she was starting her secondary education in a week's time, at the Technical and Commercial College in Gateshead. She still felt the pain of her disappointment, even after three months, the day she had found that she had not passed to go to the grammar school. True, she had done well enough to go to 'Tech', and the family had congratulated her, but she knew they were as disappointed as she was. She had honestly believed she would succeed, for she had always done well at school, and was among the top five or six in the scholar-ship class for all the practice tests they did leading to the big day. And though there was a little knot of anxiety that she had to keep pushing away, she really thought she had done well enough, when the examination itself came, in the spring.

Life seemed suddenly to be giving her knocks. She felt ashamed at her selfishness for worrying about her own future when mam was seriously ill. And it was serious, she knew, in spite of all the reassurances the grown-ups gave her. She had been taken out of school early, missed all the leaving parties and the relaxation that came with the end of the school year. Sent over to Grandma Wright's, hardly saw her dad for weeks on end. She guessed he would be boozing more than ever, being on his own. She would have been able to look after him, and the house, she was sure, with help from Dora and Alice and Rose, but he wouldn't hear of it. Nobody took her seriously, she was just a kid. She wasn't even allowed to visit mam in the nursing home. The last time she had seen her was nearly two months ago, when they had taken her away in the late dusk, in the ambulance, and she hadn't even spoke to or looked at her. It hurt her deeply. But it must mean that her mam was really very ill, otherwise she was sure she would have insisted on seeing her somehow.

Perhaps it was that sense of abandoned loneliness which had helped her to strike up such a friendship with Michael. She knew he was shy, and she made a great effort, at first to make him feel at ease. They both got so much out of their relationship, she really would be deeply sorry to leave him. She hoped he meant what he said, that he would write, try to see her again. As for herself, she would do her best to see that she got to visit him at school, and that he could spend one of his free weekends with grandma at Hexham.

Her thoughts centred on her uncle and aunt. Once again, she felt despondent at the way the atmosphere of gloom seemed to settle and spread its influence over the whole family. She was ashamed to admit that the best part of the long holiday had been when Uncle John had been away, on some business connected

96

with this funny religion of his, and Aunt Jenny had them on her own. His coming back had had a deep effect on Aunt Jenny. She had been such good fun, organizing things, trips out on the bus, picnics at the lake near to town, games in the evening. Leaving them to play alone a lot of the time, even letting them spend ages in each other's rooms when they were ready for bed, until really late at night, and letting them sleep late in the morning.

There was a tension, a totally different atmosphere, when Uncle John came back. The grown-ups' faces were closed, something was seriously wrong. One night, after Teddie had retired to her own bed in the little room right in the front of the house, over the porch, she heard her aunt's voice raised, hard and bitter. It was clear they were quarrelling, and she had been tempted to creep out of bed, to try to hear what was being said. Then she had a sudden urge to creep back along the landing to Michael's room. She pictured slipping under the blankets, cuddling in to him, and suddenly she felt herself blushing in the dark, aware of how improper her imaginings were.

Now, her aunt and uncle were sitting high up on the slope of grass and bushes behind them, with those same closed, hard expressions on their faces. Michael must have noticed. 'Uncle John and Aunt Jenny are having a row about something. It's been going on since he came.' She scuffed gloomily at the cold pebbles with her toes. She thought of her mother and father, with those closed looks, the grim lines of their mouths. The way her dad used to snarl almost at her mam when he came back in the evening. 'Why do grown-ups always have to spoil things? Why can't they just enjoy themselves?'

'*I* wouldn't! Quarrel – I mean – with you. If . . .' he could feel the colour flood up into his face, there was nothing he could do about it. He couldn't think of anything to say, couldn't look away from her.

Suddenly, she felt a great tenderness well up, closing her

throat. She wanted to cry, to hug him tightly to her. 'You wouldn't dare! I'd bash you to smithereens! Come on! I'll race you to that jetty over there!' She set off, scampering, her heels digging crunchingly into the banked pebbles, but, instead of competing, she grabbed at his hand, clasped it tightly, and they raced along side by side, rejoicing in their lithe swiftness, in the wind streaming against them, and their togetherness in the early September sun.

John watched the distant running figures with nostalgic envy, and a deep, loving sadness. Weighed down by a sense of hopelessness, he nevertheless turned back to Jenny, returning to the bitter gulf that was dividing them. 'You shouldn't have done it, Jen. You had no right to interfere like that. Not after you'd carried a secret like that all these years. You don't know what trouble you've caused. Mam and Aunt I are devastated—'

She couldn't help herself, listened with appalling helplessness to the acid of her reply. 'Oh well! We can't have that, can we? Everything's got to be cosy at the Tea Cosy, no matter what happens!'

The colour appeared in his cheeks. 'It's Teddy's life as well as Marian's that's being mucked up! You should see the state he's in. Nobody can talk to him. I don't care how many people get to know about *our* private affairs, it's not that that matters—'

'That's not what you said when you came back from Palestine, was it? "Don't say anything to mam, or to anyone else",' she mimicked cruelly. 'You weren't so keen on letting people know about me and my wickedness then!'

'I'm not *keen* on it being broadcast now. But I didn't swear you to secrecy over it. It's always been up to you whether you told anyone or not. But this thing – this business with Marian. You didn't even see fit to share it with me. Your own husband!'

'My own sinned against and innocent husband!' Her voice cut

at him like a blade. 'Maybe I felt your new-found piety had made you too sensitive to take the shock of such terrible things!' She saw that wounded, vulnerable expression, and her eyes stung with tears. She loathed herself, yet could not control that deep compulsion to go on hurting.

'The family's shattered by it. Teddy went over to Aunt Julia's in a blind rage. Nearly set about her and Dora. They thought he was going to smash the place up. So they're all in an uproar. She's written an awful letter to mam, saying some terrible things – about the way she's brought us up. Says she never wants to see any of us again. You can imagine.' He paused. 'Did you not stop to think – about the knock-on effect you'd have? Poor Marian – it could set her back—'

'Oh no! I won't have that! That's not fair! Do you honestly think I did it just on a whim, or to get a cheap shot at Teddy or something? What the hell do you think caused Marian's break-down? She's been living in a private hell for the past four years. I hope to God she hasn't been tormented by the thought of me knowing. But your Aunt Julia, and that tarty girl of hers! Marian's been petrified, dreading they'd say something. If not to Teddy, then to your mother, just to knock her down a peg or two. That's what's brought her to this point. God! The poor girl almost got herself killed trying to have another child for that drunken brother of yours! She couldn't take any more. There was never any hope for her, for either of them—'

'It wasn't Aunt Julia *or* Dora, though, was it, who let the cat out of the bag? She was wrong to worry about *them* after all.'

'All right! It was me! Bitch Jenny! But can't you see? I've been trying to tell you. There's no way out of the mess Marian's in, if the truth doesn't come out. Not a hope in hell! Surely you can see that? Secrets. That's what destroys a relationship.'

'Ah! That's why ours has survived, is it? Because we don't have any secrets.'

She was startled at his untypically brutal sarcasm. It checked her own sense of rage, like a glass of cold water suddenly flung into her face. She was almost comforted by this proof of imperfection, of his inability to turn the other cheek entirely. There was more to come.

'I'm glad you're all for honesty,' he went on. 'I've decided to take a leaf out of your book. No more secrets, eh? I told Teddy. It wasn't the first time, your affair with Castleton. I told him about Horst Zettel. He was even more stunned, as you can imagine.'

She stared at him. To her own private amazement, she felt herself crimsoning, the hot blush of shame spreading from her neck, sweeping upward. She swallowed hard. 'Fair enough.' Her voice was quiet, a little tremulous. 'I'm sure that will only confirm what he already thought about me. He made it very plain.'

'Yes. He told me he'd behaved badly towards you. Perhaps you think I should have punched him on the nose?'

She shook her head. All the anger had gone from her. 'No,' she answered wearily. 'There's not many things worth fighting for in this world, and I'm certainly not one of them.' She stood up, brushed the crumbs from the lap of her shorts, and began to gather up the remnants of the picnic meal spread on the chequered cloth. John knelt up to help her.

'I hope you're right about Marian,' he said thoughtfully. He sighed. 'You probably are. She couldn't have gone on as they were, with all that pressure inside.' He turned to her, rested his hand on hers as she passed him one of the tin containers. 'It's just been such a blow – to all of us. I don't know how Teddy will come out of it, either.'

'You mean he might cut and run again?' She moved her hand, and he took the tin, stowed it away in the knapsack, their physical contact broken.

He shrugged. He stood, picked up the crumpled cloth, and

shook it before folding it and laying it on top of the food. He turned back to her, very close, and she kept still, wondering if he was going to try to touch her again, to take her hand in a franker embrace. 'You've never been one to shirk the truth.' He sounded almost grudging, but she knew how fair he was being, how hard he was striving to overcome his hurt and anger. 'Maybe it was needed, after all, however painful.'

She felt like crying again, at his effort to be generous, to understand her, and she felt the same confused emotions, of an aching, tender love, and a kind of helpless fury at his very gentleness, his willingness to take pain, to accept the hurt. She thought suddenly of his brother's brutal mouth on hers, the bruising grip of his fingers on her arms, the violence with which he had flung her down onto the cushions before slamming out of the room. Before John could reach out, which was what she thought he might do, she turned abruptly away and moved off towards the distant figures by the dazzling lake.

CHAPTER NINE

When Sara Arad and Bernard Lightman reached the kibbutz dining hall, it was already packed. Avi, the Youth Leader, was up on the stage at one end of the long room. The faint after-smell of the evening meal still hung on the air, and there were several crashes and rattles as the duty cooks were hastily finishing off the chores before switching off the lights in the kitchen. 'This is Major Gilbau, from the Organization. He's got some important news for all of us, before we break up into our sections.'

Sara felt that wave of irritation grow at the use of the word. The 'Organization'. That way of referring to the Haganah made it sound like the criminal band the outgoing British authorities still officially regarded it as. It annoyed her as much as all those code words in current usage to denote the arms being ferried secretly to the settlements. 'Plums' and 'cherries' were bullets. 'A load of pipes' meant a cache of rifles. It made their frantic efforts to ready themselves for war sound like a bunch of boys playing spy games. So, all right, there may still be a need for a certain amount of secrecy in these movements of arms, but there was precious little secret about the whole of the kibbutz turning out for this meeting with their regional commander. She was glad that, at last, the military was taking on a national structure. And not before time, for only a few days ago, at the end of November, the United Nations had finally voted for partition.

Celebrations had scarcely ended – the kibbutz had arranged a feast and a day out at the nearby beach, and many had travelled over to Tel Aviv, or made the short trip up the coast to Haifa, to join in the festivities there. She could understand the emotive response. It was truly a milestone. After two thousand years without a country, the Jewish nation had its home again. But, like everyone else, she knew that the state, which had yet to be born, would have to fight for every inch of territory, for its very survival, from the moment of its birth.

She sat holding Berni's hand in the dim hall while the major told them of the war footing on which they were now being placed. The field armies and the garrison armies, the Gadna, the youth battalions for those under eighteen. Even those still in the DP camps of Cyprus were in the process of being trained, with mock wooden rifles, in expectation that they would be in the front line as soon as they stepped off the boats. From early in the new year, on the UN recommendation, Haifa would become a 'free port', to allow immigrants unrestricted access to their new homeland.

And they would need every pair of hands capable of holding a weapon, Major Gilbau warned them. 'The war won't start with ultimatums and declarations. In some places it's begun already, as you well know. Isolated acts of terrorism – a grenade tossed into a taxi, shootings into cinema queues. And we respond. Of course we do. And we will. So that the Arabs will go screaming to their neighbours about our atrocities, and urge them to join in the holy war. Not only here. Already Jews have been attacked in Cairo and Alexandria. It's a big battlefield, and we've got to be ready. Now!'

Late that night, when they had finally done with the fiery section meetings which dealt with their own defensive preparations against an attack, Sara and Bemi, clad in sweaters for the damp December night, walked up through the animal sheds and the long, low rows of the poultry huts, towards the slight rise at the western edge of the settlement. Beyond the mesh fence, and the recently installed rolls of barbed wire on its other side, they could see the scrubby marshland, and the pale rise of dunes in the moonlight. A twinkling point of light showed, far away, in the thicker darkness that was the sea.

'Do you wish you were on that boat, Berni?' she asked him seriously. 'Getting the hell out of here?'

He turned, stared down at her. She could see his face in the moonlight. 'No,' he answered, equally solemn. 'No regrets about being where I am. It's what I've wanted since I was a kid.' Then his expression dissolved into its characteristic wide grin. 'Besides, how do you know it's getting out of here? It might be heading in, to Haifa.' She punched his arm, and they wrestled briefly before they kissed, and resumed their walk. 'Although I wouldn't mind taking a trip soon. Just a short break. With you. I'd like to take you back to England.' He just stopped himself in time from saying 'home'.

'Why?'

'I'd like you to meet the family. Mum and dad. The rest of the tribe.' He paused, to pluck up courage to say it. 'I'd like to make you one of them.'

Sara stopped, genuinely startled by his proposal. And deeply moved. She felt the start of tears, blurring her vision, and she blinked rapidly. Her heart was thudding. She gave a kind of nervous giggle. 'This is so sudden. We haven't – it hasn't been very long. I'm not even pregnant,' she joked gamely.

They were facing each other, standing in the middle of the path. He had his arms round her, his hands in the small of her back, holding her into him. 'You know how I've felt about you for a heck of a long time. I was just too scared to approach you. Sara

Arad. The formidable founder member. One of the élite. Anyway, now we are – you know.' He nodded down towards their conjoined bodies, in delicate indication of their physical relationship. 'And I'd like very much for you to marry me? Will you, Sara?'

Again that breathless giggle. 'Are you fed up of living in sin? You might get sick of me if I – was so readily available, whenever you want—'

He groaned softly, thrust himself into her. 'It would be nice to wake up in the same bed every morning—'

'With the same person. Are you sure?'

'I want you, Sara. I want you to be my wife. Say yes.'

She gave up her attempts at lightheartedness. 'Do you think this is a good time? Don't you think we should wait to see what's going to happen? Whether we'll even have a future?'

'No!' he said fiercely. 'We've got to believe in it, not wait and see! That's the whole point! Look. I'll marry you here, if you like. You know how quick we can arrange things. If you'd rather. It's just – I would like you to meet mum and dad. And my sisters. Let them share in it all. But whatever – will you marry me, Sara? Anywhere?'

For an instant, she was very afraid – of the danger facing all of them, of the commitment, of the loss of the independence she had built around herself after the loss of her immediate family, of the whole area of personal hurt she would be laying herself open to once more, the opening of the tender wound she had healed over herself. Then she thought of his goodness, his kindness, the happiness they shared, the joy of being lovers that he brought her. He had scarcely ever told her he loved her, but she knew he did. And she loved him, too. It was almost hard for her to admit it, but it was true. Not since Carl had left, nearly three years ago, had she felt as close to anyone as this. Maybe he was right. They shouldn't wait and see. Maybe they should act on their impulses, while they were still able to do so. She nodded, smiling, the tears glinting on her eyelashes.

May sighed with exasperation and tried to restrain the anger she could feel rising inside. 'You know it makes sense, Teddy. You don't want to hold the girl back. It's a golden opportunity for her. She's bright, she'll benefit from it. And she wants it. Surely that's good enough, isn't it?'

The set expression on Teddy's ruddy features declared his stubbornness. 'Aye, she thinks she does, at the moment. If you ask me, that's because of the daft notions John and Jenny, and all of you, have been putting in her head.' He nodded through the lace of the cottage windows to the louring sky, and to the muddy lawn where Teddie and Michael Porter were playing together. 'And because of her mixing with the likes of that lad out there. He's nice enough, but he's a real toff, isn't he? Folks in India—'

'Oh, for God's sake, Teddy!' Iris interrupted scornfully. Her features, too, were florid, her colour heightened because she was very well aware that she was part of the 'all of you' Teddy had flung in accusation. 'Don't be such an inverted snob! It's something your ma and I want to do for her, when it will do most good. Better than hanging on, making her wait till we're dead before she can get any benefit from our money.' She boomed with laughter, trying to dispel some of the growing tension. 'Good God! We might both live till we're octogenarians and she'd be forty before she sees a penny!'

'How can you be sure she'd be accepted, anyway? I thought they had to sit some kind of entrance exam? What if they wouldn't have her? It's not like she's from blue blood, is it? Her dad a draughtsman at the shipyard. Not quite your aristocracy!'

His gaze held Iris with steady challenge, but she met it squarely. 'Well, I can always fling my "Honourable" at them, even if I'm not blood related. But there's no need to worry. She'll sail through the entrance test colours flying. John can give her a bit of coaching, just to make abso-bloody-lutely certain. Come on! She'll love it. And it's easy for her to travel in from here. The train's full of Convent High girls—'

'Well, looks like you've got it all worked out then, doesn't it? She's going to think even less of me now if I start playing the heavy parent and saying no.'

The anger flowed out of May like water from a sink at the hopeless bitterness she heard in her son's tone. She wanted to go over and fling her arms round him, squeeze him tightly to her. 'You're her father, Teddy. It's entirely up to you what happens. And Marian, of course. If she's fit to make such decisions. We only want to do what's best – for you, as well as for Teddie. I'm sure you know that.'

He sighed. His voice was bleak. 'I hardly ever see her as it is. She's more at home here than she is at Low Fell now.'

'You're always welcome here, Teddy.' May's voice quavered with her emotion. 'It's your home, if ever you need it. Always will be. You can move back in here tomorrow – today, if you want to. Stay as long as you like.'

His mind filled nostalgically with the memories of cosy comfort, the warm, happy times he and John had known as they grew up here. Meals cooked, clean linen – he pushed away the temptingly rosy picture. He cleared his throat. 'I suppose – the money that comes through from Grandma Wright's will – we could use that for the school fees. It should be cleared any day now—'

'Don't be daft, Teddy!' his mother said. 'You don't know what you'll need that for.' He knew she was thinking of what lay ahead for Marian, who, after six months, was still a patient in Winyard House. 'First thing is to pay off the rest of the mortgage, then see how you go on from there.'

How indeed? Teddy wondered grimly. Any day now, they were

going to tell him that Marian was fit to be discharged, that any further treatment she might need could be administered at the outpatient clinics. Already she was allowed out regularly during the week, and had spent several weekends on release. Dr Hennessy had hinted that it was Marian's own unwillingness to take the decisive step back into the outside world which was holding her back. Teddy strongly suspected that if she had remained in a local authority hospital she would have been tossed out weeks ago, in spite of the new National Health Act Nye Bevan was still struggling to bring through Parliament. The private sector was far more genteel and lenient, as long as their bills were being met.

And now his mother and Aunt I were aiming to drag him into further indebtedness to them, by paying for Teddie to become a day pupil at the prestigious Convent High School, in the city. It made sense. Of course it did, not only for his daughter herself, but also because of the uncertainty that lay ahead for their home life.

When he awoke, late and badly hung-over, the day after Jenny had delivered her bombshell to him, he had been very strongly tempted to grab a bag, stuff some clothes in it, and head off, anywhere. It was perhaps as well that he was too ill to make such a move. It took him several more hours to rise and make his shivering way downstairs, to grope for the kettle and the teapot in the silent kitchen. He was certainly glad then that Teddie was still away, staying over at his mother's. Finally, he managed to wash and shave and get dressed. He went up to the George. His hand was still shaking as he lifted the first pint, and, for a second or two, the smell and the first taste of the cold bitter made him nauseated, then it was down, and he was better, except that his need now, and a desperate one, was for yet another beer.

He moved on to the club next door; came out to a cool, cloudy night, much later. He had purchased a bottle of whisky, put it in his coat pocket. He concentrated on the short walk home, talking and singing softly to himself all the way. His sudden urge to start roaring out the old army songs at the top of his voice when he met the closed curtains and lamp-lit respectability of the Chow Dene estate was almost irresistible. He sniggered softly to himself at the notion. But as he stood swaying on the top step, and made to stab at the front door lock with his key, he felt a great reluctance to enter the lonely silence of the house; so great that he hesitated, looking up at the night sky. Through dark clouds, he saw a few stars.

His mind went back to the foreign warmth and the immensity of a star-filled Spanish night, the dark eyes and gypsy features of the Irish girl, Rosie Connelly. He remembered the paleness of her breasts and body, in contrast to the dark tan of her limbs as she scrambled out of her clothes, reached out for him with her hand, pulled him towards that black water . . .

Once inside the house, curtains drawn, he quickly scrunched up newspaper in the gate, flung a few sticks on top, then went out to the chill of the shed that ran alongside the kitchen to bring a shovel of coal from the coalhouse. He laid the pieces carefully on the sticks, lit the paper, held a sheet across the front of the chimney breast as a blazer, until the sticks crackled and the new fire roared and the sheet he was holding stretched tight began to scorch. He crushed it, and flung it in the flames. He sat on the rug, huddled, staring into the fire, savouring its heat, until the hardness of the bottle in his pocket brought him to awareness, and he eased himself up, slipped off his coat, unscrewed the cap from the bottle.

He was struggling to absorb the fact of Marian's unfaithfulness. All the time, all that arid loneliness and enforced celibacy of the POW camp, when he had been tormented with remorse for his own past failures towards her, she had been betraying him, with this bastard stranger, this Jim Moody. The irony of it kept coming home to him, as the level of the whisky dropped. Every now and then he would give a quick shake of his head, and a bark of harsh laughter, staring into the glowing coals. Where had they done it? Up there, in the room and the bed where she had tearfully welcomed him back into her arms, into her body? Here? On the rug, in the flickering warmth of the fire, at it, writhing, while Teddie slept above? His grip on the glass tightened. He stopped himself from hurling it into the hearth. He'd only have to pick up the shattered pieces.

And Jenny. Smooth, smart, cool, cocky, superior Jenny! She was at it, too, with some bloody pongo – an officer, of course! While John was risking his life out in the desert. What a laugh! What a meaningless shambles of a maniacal laugh! The Wright Brothers! Famous as their American namesakes! Famous for their wives' bitch-on-heat infidelity! Above and beyond the call.

He got up once, to fetch more coal from the back, more steadily sober than ever, despite the bottle being half-empty. Or, thank God, half-full! It all depends on how you look at it. But how do you look at a wife who's carried another man's bastard inside her, and killed it, and now can't have any more? And who's cracked up because of it? Welcome her back, his own arms open? Like brother Johnny? Love thine enemy? Do good unto them that despise you? Christ, no! He couldn't do that. Couldn't lower himself.

It pained him to realize there was no one with whom he was close enough to talk to about any of this. Discounting family, of course, who were too close. He had never felt more alone. All at once, he remembered the endless circuits round the dusty track of the German compound; the sparse tufts of grass beside the hut where they would sprawl in summer, and he would get out the photos, pass them over, read bits of the precious letters to Young-un. He found himself moving to the writing bureau,

110

taking out a pad and pen, sitting at the table, writing Tony Ellis's name, his number, the prison address at the head of the paper.

Next day at work he asked to leave early, managed to hold in his anger at the chief draughtsman's churlish reluctance as he granted the request. At Winyard House, he had to wait three quarters of an hour, though he had telephoned ahead to make an appointment to see Dr Hennessy. 'I know what's behind Marian's breakdown,' he announced bluntly, as soon as he was seated in front of the doctor's desk. He told him, equally bluntly. The doctor looked uncomfortable, irritated even, and Teddy wondered if he felt cheated somehow that he had not got to the crux of the problem for himself.

'Don't confront her with it right now,' Hennessy advised. 'Give us a chance to prepare her a little.'

'How? You mean *you* want to tell her?'

'If you wouldn't mind, Mr Wright. I know it must be an awful shock for you. Not easy. But we've got to know her. I think she trusts us here. I could—'

'I don't know if I can hide it. She'll know something's wrong.'

'Please, Mr Wright. Try. She's made a lot of progress. This might do all kinds of damage.'

It hasn't done *me* any good, either! Teddy thought angrily. But somehow he managed. Maybe Marian just thought his surly uncommunicativeness was normal. 'I mightn't be able to get in during the week,' he told her. 'Panic on in the office. Overtime every night for a while.' Then Dr Hennessy sent him a letter, asking him to postpone visiting for a further week. Marian had been told what had happened. Meanwhile, following Teddy's raging visit to his Aunt Julia's, her letter to his mother arrived, and the family was caught in a maelstrom of violent emotions.

It was almost a relief, even though Teddy's nerves were tautly stretched, when he finally faced Marian. Her eyes were puffed and red, she had clearly done a lot of weeping, but she was calm enough, at least on the surface. But the look she gave him was of such sadness he could not help but feel her pain, to take it in with his own. He noticed how stolid and unappealing she looked. He had not seen her for over two weeks. Her face was fleshy, unhealthily pouched, her body's plumpness bordering on fatness now. Her hair, neat and clean enough, was styled and cut in a kind of girlish, inappropriate way he found very unattractive. The cardigan and pale, striped, buttoned dress had a dull, institutionalized air. The nails of her right hand, which lay with its companion in her lap, the fingers picking and twisting, were short and bitten down.

'I'm really sorry, Teddy,' she said breathlessly, like a child being forced to apologize for a minor infringement. 'I should have told you.' The pathos of her understatement left him groping for an answer. 'You'll be wanting a divorce, I expect.'

'Whoa!' he said hoarsely. 'Slow down, lass. It's early days. Let's get you out of here first. Let's not rush into anything.'

'Does everybody know about – what I did?' Her voice trembled.

'A few. Mam. Aunt I. John.'

She nodded. Her lip trembled, too, now, but her words surprised him. 'Good. I'm glad. It's better that they know.'

And oddly, frustratingly for Teddy, more and more, in the weeks that followed, this great tragedy in their lives was once more gently put to one side, eased out of their conversation, though never out of their minds. Even with his daughter, it was never referred to. Ashamed as he was, Teddy could never find the courage to find out how much, if anything, she knew.

But it couldn't go on. As he sat months later in the December dusk of afternoon, in his mother's house, discussing Teddie's future, reluctantly acquiescing in their plans for her to stay in Hexham and to attend the private school in Newcastle, he felt that, with the end of this bleak year, only the second of peace, something concrete, some momentum, must be given to his life, to end this helpless, lonely sense of stagnation, even though he had little idea of what the outcome would be.

CHAPTER TEN

'Porter loves her hands and face,
Her eyes and long dark hair,
But best of all in bed at night
He loves his Teddie bare!'

Roger Lloyd and his three friends snorted with laughter. 'Get
it, Porter? B-a-r-e. Teddie bare!'

'Shut your mouth, you slime bag!'

'Oh-ho! Don't tell me you've never done her, Porter? All those
cosy weekends you spend together? When old Wrighty and Juicy
Jen are tucked up and at it hammer and tongs? Mean to say you
don't creep along to Teddie's room and slip her—'

'Filthy sod!' Crimson faced, Michael launched himself at his
chief tormentor, who was caught napping by the sudden violence
of the response. His fear entirely overcome, Michael rejoiced
savagely in the grip of his clawing fingers on Lloyd's blazer, and
the ease with which he swung the heavier figure round and
dragged him to the ground. He tucked his chin down and began
punching frantically, getting in a barrage of blows, deeply satisfied at the feel of the first of them smashing into the startled
features, the yelp of pain. He clung on, pressing his body over
the buffeting form under him, his hands now settling on the
neck, seizing the tie, throttling as hard as he could.

He was weeping now, but so was Lloyd, who eventually succeeded in rolling away, squirming out from under the transformed boy. 'You bastard!' sobbed Lloyd, coming back at him as they both scrambled to their feet, swinging his own punches now, battering at Michael's raised arms and shoulders. Belatedly, Lloyd's two cronies joined in. One of them tripped Michael, kicking at his feet from behind, and he went down again. This time, he was the one trapped beneath his opponent's weight. Lloyd's knees drove crushingly into his ribs and midriff. Desperately, still transported with his righteous fury, Michael reached up, got his fingers into that red, open face, and raked, and his enemy reared back, with another squeal of pain. 'You – fight fair, you dirty little nigger lover!'

Lloyd's crude reference was to the fact that Michael had spent most of his infancy in India, that his family was still out there. Just a couple of months ago, with the assassination of Mahatma Gandhi, there had been more rioting, hundreds of deaths. Lloyd had gone on and on about it, with that relentless cruelty which baffled as well as sickened Michael. His anger welled up again at the torment he had endured. To hell with the rules of fair play! Lloyd's hands had gone up to protect his face, and his weight was withdrawn. Michael twisted free and jabbed out with all his force. His heels crashed into Lloyd's belly and bowled him over on to his back, cutting off his bellows of protest. The two henchmen fell back, alarmed at the untypical wildness of the attack, and Michael scrambled to his feet again, weeping, but filled with a murderous desire to charge in, fists and boots flailing.

A fierce grip on his collar and a force which lifted him off his feet and shook him like a rat caught by a terrier, cleared the mists of rage. Mr Fallon gave him another shake, and dumped him down. 'What do you think you're doing? Pack it in!'

Roger Lloyd was getting to his feet, doubled-over, still half-winded. 'He – he scratched me, sir! Clawed my face. Kicked me!'

'*I'll* kick you if you don't shut that row. Get along to the staff room, the pair of you. You're on detention, right away!'

As they both stood in the hallway, at the foot of the wide staircase, Lloyd wiped at his tear and dirt-stained face, and tried to rearrange his shattered dignity as he straightened his ruined tie and unbuttoned shirt. 'I'll get you for this!' he promised, in a venomous whisper.

Michael felt light-headed. He had surprised himself. He felt proud, imagined himself as a noble knight, bloodied but valiant, defending his lady's honour. 'You come near me or talk any more of your filth in front of me, and I'll kill you,' he said simply. Lloyd's face closed in an evil scowl, but he did not answer, and stared down at his muddy shoes.

He would, too, Michael vowed. Teddie had come to visit that afternoon. She wore her school uniform, the brown blazer over the brown gymslip, the brown woollen stockings, brown shoes. The grey brimmed hat, with the thin bands of black and yellow on the ribbon. 'You look great,' he told her, and had noticed her cheeks turn pink.

'Grandma and Aunt I made me wear it.'

'I like it,' he assured her again. She came quite often, on a Saturday or Sunday. The boys were quite used to seeing her, she knew a lot of them by sight and by name. They hovered around, wanting the chance to talk to her. He was proud of the way she was able to chat, her friendly manner, and also a little nervous, and jealous, making sure they got away on their own as soon as he decently could. Not that she ever gave him cause to be jealous. She always made it perfectly plain that he was her special friend, that she had come to see him, as well as her aunt and uncle. That was why Lloyd was so narked. He, and a few more of the senior form, thought they were God's gift, looking sneeringly down from the height of their thirteen-year-old superiority. Thank goodness that, after the summer, they would be gone, off to their public schools. Then, from September, Michael himself would be among the élite seniors, with Common Entrance looming on the horizon. His last year at Beaconsfield.

He hoped Teddie would still want to keep in touch with him. She had come to mean a great deal, his best friend, far closer than anyone here at school. And she was a girl! This had amazed him at first, then delighted him, as they learned more and more about each other. Far from inhibiting their relationship, it seemed to him it was an added bonus. They could talk about so much, feel so close to one another, were so sympathetic in so many ways. He only hoped she wouldn't change as she grew up. His very limited experience of older sisters of school chums, and his own cousins, had given him an unfavourable impression of girls in their teens.

He felt himself wanting to smile as he recalled how apprehensive Teddie had been at Christmas about starting her new school. 'I bet they'll all be terrible snobs,' she confessed. 'I wish I could talk nice, like you do, and Aunt Jenny. And Uncle John. It's queer, isn't it? Even Grandma speaks real nice – and yet my dad's a real Geordie. Like me.' She pulled a humorous face. 'Uncle John and Aunt Jen have been giving me some elocution lessons. "George ought to swallow four quarts of warm water every morning!" ' She dragged out the greatly lengthened vowels, and sniggered self-consciously. 'The'll nivver larn us to taak proper, man!'

'You'll be fine.' And she *had* been, was settling in after a term there, playing hockey for her house, and able to laugh, and make him laugh, too, with her accounts of some of the more pretentious of her schoolmates.

He thought again, with wonder, of the way he had gone for Lloyd. He could visualize her grin, her wholehearted approval of his all-out attack, if she had known of it. His face grew hot once more as he recalled Lloyd's filthy rhyme, his sniggering sexual references to Teddie and, just as bad, to Mrs Wright. Michael had never sullied his friendship with Teddie by thoughts like that. It sickened him to hear Lloyd's foul desecration ... but then a burning shame consumed Michael, the pain of his guilty secret gnawing at him, when he thought of Teddie's aunt.

Powerless against his own lust, no matter how hard he strove to banish it, he could hardly ever think of Mrs Wright *without* sexual feelings stealing in upon him. Jenny. Even the mental use of her Christian name was an unforgivable familiarity. Just the whiff of her scent was enough to start that strange tingling heat all over his body, that secret, shameful beat in his loins. She was so wonderful and kind to him, so understanding. How could he be so gross, so stained as to think of her in that way? But, helplessly, he dwelt on her physical beauty, her rounded breasts, the silk clad legs, the shape of her in those dark slacks she wore. And now even in his sleep his thoughts were shockingly evil. Twice he had woken, horrified at his unspeakable fantasies and the worse shame of his aching, straining body, the sticky wetness on his pyjamas and sheet the stigmata of his sin. He must be really sick, inside his head. But how could he ever tell anyone of a sickness like that? Even his true and loyal friend, Teddie – she least of all, for he knew how much she doted on her aunt – she would be aghast at his perversity.

An hour later, after punishment had been assigned for the following day, he found himself facing the object of his illicit passion and innocent adulation when Jenny sought him out after hearing of the fight from her colleague. 'Come on up to the flat. John's out this evening. He won't be back till late.' She put her hand on his shoulder, and he felt the heat spreading over him. John. He almost wished she wouldn't be so friendly, so relaxed, like she always was when they were away from school, or, like now, on their own. And he almost wished – but not quite – that she wouldn't touch him the way she often did, as now, when she patted the settee, which was only just big enough for the two of them, and sat with her arm draped round him again. 'Come on, now. Tell me what's been going on between you and Lloyd. Mr Fallon said you told him you started it. You went for Lloyd. He's got scratches on his face.'

Michael blushed. 'He's bigger than me, miss. I had to – I—' he sighed, gave up. 'Yes, it was me that started it.'

'Why? What did he do? Was he bullying? Picking on you?' He shrugged, she felt the movement of the thin shoulders under her hand. 'Was it about your family again? Teasing you about them?'

'Yes. That – and other things,' he went on reluctantly, uncertain why he had spoken.

'What other things?' She waited. 'I'm asking as a friend. Between us. We're good friends, aren't we? It won't go any further. Not even John, if you don't want me to.' Again she waited, glancing sideways at him. He was slumped, his hands loosely linked between his slack, bare knees, the fingers twisting. 'Was it about this afternoon? Something to do with Teddie being here?' She felt him start, knew she had touched the nerve, felt a sweet impulse to smile and hug him to her. 'Is he jealous? Did he say some rotten – nasty things?'

The red, tragic face turned to her, the mouth open in surprise, so obvious and innocent that again she wanted to hold him to her. He was floundering. 'Well – yes, he – was being rude—'

'About Teddie and you?'

All at once, to his horror, the tears flowed, gushed hotly out of him, he was sobbing, his entire body racked with grief. 'Please – don't say anything – don't tell anyone –' Juicy Jen. Juicy Jen. The evil phrase rang over and over in his head. Now Jenny *did* squeeze him, hugged him tightly to her, held his shaking body, felt the wetness of his tears on her blouse, the hot face pressing into her breast. Her fingers spread on the back of his hair, holding him to her, closer still, embracing and gently moving in a rocking motion while he wept abandonedly.

119

'Isn't it nice to have the place to ourselves for a bit?' May smiled tiredly across at Iris as she lowered herself into the depths of the armchair and raised her feet on to the leather pouffe. She kicked off her slippers, waggled her stockinged toes.

Iris pushed the dark rimmed glasses up on her broad forehead. 'You look tired, love. Are you all right?'

May nodded. 'Just old age, my love.'

'Get away, you young sprog. I wish *I* was fifty-three again.'

'Fifty-four in a few months. And don't come the old crone! You're only two years older.' The pain in her arms was easing now, though they still felt heavy. She let them hang on the wide arms of the chair, tried to relax her muscles, to breathe evenly, deeply. She strove to will away the fear, whose edges were fluttering shadow-like in her mind. She remembered her mother's symptoms, which had been there, warning her for several years before she died at sixty-two. May had been with her when she died, in the hospital in Gateshead. She would never forget that intense, burning look, the agonized expression and fierce grip, which only death could relieve. She must go to the doctor. She had felt twinges before; breathlessness, tightness at her chest, the ache in her arm. It was no good putting it off. It was twelve years now since her mother had died. There were probably all kinds of new medicines available now. And she had had nowhere near the hard life Robina had led, bringing up five children in the cramped conditions of Sidney Terrace.

In fact, her own life was seen as the lap of luxury by some folk, she reflected. She thought of her sister's bitterness towards her. Although it was getting on for a year since she had received it, the letter Julia had written to her revealing the truth about Marian was still etched deeply in her consciousness . . . *you with your swanky house and your motors and your posh girlfriend and your servants* . . . Ruby would be spitting mad to hear herself described as a servant. 'Help', 'treasure', were much nearer the mark, and ever ready to give her opinion, whether called for or not.

It had been a great shock, and a hurt, too, to think of all that happening without her knowing the slightest thing about it. The infidelity, the abortion. She could imagine the loneliness and the pain Marian must have suffered, keeping it all to herself, terrified that Julia or Dora would let slip the secret which had eaten away at her nerves for so long. It had surprised May that the secret *had* been kept all that time. Reluctantly, she had to admit to an admiration for Julia and her daughter for not betraying Marian's trust – and, she supposed, for being on hand to provide the practical help and solution to the problem the distraught girl faced. With painful honesty, May doubted if she could have given that support herself – but then, what mother *would* forgive the breaking of the sanctity of her son's marriage under such circumstances?

She had even made the effort to heal something of the breach between herself and Julia, driving over there not long before Christmas, when Marian was due to be discharged from Winyard House. Iris had insisted on accompanying her, even though May had volunteered to travel out to the pit village on the bus. 'Nonsense! Dear Julia's had plenty to say about me. You know what she thinks about us.' Iris did not fail to observe the pinking of May's features even now at her reference. 'Mind you, I give you warning, I might well be tempted to clock her one if she starts on that tack again.'

She didn't, but the meeting was far from a success from the point of view of a reconciliation. 'I know you did what you thought was best,' May offered. 'What's done is done. The main thing is to see that Marian's all right. I know how much she relied on you when – while Teddy was away. You and Dora. I'm sure she'd like to see you – to carry on, as friends. Whatever Teddy said – he was upset, badly hurt, you must understand that. But, well, Marian will need help, in all sorts of ways. And you're near to her. You could look in, during the day—'

'When Master Teddy's not around to chuck us out, you mean?'

'Well, I don't know what Marian will be like at coping. With even ordinary things. The house, shopping.'

'Hah! I get it! You mean it's OK for me and our Dora to come round skivvying for her, is that it? Mebbes you could send your maid over to clean for her, if youse two don't fancy getting your hands mucky!'

'Still as understanding as ever, I see,' Iris intervened crisply. 'Come on, old girl. Time we were off. No point wasting our time here.'

'Listen, you!'

'No! *You* listen, for a change! You were a thankless, lazy young baggage years ago when May gave you your chance at the Tea Cosy, so don't go on about skivvying to us!' She glanced significantly around the cluttered, untidy room of the cottage. 'And from the look of it, marriage and children have merely reinforced your natural inclination!'

Julia was spluttering inarticulately as they left. 'I'm sorry,' Iris muttered grimly, 'but that woman really gets under my skin!' She glanced a little sheepishly across at May, but her friend was leaning back, shaking with laughter, in which she presently joined, until their eyes were streaming.

CHAPTER ELEVEN

Jenny edged past John, coming close to the mirror over the mantelpiece, and made a fractional adjustment to the small hat perched on top of her newly styled, shining hair. She slightly increased the rakish tilt of the raised wing towards her left eyebrow, and with her fingertips fluffed up the wisp of veil, touched the pale pink blossom beneath it. 'How's that?' she asked, gazing at herself critically. 'Not too much make-up?'

'You look beautiful.' John took hold of her arms, below the short sleeves of the dark, polka-dotted silk dress. He held her lightly, felt her resistance, that start which presaged the quick, embarrassed turning away from this unlooked-for intimacy. He refused to let her go, and she stood very still, her eyes flickering to his, then down.

'Not like the tart I really am?' She smiled, striving for the light jokiness she failed to achieve.

'You could never be that, no matter how hard you tried.'

'Oh, I dunno.' She gave another breathy laugh. Now, she moved again, politely, against his pressure, and he had to let her go. 'The car will be here any minute. Are you ready?' She moved round him, reached for her short jacket and her shoulder bag, the thin gloves. 'Listen. Have you had your chat with Michael yet?'

She had told him soon after Michael's fight with Roger Lloyd about the boy's tearful outburst, his confession of the reason for the fight. 'He's reached that age now, John. He needs the man-to-man bit. Help him to understand what's happening. Or going to happen. He ought to know.' It had taken a lot more prodding before John could be stirred to action. 'I'll tell him myself,' she had threatened. 'Think how mortified the poor lamb will be!'

Now, as they made their way down the stairs towards the front entrance, John nodded. 'Yes, we had our chat.'

'Well? How was it? Did it go all right?'

John chuckled. 'I guess so. We were both embarrassed as hell. He had an idea about most of it. One or two things a bit mixed up, though. For goodness' sake, don't ever let on you know, will you? About our talk? He'd probably run away and never be seen again!'

'Don't be daft! I'm not *that* thick!' They stood at the top of the steps, gazing down the curving drive, waiting for the vehicle to come into sight. She went on thoughtfully, 'I wonder if anyone's doing the same for Teddie? Poor kid. She'll be starting the curse any time now. I can't imagine Marian telling her much, can you? And as for her dad!' She laughed scornfully. 'He'd be shocked rigid at the very idea. "That's a lass's job!" '

Though John grinned at the exaggerated impersonation of his brother's gruff speech, he couldn't help feeling that such an atti-tude would be fair enough. Surely Jenny didn't imagine a father should talk to his daughter about the mysteries of sex? John's own stilted talk with the blushing Porter had been difficult enough, brief though it was. Suddenly the unkindly disloyal thought came to him that his wife might be ready enough to deal with the sexual problems concerned with adolescence, but she was far less ready to face up to the physical problems within their own marriage. But then so was he, he admitted, ashamedly. They had let things slide, for months now, in spite of his constant

124

resolves that he would do something, would sort out the sterile mockery of their private life.

With relief, he saw Uncle David's elegant Humber approaching. Determinedly, he pushed his gloomy thoughts to one side. He would not let them intrude on the happiness of the day. They were going to the wedding of Sara Arad and her fiancé, a fellow inmate of her kibbutz, a British Jew whose family were all over here. They lived in Sale, which was where Uncle David and Aunt Cissy were taking them for the ceremony, and for an overnight stay in a hotel. The drastic petrol rationing, which rendered John's small sports car almost permanently immobile, was no deterrent to David Golding, who obtained supplies for his business interests.

John had been delighted at the prospect of seeing Sara again, after a gap of four years. 'You'll like her,' he had told Jenny enthusiastically. However, he was not surprised when Jenny declared that she did not want to attend the wedding. He knew why.

'I'm sick of it!' she said bitterly. 'Every time I meet up with one of your bloody family, I'm wondering, "Do they know?" I hate it. I feel such a fraud.'

'Look, you know by now Teddy hasn't said a word. As for Marian, the poor girl's probably forgotten about it. And she won't say anything, anyway. Teddy will have told her not to.'

'Not like me, eh? The original big blabbermouth!' Her voice shook. She blew her cigarette smoke at him like a weapon. 'I suppose I'm being paid back. I know how Marian must have felt, waiting for one of us to open our mouths. I wish they all knew! Especially your mother! We should have told her!' But he guessed she was more relieved than angry at his urging that they should remain silent.

Now, his hypersensitivity detected the faint colouring beneath her flawless make-up, the deceptive front of Jenny's breezy manner towards his aunt and uncle. Cissy, glamorous in her summery outfit, was already sitting in the back, and Jenny climbed in beside her, while John got into the front passenger seat. 'We'll stop at a roadhouse for some lunch,' Cissy announced after greeting them. 'The ceremony's not until this evening. There's something at the synagogue first, but that's strictly for the chosen ones.' She laughed dismissively. 'Though I guess they'd let you in on that, wouldn't they, David? Even though you're lapsed. He's got his little hat, you know,' she chuckled tauntingly. 'Those skullcap things they pin on.'

Soon the women were chatting and laughing in private conversation, and John and his uncle talked together. 'I think the groom's family were hoping that Sara and Bernard could be persuaded to stay over here. Not to return to Palestine. But Sara's absolutely determined to get back as soon as they can. They're all just waiting for the balloon to go up. She says they're all ready for it. They've been training for months. All the settlements are armed.' He shook his head. 'God knows how they'll manage, though. Half of them are in the proposed Arab territories.'

The evening reception was in the ballroom of a hotel on the outskirts of the city of Manchester. The wedding had actually taken place already, but for the two hundred and more guests, the *choopah*, the wedding canopy, was erected again, and the glasses, wrapped in paper, were resoundingly crunched underfoot by Bernard. '*Mazel tov!*' The cries rang out, everyone shook hands, hugged, the band struck up the music for the bridal dance. Sara looked blooming, John thought, her full figure voluptuously desirable in the frothy white wedding gown, as she led the bridesmaids and other friends on to the dance floor.

'My God!' Jenny's voice breathed in his ear. 'You never let on she was such a dish! She's *gorgeous!*'

John had not had a chance to get near, let alone talk to her, but later she came sweeping along to their table, still in her flowing lacy finery. Her tanned face and shoulders looked even exotically darker against the whiteness of the dress. 'John. It's lovely to see you again. Thank you for coming.' He stood, and she embraced him, her lips brushed his cheek, her arms were around his shoulders. 'At last I get to meet you, Jenny.' Jenny stood also, and they hugged lightly, their cheeks brushing in fleeting contact. 'I heard so much about you. I remember how proud John was. He showed me your photograph. In your navy uniform. Please. Tonight I dance with all my friends. May I?' Jenny smiled, nodded as Sara took John's hand, led him towards the crowded dance floor.

Her dark eyes shone as she gazed at him, while they shuffled, holding each other in the crowded anonymity. 'I was never good at this modern dance,' she smiled. 'So, my dear friend. How are you? Is everything good for you?'

He nodded, turned aside her enquiry. 'It is for *you*, I can see that. He's a very fortunate man, your Bernard.' He paused, then said, with almost abrupt awkwardness, 'Are you going back? Can't you stay a while? In England? We'd love to have you – show you where we live.'

He felt her hands press more tightly on his shoulders, drawing him even closer, so that he was staring down at the deep divide of those brown breasts, the cleavage of the tightly fitted satin bodice. He forced his gaze away, upward, to her eyes. 'Not you, too.' She was smiling, but he could see the seriousness behind her gaze. 'Berni's parents. Everyone is putting pressure on us. Even your uncle.' Her hands pressed, she leaned even closer against him. 'I have to, John. You remember. You know what it is like. I have to. It's our home. Soon we will be fighting for it. Our own homeland. I belong there.'

He told her then about Haifa, about the simple shrine on Carmel, about his discovery of faith. 'I hope I'll get back there one day. Soon.'

She nodded, her dark eyes holding him. He was startled at the warmth and compassion he could see there. He felt as though she could see into his inner mind, the sadness. 'You will, I am sure of it. We will walk on the mountain again, yes?' Her lips were shining, full. They moved to his, touched, and they kissed, holding each other for a long, private moment in the dimness of the shapes all around them.

When John came back along the corridor from the bathroom, Jenny was still lying across the foot of one of the twin beds in their comfortable hotel room. She was lying flat on her back, her arms resting above her head. She had removed only her shoes, and her stockinged feet were resting on the rug between the beds. John put down his wash bag, slipped off his dressing gown. He had seen little of her during the later stages of the party. He knew she had been drinking quite a bit, but she had spent a lot of the time up dancing, so he was surprised at the obvious effect of the alcohol on her now. 'Come on. You'd better get into bed. Let me help you.' He tried to pull her up by her arms.

She giggled. 'Somehow I think that your Sara isn't altogether ignorant of the mysteries of the boudoir. I'd say she and her bridegroom knew each other pretty well by now, wouldn't you? In spite of the white wedding.'

For a second he wondered just how drunk she was, for when he got her to her feet, easily enough, she draped her left arm round his neck and hung there, the front of her body leaning suggestively into him, while he groped for the fastener at the back of her dress and drew it down to the hollow of her back. When the upper half of the dress was clinging about her hips, she flopped back on to the bed and lifted her legs for him to slide it off her limbs. The lace-edged silk slip was tight against her thighs. He could see the straps of the suspenders, the ridge of the stocking tops under the shining material. He reached up, under the lace, unclipped the stockings, his senses responding to the cool smoothness of her skin. Carefully, he rolled the stockings down, dragged them off her feet.

He was roused now, his pulse racing, his penis hard, threatening to project through the flap of his pants. He felt ashamed, knowing that this drunken wantonness, this abandonment on her part, was far from the norm, and that he was taking advantage of it. But then, he thought ignobly, so was she. And more shame, and anger, followed as he reflected that this was sexual lust, not love, and that he could well be any man, any rampant male and she could enjoy him. It. And all the while, with a kind of fastidious disapproval, he observed his fingers sliding up, under the silk, over her skin, feeling the satin-clad smoothness of the girdle, digging in to its waistband, tugging at the rubbery material, pulling it down, hauling it with some difficulty over her hips, folding it down over her buttocks still resting on the bed. All at once, he was struck by the unyielding ugliness of what was supposed to be a dainty undergarment. The suspender straps, with their hard rubber fasteners and metal buckles, jiggled and flapped. The restrictive girdle itself was like a bond around her calves and ankles as he fought it off. Under the fragrance of her perfume, he could detect that faint smell of rubber. The delicacy of the panties, their legs trimmed with narrow lace, looked crushed, creased into a myriad of tiny folds.

But now the sweet smell of her, of scent and talcum powder and the odour of womanhood, caught him with strident urgency. He pulled roughly at the silk panties, and they came away easily, he stripped them from the long pale legs. He was kneeling, his head dipped, and suddenly she was clutching at him, drawing his face up, away from her belly, and he saw her tousled head lift, she struggled up on to her elbows, staring at him with a tragic expression.

'Oh God, Johnny! I wish you weren't such a good man! I wish

you weren't so – pure!' She dragged him up on her, her fingers like claws in the back of his head, and plastered her mouth wetly, savagely, against his. Gasping when the kiss ended, he lay on her, his face pressed into the sweetness of her neck and shoulder. He felt its fragility, felt the buckled strap of the brassière, the thinner silk of the slip, across his mouth.

She groaned again, deeply, shudderingly. 'I don't want you to love me, Johnny. I want you to have me! Take me! I want – oh, Christ! I can't even *say* the word I really want to use. But you know it, Johnny! You know it, don't pretend!' Her nails raked agonizingly, sought out his throbbing penis, seizing, pulling him.

'Bitch!' He was half sobbing as he battered her seeking hand away, clawed up the silk from her belly, and pushed his way inside her, pounding her, and she grunted, her knees drawn up high about his thrusting body, her chin digging into his shoulder, the tears trickling down her temples at the hard, clean fusing of their pain.

'We've got something to tell you, mam. And Aunt I,' John gazed at both his listeners, the momentous happiness on his shining face clearly telling them that the news was good. 'Jenny's going to have a baby!' He watched the shock and delight dawning simultaneously.

'Oh, son! That's – wonderful!' May gripped him tightly to her, felt the tears come with the sob of laughter that bubbled up from within. Iris's meaty arms came round both of them, and all three huddled in a loving scrum, then broke, red-faced, the women sniffing and searching for handkerchiefs. 'When – when did you find out? When's it due?'

'February, they think. We've known – hoped, for some time. But we wanted to be absolutely sure. It was confirmed this morning. Over two months now. It's definite. We wanted you to be the first to know.' Not quite true, but he dismissed the white lie.

Jenny must have told her parents by now. She had phoned him from Keswick over an hour ago. He was staying up at Beaconsfield for an extra week, taking advantage of the long summer break to help sort out the administrative tasks they never seemed to have real time for during the term. Jenny had tried to break the news lightly, but her voice was shaky, the emotion clear. The uncertainty in her tone made John long to be with her, to hold her reassuringly. He had swallowed hard. 'It's the most wonderful news in the world. I love you, Jenny.'

'That'll teach you to get me drunk in Manchester!'

He strove to push away the image of their congress in the hotel room, but he knew as surely as Jenny that that was the night when she had conceived. They had taken none of their usual careful precautions; it had been a congress of unplanned, urgent lust.

'Oh, John! You should be there, with Jenny! She'll want you with her. You're going right away, aren't you?' His mother glanced across at Iris. 'Look, we've got some petrol, haven't we? Why don't you take it? We can—'

'No, it's all right, mam, honestly. She's coming up by train tomorrow. You'll see her then.'

'Come on! Let's crack open a bottle of wine! Shame we haven't any bubbly! Oh hell!' Iris gazed at John with comic despair. 'Suppose you don't get any dispensations for special events? We could say it was for medicinal purposes. We've all had a shock!'

John laughed. 'A glass of lemonade will do me fine, Aunt I. I couldn't feel more lightheaded than I am at the minute.'

They took their drinks out into the garden. The penultimate day of July was one of sunshine, a light breeze, and high fluffy wisps of white cloud. May looked lovingly at him and raised her glass. 'This is a week for good news.' They had been listening on the wireless to the opening day of the Olympic Games, the first since the outbreak of war, at Wembley. 'And this is the best we could ever have dreamed of!'

'Better even than the end of the bread rationing!' Iris pronounced, and lifted her glass, too, in salute.

Teddy answered John's knock. He was dressed neatly, in sports jacket, collar and tie. His face glowed ruddily, his hair was carefully brushed, the wave rearing high from his brow, the parting immaculate. 'Good job you left a message for us at work. Otherwise you mightn't have found us in. Making the most of being a bachelor for a while.' He ushered his brother into the living-room. John glanced around, taking in the neat orderliness, the lightness from the large windows at both ends. He knew that Marian was away, staying with her mother, and that Teddie was with her. 'What is it then? To what do we owe the honour?'

His brother's eyes glittered, his face, for all its brightness, had that hard, glassy wariness, and challenge. John met his look. 'I've got some good news. I'm returning the compliment. Making you an uncle. Jenny's pregnant.'

'Is it? Good news?'

John felt the spark of anger, and hurt, at Teddy's cruel question, though his attitude was far from unexpected. 'Yes,' he answered strongly. 'The best, as far as I'm concerned. *And* Jenny.'

'Well, that's fine, then. Congratulations, the pair of you. Not before time, mind. You're getting a bit long in the tooth. Where's the good woman, then? The pair of you should be out celebrating, shouldn't you? Or have you already done all that?'

'She's at Keswick. She's coming over tomorrow. I thought I could buy you a pint up at the George.' He noticed Teddy's slight hesitation. 'It's all right. I can have a ginger ale. I'll not show you up. Everyone will think it's a whisky.'

Teddy led the way along the narrow corridor of the pub to the 'best room' at the back. It was a gloomy little place, even on a fine summer's evening. The heavy chairs and wrought iron tables, the dark brown wainscot and the nicotine-yellow of the upper walls and ceiling, the fly-spotted lampshade, and, worst of all, the overpowering, cheap scent and suspicious stares of the huddle of abandoned wives whose husbands were gathered in the rowdy congeniality of the bar, smothered any atmosphere of levity. 'It'll be more private in here,' Teddy said, moving to the table furthest away from the staring women.

John cleared his throat. 'I want you to know how much we appreciate you keeping quiet, about Jenny. Not letting on to anyone. Not even mam. And we're grateful to Marian, too. For not saying anything. All this time.'

'Well, it's not the sort of thing you want people going round blabbing about, is it? I hope your lass hasn't been going and getting herself all hot and bothered over it. You know we won't go blethering about it. Your secret's safe with us.'

The colour mounted in John's face. 'Look. Jenny's tried to explain. She did what she thought was best. And I think she was right. I know Marian's still not well, but—'

'Why no, man! Everything's A1. Sometimes a whole day can go by without her blubbing more than once or twice. Things carry on like this, we'll be sleeping in the same bed again, in a year or two.'

'I'm sorry. Look, I wish there was something I could do – to help—'

Teddy's laugh was savage. 'Me and you, kidder? We can't even help ourselves, eh? Still, you must have got round to it, somehow. Jenny up the spout, eh? Keep her out of mischief for a few months!'

'Teddy!' The pain showed on John's face so plainly. 'Don't be like this. I know what you've gone through. It—'

'No, you don't! You've no fucking idea!' The obscenity rang out, and John flinched. Teddy stood, flashed his shark's grin over at the gawping wives. 'Sorry, ladies. Wash my mouth out! Just a little tiff. And we're brothers, in case you're wondering. Not poufters!'

133

He strode out, leaving his pint unfinished. John scrambled after him. Outside, the sun was just setting, the clouds bruise-dark against the pale expanse of sky. 'Get off home, John. I wish I could be happy for you. But I can't be like you. Forgive and forget and all that.' He turned to face John, his face bleak. 'I don't even fancy Marian any more, to be honest. I'm glad there's none of that between us. You know. In bed. I don't think she wants it, really, either. It's bad enough living in the same house. Stuck together. Seven months now since she came out of Winyard House.' He shook his head. 'I can see now why she didn't want to leave. Tell Jenny all the best. I mean it. So long.'

He turned down the hill. John guessed he was going no further than the club, just a few yards down the road. For a second he thought of pursuing him, then Teddy's hopelessness struck him, and he turned in the opposite direction, his eyes stinging.

CHAPTER TWELVE

'Come on. You must come in and have a cuppa. Marian's expecting you.' Teddy held open the door of the low, rakish car, and Jenny eased herself out from behind the wheel, tugging the summer dress down over her bare knees. She laughed nervously as Teddy held out his hand to help her. 'There's no dignified way of getting out of this thing. Thanks.'

'I'm surprised John lets you drive, still.'

'I soon won't be able to get behind the wheel. I'm making the most of it.'

'Rubbish. You're still as skinny as a rake. Doesn't show at all.'

She felt herself blushing at his boldness, and was glad to avoid his gaze, moving in front of him up the narrow path of the front garden. Marian appeared in the doorway, at the top of the three steps, and Jenny felt herself reddening even deeper. 'Hello, Marian. Long time no see, eh? How are you? You're looking well.' They embraced, laid their cheeks together, the awkwardness heavy between them. Teddy's heartiness did nothing to alleviate it.

'She is, isn't she? Blooming, eh?'

Marian laughed in breathy embarrassment, while Jenny noted how much weight she had put on. Her hips were heavy, her bosom overripe, her bare arms softly fleshy.

'Get the kettle boiling, lass!' Teddy ordered, grinning. 'Come on in the room. Teddie!'

Teddie came clattering down the stairs, dressed in green shorts and a loose blouse. She had white ankle socks on, and a pair of canvas sand shoes. 'Hello, Aunty Jen. I'm all packed.'

Jenny had come to Low Fell to take Teddie back to Hexham, from whence they would set off at dawn the next day to drive over to Keswick, for a two-week stay. Teddie was full of eager excitement, for Michael Porter, whose mother and sister were home now from India, would be joining them. She had not seen him for over five weeks, though they had written regularly to one another. Her father teased her relentlessly for the way she waited anxiously for the post each morning.

'You're driving over to Keswick,' Teddy observed, when he and Jenny were seated at the dining table, by the window, which looked out on to the rear garden. A clean floral cloth covered its surface, and the best cups, saucers and tea plates were already set out, to Jenny's private consternation, for she had been hoping that she might be able to get away quickly, without the awkwardness of prolonged conversation with both Teddy and Marian. She had scarcely seen her sister-in-law since Marian had been discharged from Winyard House at the beginning of the year. Nor, thankfully, Teddy, which made her embarrassment all the more acute now, as she struggled to make small talk.

In her hypersensitive state, Jenny detected a mocking criticism behind Teddy's remark. 'Yes. Your Uncle David's given us some extra petrol coupons. I managed to persuade John to set aside his principles for once and take them. Your mum and Aunt I are always offering them. They still get them for the café, but Johnny always says no.'

'Well, now that you're in a delicate condition, as they say, he'll have to be a bit more easy-going with his conscience. When are you due? February, is it? Fancy you letting the princess pip you at the post! Hers is due November, isn't it?'

Marian came in from the kitchen on this last remark, carrying a tray on which stood the cosied teapot and a plate of scones and biscuits, and Jenny prayed that Teddy would leave the painful subject of pregnancy. To her dismay and anger, though not to her surprise, he refused to do so. 'I was just saying, love, Jenny's still as thin as a lat, eh?'

'For God's sake! I'm not four months yet!' Jenny's voice was sharper than she intended. She saw Marian's face pink, the obvious effort the poor girl had to make to carry on the casual tone.

'And how *are* you feeling? Sick or anything?'

Silently Jenny cursed Teddy's cruelty in putting both the women on this rack. 'A little bit. And wicked heartburn.' She went on quickly, 'So, Teddie. Have you heard from young Michael at all? He sounded pretty keen on the phone. We'll be able to meet him off the train on Monday. He'll be arriving about one o'clock, his mum said.'

The conversation limped along. Jenny forced down a scone, though every piece stuck grittily in her throat, washed down with sips of scalding tea. Her inner anger increased as she sensed that Teddy was fully aware of the tension, and her embarrassment, and was deriving a mean pleasure from it. 'Life's funny, isn't it?' he announced. 'I was listening to the cricket on the wireless. Poor old Bradman. His last test at the Oval. Everybody wanting him to go out in a blaze of glory. And what happens? Out for a duck! Talk about an anti-climax! But it's true, isn't it? I mean, life *is* really like that. Things rarely turn out the way you expect, eh?'

All at once, Jenny's anger bobbed to the surface. To hell with him! She looked over at Teddie, her voice incisive. 'Why don't you get your things ready, sweetheart? You can stow them in the back of the car, if you like, then we'll be off. Just give us five minutes, all right? I just want to chat with your mum and dad.

137

Grown-up things.' Teddie flushed deeply, but she rose at once and left the room.

Teddy was staring at her, his head tilted, that hard, challenging expression set on his features. Marian was red, and looked frightened. Her voice was faint, she stared down at the table. 'If you want to talk to Teddy, I'll just go and get—'

'No, Marian! Stay! Please! It concerns you as much as Teddy. Listen! We've never talked, properly, since – I want you to know, especially you, Marian. I didn't do it to cause bother, out of maliciousness. When I told Teddy – about the abortion. It wasn't just wickedness. I know you won't believe me—'

Marian gave a kind of whimper, her hands jumping from the tablecloth to her breast, the fingers twisting, almost in a prayer clasp. 'No! No! I know that. I told Teddy. It's better – I'm glad it's all come out.'

'And all this time, neither of you has said anything to anybody. About what you know of me. My affairs – God, no! They weren't even that. I don't know what the hell they were! My lapses, with Horst Zettel and Martin Castleton.' Even in her heightened emotion, and the tears which had risen to her eyes, she noticed Marian's eyes widen, the shock at the mention of the German boy's name, and she realized bewilderedly that Teddy had not even told his wife the secrets which his brother had revealed. She found herself gazing at him, unable to read the depths of his disturbingly penetrating look. 'I want to put it all behind me. But I don't know if I can. Not with things being like this. I feel I ought to tell your mother, at least.'

'And what good will that do?' Teddy's question was bluntly aggressive. 'It'll only cause more upset. There's been enough of that already. For all of us.'

'Do you wish I'd kept my mouth shut? Do you?' Her question was to both of them, but Marian ignored it. Head down, she began to collect the tea things, indicating that for her this moment of truthfulness was over.

'No good wishing that now, is it? You do what you think's best. Nobody will hear anything from us, I can tell you that.'

'No. I know that.' Her voice was quiet. She moved forward, compelled to reach out, to put her hand briefly on his bare forearm.

In the car, on the drive back across the Tyne to Hexham, Teddie sat silent, her ebullient mood vanished. The long legs, tanned by the days of summer, were stretched out, the bony knees jutting upward because of the low slung bucket seat. 'Make the most of it!' Jenny grinned. 'You'll be squashed up in the back with the cases tomorrow!' She paused, went on carefully, 'Everything all right? You're a bit quiet. You do want to come, don't you?'

'Yeah, of course I do. But – I'm not a kid any more – not a little kid, anyway! I'm nearly thirteen. Sometimes they seem to think – I know things aren't right at home. I don't just mean mam being ill. Or maybe it *is* that. I dunno – her and dad. What's wrong, Aunty Jen? Why won't they tell me what's the matter?'

Jenny swallowed hard. She felt the sting of threatened tears once more. 'Oh, Teddie, my love! I know you're growing up. You're right. There are problems. But—' The blabbermouth strikes again! Jenny thought savagely. Yet she had to fight hard against her deep wish to tell the girl the truth, plainly, kindly. She was sure Teddie would be mature enough to understand. 'They're doing their best to work things out. Just be patient. It's because they love you and don't want you to worry. That's why they haven't said anything.'

'Is it something to do with the war? When dad was away? With mam – and Dora?'

'Please, Teddie! One day it'll be sorted out. Soon, I expect. But it's up to them if they talk to you about it.'

'*You* know, though, don't you, whatever the big secret is?'

139

'Teddie, love!' Helplessly, Jenny reached across, put her hand on the cool knee.

'You think I'm just a child still, too. But I'm not daft. I know a lot already.' She moved her leg deliberately, away from Jenny's touch. 'It's not such a big deal, grown-ups' secrets!'

In spite of her distress, Jenny's lips twitched in a smile at the Americanism. Yes, we have our secrets, Teddie, dear. And I wonder if you'd be so dismissive if you knew mine. Would they be 'no big deal', too?

'What's this then, ducks? Secrets, eh? Not another billy-do from your boyfriend!' Charlie Lewis had finished buttoning up his uniform jacket. Tony turned, lifting his head from the washbasin, where he had been swilling his face under the tap. He groped for the thin white hand towel, wiping the water from his eyes, and saw that the warder was already taking the envelope from the pocket of Tony's shirt, which still lay with his thick serge trousers on the top of the bunk.

'That's private!' In spite of his agitation, Tony's voice remained soft, governed by the inbuilt subservience which had been a part of his life for so long, almost since he could remember.

Lewis's smile was full of the power he knew he held over the thin figure, standing shivering in his vest and drawers. 'Put your clothes on, Ellis. Don't want you catching your death, do we? You don't have any secrets from your Uncle Charlie. Nothing's private in here, sunshine.' His gaze fixed eloquently on Tony's frame, then he sat casually on the unmade bottom bunk and began to read the letter.

Tony made no further protest, but finished dressing quickly, while the warder continued to read with avid interest. Lewis's thick lips were moving slightly, his eyes scanning quickly the closely written lines, and Tony felt that hopeless, bitter contempt

140

that he was so used to hiding. Lewis was one of his chief protectors, as well as his tormentor. Tony knew all too well how hellish life could be without the warder to take care of him, which was why they were here now, hidden away securely in the unoccupied cell, where Tony had been paying his dues. It was a service Lewis demanded regularly, and which Tony loathed, though he could disguise that effectively, too, as he went through the mechanics of satisfying the sadistic figure's desires. There was no iota of tenderness in these transactions, though again Tony was used to that. He had endured many such during the three years since his sentencing.

He could feel the sickness churning away inside at the warder's grin, the gaze that defiled the warmth of the words Teddy had penned. When the first letter had come – the first, that is, which contained the news of Teddy's personal grief at his discovery of his wife's faithlessness during the war – he had shed tears for his friend, in the privacy of darkness, as he lay on his bunk and listened to his snoring cell mate. He could imagine, vividly, the sense of shock, the hurt, the double pain of learning about the abortion, for, through the long months in the POW camp and during the three years of his imprisonment in Britain, Tony had attached himself to Teddy's family. To the pretty, blonde wife, and the little girl, even to his officer brother, and his mother. He had never met them, doubted he ever would, yet he held them in his heart as an ideal picture of the warmth of kinship. He could share Teddy's pain, his feeling of outrage. Ashamed though he was, there was a part of Tony that was ignobly glad that Teddy's tragedy had brought him closer, that through the letter, and those that followed, there was a feeling of real closeness, an intimacy which they had never before acknowledged, even in the insulated atmosphere of the wartime prison camp.

When that first letter had come, Tony couldn't wait to make use of his precious, sparse private time to sit down and write a reply. He tried, unsuccessfully he was sure, to let his heart pour out on to the notepaper.

Don't give up, Teddy. Remember how you used to keep me going in camp when I was down in the dumps. Everybody looked up to you, Teddy. I wish I could be with you now, wish 1 could give you a bit of that help. I want you to know how much I'm thinking about you, and hoping things will work out for you. And I don't mean that in any puffy sort of a way. I know you're not like that. You know what I am, but I hope you also know that I'm your friend, always will be.

It seemed that his uninspiring words had done something – at least Teddy had written back, still in that new, more intimate manner, which had meant so much. It made Tony burn all the more with helpless inner rage at Lewis's brute trampling on such sensitivity, as the warder tossed the thin sheets of paper back on to the table.

'No wonder your brown-hatter friend can't get it off with his missus! I reckon he still fancies you, eh? *Young-un!* That's a good one, eh? I must remember that. One thing's for sure. By the time you get out the nick he won't be able to call you that no more! Never mind! You'll be able to take your false choppers out and give him the thrill of a lifetime, eh?'

'Can I go now, Mr Lewis, sir?' Tony stuffed the pages back inside the envelope, slipped it back into his breast pocket.

'Yeah, you do that, Young-un. You run along and write your love letter.' Lewis gave a deep, lascivious chuckle. 'I know where to find you when I want you again.'

'Aren't you going out tonight? It's quiet with Teddie not being around, isn't it?'

Teddy could tell from Marian's over-pitched tone how uneasy she was. It was something he was accustomed to whenever they were alone. It showed also in the unnatural tension of her body stance, the anxiety behind her eyes, which never stayed on his for more than a second or two. 'I thought I'd have a night in. Just the two of us. On our own.'

'Well – shall I make a pot of tea? How about having an early supper? I could do with a bite. I'll have an early night, I think. Bit of a headache. Better take one of my pills.'

The sleeping pills the doctor had given her would knock out a horse, Teddy thought. Within half an hour of swallowing one she would be dead to the world, snoring like a saw-mill. Several times, when she had taken one too early before retiring, he had been forced literally to drag her upstairs and undress her, while she lolled and mumbled like a hopeless drunk until she hit the pillow. 'Sit still,' he said now, reaching out, touching her knee. He saw the flashing glance of fear, the knuckles tighten on the arms of the chair. 'We have to talk, love. It's been months. We never get anywhere.'

'But we *do* talk. Dr Hennessy—'

'Hennessy!' The explosive sound indicated Teddy's frustration. 'We go round and round with him, love! You know we do! Week after week. Same old things. "Give it time". "We're making progress". You and me – on our own – we're the only ones who can get it sorted.'

'No!' She was sitting forward, clearly distressed. 'I can't! You know how it makes me—'

'I can't go on like this, Marian. It's no good just running away from it all the time.'

She slumped back in the armchair, began to cry quietly. He felt the rage growing, welling up inside, even though he was disgusted at himself. 'I don't want to upset you, love, but it's not easy for *me*, either. I'm up to here.'

She held her hand over her eyes, hiding her face. She sniffled noisily, her body heaved in a great sigh. 'What is it you want, Teddy?' Her voice now was flat, almost toneless. 'Do you want me to leave?'

143

'No, no! Course not! It's just – we've got to do something! Move forward. We don't even sleep together!' His plaintive cry sounded feeble and pathetic, even to him, and his self-disgust rose like bile. 'Don't you want – don't you feel like it – some-times?'

She seemed calmer suddenly. She groped and found a dainty handkerchief, blew into it, and sniffed. 'You should have said. You know it was the doctor suggested sleeping separate, that it would be better —'

'I'm asking *you*! How do *you* feel about it? Don't you want – to do it, you know?'

She shook her head. He was startled at her untypical direct-ness. Her clouded eyes met his, did not flicker away immediately. 'No. Not now.'

'What?' For an instant, surprise replaced every other emotion. 'Never? Not even—'

'No. It doesn't bother me. I don't think I could, now, after—' She seemed to realize all at once what she was saying. She blushed, went on awkwardly, after a pause. 'If you still want it, then that's all right. I mean you can.' Then she truly amazed him, as she fixed her gaze on him, with an earnest, almost pleading expression. 'Or maybe you could find someone else. Someone nice and attractive. Someone you can be – friends with. Sleep with. I wouldn't mind. Honest! It wouldn't – I'd be happy for you, I swear I would!'

'Christ! This is ridiculous! I can't believe you're saying this to me.' He stood up, boiling over with rage, and gazed down at her. 'You're saying you want me to go to bed with another woman?'

'I want you to be happy. To feel better. That's all.'

'And that's your solution, is it? For me to take up with a fancy woman?' He thought suddenly of his Uncle Dan, and the hidden Jesmond love nest in which he had ended his life. Perhaps Aunt I had given him her seal of approval, too. Somehow he could never imagine her being an enthusiastic participant in what went on under the marital sheet. But Marian was not Aunt I, not by a long chalk. The trouble was, he could remember far too well the passion they had shared when they had first loved together, in Marian's grandmother's house.

He fell to his knees in front of her, put his hands on her legs, pressed his chest against her limbs. 'Tell me about this feller. Jim Moody,' he said desperately. 'We never talk about it. What really matters. Did you love him?'

Marian looked at him helplessly, her face red, the tears shining on her cheeks in the dim light of the evening. She shook her head hopelessly. 'He was – he was very kind,' she answered simply.

'Did he love you? Did he want you to leave – to go with him?'

'He said he did.'

Why didn't you? Teddy didn't say it, but the question resounded in his brain. Why didn't you just go off together, instead of breaking yourself on this lie for four long years? How much easier it would have been, for all of us, than this.

All at once, the anger and tension seemed to drain from him, leaving his body slack and weary. He released his hold on Marian, pushed himself to his feet. 'I think I will take a bit of a stroll, after all. You get something to eat. Have an early night.' He moved towards the hallway. 'Don't worry. I won't bother you,' he couldn't help adding bitterly, before he left.

PART II
A CROWNING MERCY

(Oliver Cromwell)

CHAPTER THIRTEEN

Sara and Berni flew back to a war which, official or not, had been going on for seven months, during which time, already, thousands of Jewish and Arab lives had been lost. They themselves had been blooded. The kibbutz had come under attack several times, mostly sporadic small arms fire, of brief duration, but in March, at dawn one morning, shells had come screaming down on the compound, taking them by surprise, despite the posted sentries. The raid was from a considerable force to the north of the settlement. Later it was said that this force was a unit of the Arab Legion commanded by the celebrated Glubb Pasha. Ironically, the settlement might well have been overrun had not a nearby contingent of British army troops come to the rescue and replied to the shellfire with their own bombardment, which staved off an assault.

Sara was ready to call off the arranged wedding in England. 'We can't leave now!' she had protested vehemently, and a great many of their fellow kibbutzniks agreed with her. Operation Nachshon began, the largest organized Jewish offensive so far, to open up and maintain a corridor from Tel Aviv to Jerusalem. Sara and Berni were part of the group which unloaded a large consignment of arms smuggled in on a Polish ship. It was far easier than expected to get the weapons, truckloads of them, safely away from the port, and reinforced the idea that the British were scarcely more now than bystanders, counting the days when their soldiers could finally pull out of this powder-keg country.

Sara and her fiancé were part of the convoy ferrying the arms to the front-line Hagana fighters, who, in April, finally broke through into the city of Jerusalem. Berni still had not cancelled the tickets for their flight out, fixed for a week's time, though Sara, eyes flashing with the light of battle, and looking every inch the *sabra* in her grimy khaki drill and beret pulled rakishly across her oil-smeared brow, assured him she would not be on the flight. Then, as the final Arab resistance was overcome, and the way to the ancient city lay open, the trucks were diverted to the west of Jerusalem, to a small village named Deir Yassin.

The thin columns of smoke rising from the hillside could be seen a mile away. There was no building left intact, all were smouldering in the sunshine. The stench of burning, and of something worse, far more sinister, hung thickly enough on the air to make them gag. As they drove through the heaps of rubble, the scene of carnage in the vivid brightness of the day became a nightmare. Bodies, and bits of raw, red, pulverized flesh, were heaped everywhere. Children, women, old men . . . the slaughter had been indiscriminate. Many were not the victims of shelling, but had clearly been gunned down at close range. They soon learned why.

A gaggle of inhabitants was already being assembled on the rocky slope on the far side of the village, overlooking the city a few miles distant. The distinctive uniforms of their guards, and the brutal manner with which they treated their captives, proclaimed them as members of the Stern Gang, still outlawed, and responsible for many atrocities against the Arab enemy, as well as the continued killing of British troops. The young detachment from the settlement watched in appalled silence as the hopeless column set off, to be paraded through the streets of Jerusalem, like part of some barbarian triumph. Approximately two hundred and fifty villagers had been killed. Sara was too shocked to cry, but she moved away behind a bush and was violently sick on to the rocky soil. That night she clung to Berni, and the tears came. 'Let's go,' she said simply, and they did.

The Declaration of Independence was signed by David Ben-Gurion the day before Sara and Berni's wedding. Until then, many people did not even know what the new nation's name would be. By the morning of the wedding day, the British had left Palestine, except for a small garrison at Haifa, to supervise last-minute evacuations. The war was now official. Five Arab states lined up to announce themselves as enemies of the newborn territory, and crossed its borders from north, south and east.

In spite of the horrors they had witnessed at Deir Yassin, both Sara and Berni had no doubts about returning to help fight for the survival of their adopted country. On their last night in England, in bed in the comfortable home of her in-laws in Sale, Sara asked solemnly, 'You don't regret anything, do you? You don't wish we were staying here?'

'I belong with you, Sara Lightman. And we both belong back home – in Israel.'

Even the magic sound of the country's name set her skin puckering with emotion. 'I love you, husband!' she whispered unsteadily, and nestled into him, her lips moist against his throat. After a long pause, she said, 'Are you afraid?'

'Scared stiff!' She could sense his grin in the darkness. 'But speaking of stiff!' He moved, rearing over her, pulling at her silk nightgown and opening her limbs.

'Sh!' she admonished joyously. 'We don't want to wake the whole house!' and welcomed him rapturously to her eager body.

The battle for the Jerusalem corridor was once more raging. The Arab Legion had occupied the fort at Latrun, thus closing the road into the city, where conditions in the Jewish occupied section were growing more desperate daily. Food rationing was severe, the shortage of water acute – a gallon a day per person, for drinking, washing and cooking. The day the Lightmans arrived back in Israel, an assault was launched on Latrun, which failed. The plight of the inhabitants of the Jewish area of Jerusalem was now critical. Although the kibbutz defence force was mainly concerned with patrolling their section of the Tel Aviv–Haifa route, as well as protecting the settlement itself, its members were part of the national military forces. Sara and Berni were again drafted to a transport unit involved in the all-out effort to open up the Jerusalem road once more. Word came down that yet another attack, the third, was to be mounted against the fortress of Latrun, and the formidable Arab Legion. At the same time, frantic efforts by the UN to bring about a ceasefire, or at least a temporary truce, appeared to be succeeding. 'I hope to God they get an agreement before we attack,' Berni said soberly. They were bedded down for the night around their trucks near an Arab village, Beit Jiz, in the foothills to the south of the Jaffa–Jerusalem road, and uncomfortably close to the artillery of Latrun. Its flashes lit the sky, and the dull, reverberating booms declared its stranglehold on the vital route. 'Don't worry. We're out of range,' the lieutenant assured them cheerfully. But the feeling about the forthcoming assault on the fort was not good. Casualties had been high on both previous attempts, and there seemed little reason why this should be any more successful.

'They're sending up a batch of recruits fresh from the boats,' someone observed gloomily. 'They were in Cyprus a few days ago.'

'Sufficient unto the day.' Sara rose, put her hand on Berni's shoulder, leaned heavily on him for a second, and kissed him swiftly on the ear. 'Goodnight, Private. Don't forget to wake me early.'

He appreciated the restraint of her behaviour in these public circumstances. It was odd, but marriage had made them shy in front of the others. She was sleeping with the four other females of the detachment. They had made themselves their own little enclave, complete with ablution and latrine area – a shallow trench dug among the scrub at a discreet distance. No one would do more than remove boots and army blouses, and lie out in the open under a blanket, but the conventions were observed. Not that there weren't nudging, jovial remarks from their colleagues. 'Why don't you two crawl into the back of one of the trucks?' And from one of the girls, 'My God. You're going to miss it, aren't you, Sara?'

They were woken before dawn. A large contingent of the promised recruits arrived, and with them the exciting news that an alternative route into the Jewish quarter of Jerusalem had been found, passing through the very area where they were now encamped, and out of the range of Latrun's guns. They themselves were now to be part of this new column of a hundred and fifty men or so, and would follow the proposed route, on foot at first, then help engineers to organize a passable road for the trucks.

They set off as daylight was breaking. They had not gone far before they heard the noise of straining engines, and two jeeps came bouncing along the rocky track. They ploughed on ahead, raising clouds of dust but fortunately drawing no other attention to themselves, and the men trudged on in their wake. They found the vehicles at the head of a high bluff, where the track petered out at the crest of a steep hillside, scattered with olive and other fruit trees. The orchards were deserted. The Arab villagers in this region seemed to have fled *en masse*. These migrations had been mirrored in many other parts of the country. Thousands of future refugees were on the move, and villages stood virtually empty all over the territory.

For a while, dismay assailed the pioneers of this new route, but they pressed on, slithering down the slope in their own dust clouds, leaving the jeeps stranded above. Once down the hill, progress into the city was easy, apart from the sporadic shelling from Jordanian troops, who did not appear to be aware anything untoward was happening.

The inhabitants greeted the new arrivals with cheers and hugs and much back slapping, even though they had brought nothing with them except the rations each one carried in his knapsack. 'We'll be back,' their commander promised, somewhat optimistically, Berni thought. But that night, bulldozers ground their way along the tracks. The Arab villages along the route were flattened, the few women and children and old men drifting in silent resignation with their animals into the hills. The road was widened, and the first of a long convoy of laden vehicles came slowly in the wake of the road builders. Only at the head of the bluff over the orchards did it halt.

Berni and Sara's unit became part of the large band of porters who laboured through the remainder of the night, then on into the new day, ferrying much-needed supplies on their backs, down the steep hillside, until, drenched in sweat, caked in dust and weary to exhaustion, they sank down among the gnarled trees, trembling with fatigue. The NCOs left them in peace for a while. Then they were round, bawling, kicking at boots, stirring them to groaning movement, herding them like the lines of cattle that were being carefully led down the slopes as part of the rescue mission.

It was a remarkable achievement, and carried out with the loss of only one life, and four wounded, the casualties occurring in the city itself, as a result of the Jordanian attacks. The route soon acquired the name of the Burma Road, and the efforts made to establish it were greatly appreciated by the inhabitants of the beleaguered city. And by those like Berni and Sara, who had taken part in the arduous trek, when they learned that the assault on the Latrun fort had been planned to go ahead on 10 June and had been called off at virtually the last minute when the new route into Jerusalem had been pioneered. The next day, a four-week truce negotiated through the UN was agreed by both sides.

'Beasts of burden, that's all we are!' was Berni's summary, when the tale of their exploit was told back at the kibbutz. 'Here she comes!' Sara came over with her plate and sat down beside him at the crowded dining table, raising her eyebrows in an enquiring smile. 'My little she-ass!'

'And as asses go, they don't come any prettier!' someone offered gallantly.

Berni chuckled. 'Yes. Well, you can keep your hands off *my* ass, all right?'

John was sitting by the fire in the staff room listening to the wireless when a telephone call came from his mother. There was a general feeling of disillusion, in keeping with the weather's rapid deterioration from autumnal Indian summer conditions to dank, wintry chill. Dr Bronowski had made a bleak but accurate summary in his Home Service talk earlier. 'We sit under the shadow of the Nine O'clock News, nursing our sense of doom.' The Berlin Airlift was entering its fourth month, and the 'Iron Curtain' Mr Churchill had prophetically described soon after the war's end was locking ever more firmly into place.

John found it hard to argue against the embittered cynicism of the majority of his colleagues, whose chief spokesman was the deputy head, Maurice Nicholls, dispensing vitriolic negativism along with the wreaths of cigarette smoke that almost permanently surrounded him. 'What price your new world order now, Wright? They estimate that by the mid-fifties the Reds will have the capability to produce their own atom bomb, so I reckon that means we've got another five or six years before we wipe ourselves out of existence. And don't tell me that that bunch of jabbering politicians at the UN is going to come up with a solution. They can't even agree on who should sit where during their endless debating!' He gave a scoffing bark of laughter and glanced about him for acclamation. 'Or perhaps that's what your Maker intends, eh? Wipe us all out and start again! Perhaps that's the only way.'

John smothered his irritation. 'He's not just *my* Maker, Maurice. He's yours as well, you know.' He was ashamed of the feeling of entrapment which came with his religious beliefs. He was no longer 'one of the boys'. The alcoholic bonhomie of trips to the pub was a thing of the past. His infrequent visits to the Angel, sitting nursing a ginger ale, merely served to distance him further. Even Jenny was embarrassed, he could tell, though she never said anything directly to him. He was embarrassed himself. Part of him resented the killjoy image with which his faith appeared to brand him. And if not that, then someone too naïve to see what was going on all around him in the real world.

Maurice Nicholls was becoming very skilled at needling him. The other day, he had made an offensive remark which had infuriated John. It followed from some argument about nationalism, during which Nicholls had cleverly drawn John, as he so often did, to elucidate the Baha'i standpoint. 'My God, Jenny,' the deputy head declared in that bluff, avuncular manner he assumed with her, 'I swear I begin to wonder how you became *enceinte*, if you'll forgive my indelicacy. Your old man is so saintly I expect to see a bright star hovering over Beaconsfield any night now, and a queue of wise men and shepherds in the drive.'

'I can assure you there's nothing immaculate about what we get up to, Maurice. But if you're curious or ill-informed about such things, there are several books I can recommend.' Jenny's reply was crisp and effective as a put-down, but John could detect the tinge of pink under her skin, despite the poise she displayed.

She made light of it when John referred to the incident in private. Jenny's pregnancy was no longer a matter for conceal-ment. Not that it had ever been so, as far as their friends and colleagues were concerned. Now, five months along, her rounded pot and generally more fulsome figure could still be discreetly hidden beneath loosely flowing clothing, but it was common knowledge among the pupils, too, that Mrs Wright was going to have a baby. She had told Michael Porter soon after she had had her pregnancy confirmed. She had no fears that he would betray her confidence.

'I'd like to keep working, if I may,' she told James Challoner forthrightly. 'As long as I can.'

Unlike some of his staff, notably his deputy, the head had been as enthusiastic in his accord as he had been in his congratula-tions. 'Splendid. It's such a wonderful thing. We'll all be so proud to share in it. So good for the boys. Makes us feel even more of a family. I just hope we're not going to lose you. It would be wonderful if you could stay on here, after the happy event. Though I know we'll have to make some arrangements for accommodation. You can't stay up in the attic. We'll manage something, I'm sure.'

With the baby due in early February, Jenny had decided to carry on teaching up until the end of term, in December. 'That's leaving things a bit late, isn't it?' Maurice Nicholls had remon-strated. 'I mean – it'll be difficult. You should be resting, shouldn't you?'

'I promise not to give birth in Big Hall, Maurice!' she teased maliciously. 'I hope I won't take up too much room, though.'

'It'll all add to the festive jollity,' he rallied. 'Perhaps we can organize a nativity play. You can have the starring role.'

When the phone rang that October night and someone called out, 'It's Mrs Wright. Your mother,' by way of further identifica-tion, John was for an instant quite relieved at the opportunity to break off yet another tedious argument with Maurice, though already anxiety was beginning to surface. He wondered what had happened to make his mother take the unusual step of ringing the school.

'Hello, John. Sorry to bother you, but can you call in some time soon? I'd like to talk—'

'What's wrong, mam?'

'I don't want to talk over the telephone, but it's that brother of yours. He hasn't been in touch with you, has he?'

'No. I haven't seen him since the summer. Or heard from him. What is it? Is Marian all right?'

'As right as she'll ever be, I suppose. But he's proposing to up and off again. And you'll never guess where. Your Aunt Cissy rang me. He's been over to see David. He wants to go off to Palestine and fight for the damned Jews!'

CHAPTER FOURTEEN

'Where's Jenny? Is she not with you?' John was aware of the criticism in his mother's enquiry, but he ascribed it to her overwrought nerves.

'No. She couldn't get away. So what's this about Teddy?'

'Do you know, it's months since we've seen her? We're wondering what we've done to offend her, aren't we?' May looked across to Iris for support. 'Is she still keeping all right? Isn't it time she stopped working now?'

'She wants to carry on until the end of term.'

'Good heavens! She can't do that!' May's tone was sharp with outrage. 'That's what? Hardly more than a month before the baby's due! I mean – she'll be starting to show now. Or soon, at any rate. It'll be embarrassing for her. The boys . . .' her voice faded eloquently.

'It's nothing to be ashamed of, mam!' He made an effort to curb his irritation. Part of his problem was that he could understand all too well his mother's shock at Jenny's decision to stay on at Beaconsfield, for his own initial reaction had been identically conventional – embarrassment at the idea of his wife publicly proclaiming her advanced state of pregnancy in the masculine environment of the school. But he had swiftly mastered his own narrow-mindedness and acknowledged Jenny's far more honest

159

approach. Even James Challoner had shamed him by his enlight-
ened attitude. 'It's not exactly unnatural, after all!' John added
now, with a smile, in an effort to lighten the confrontational
atmosphere.

He was sure his mother had been further upset by Jenny's
arranging to have the baby in Keswick, and, once again, he had
to acknowledge a similar disappointment on his own part, again
quickly countered by his appreciation that for such a momentous
event she should wish to be with her own family. He and Jenny
were to spend Christmas with her folks, and he would return
alone for the start of the new term at Beaconsfield. Of course, he
would have liked to be close at hand for the birth, but it couldn't
be helped. And he was sure James would allow him a day or two's
leave – a long weekend, so that he could get across to Keswick to
see Jenny and the baby as soon as possible.

'We *will* see her before she goes off to the Lakes, won't we?'
May asked pointedly, ignoring his attempt at light-heartedness.

'Coffee's ready!' Iris lumbered off gladly towards the kitchen
to bring the trolley in, for Ruby had long since departed for her
home.

'Now then, mam. What's going on with Teddy? What's he up
to now?'

At last, May launched forth upon the reason for his visit, and
quickly sketched in the details of Teddy's proposed defection. It
was easy for John to see how deeply troubled his mother was. 'It
was Cissy who first let me know what was going on. She telephoned – yesterday morning. He's been over to see David. He'd
already seen him before, apparently. At his office, or in town
somewhere. I don't know.'

Her voice was taut, and, as so often in the past, so that it was
hard for John to think of them as anything other than a couple,
he saw Aunt I take May's cup to her, then stand behind her and
put her hand on May's shoulder. May reached up almost uncon-

sciously and placed her own smaller hand over that of her companion. John felt a stab of love for both of them.

'That blasted man!' May uttered feelingly, and John knew she was referring to David Golding, and his own involvement with his uncle before the war, which had led to John's brief detention in a Berlin cell, after his efforts to aid the family of Sara Arad to get her out of Germany.

'There's some organization in Britain – some Jewish thing – recruiting for people to go out to fight for them in Palestine. They'll take anybody. Anybody fit enough. You don't even have to be Jewish!' May coloured slightly. 'I'm not saying it's wrong. Of course we all know what they've gone through. Suffered. But—' she clenched her hands, stared at John, her eyes eloquent in her despair. 'Why on earth has Teddy got to go off again and risk getting himself killed in somebody else's fight? Hasn't he gone through enough? Even if he can't live with Marian any more – why does he always have to run off to war? Go off fighting other people's battles? It's just like Spain all over again! He's running away from his own mess.' Her lips tightened, set thinly. 'Well, not *his* mess this time. What Marian did to him – I can understand how badly hurt he is.'

John felt the urge to interrupt her, to speak in Marian's defence. But he knew how deeply set was his mother's moral code, and how profoundly she was shaken by the revelation which had come out in the last year. He let her continue.

'But there's a proper way of doing things. If necessary, he can get a separation, do things legal and proper. Even a divorce, if it comes to that.' He knew the effort it cost his mother even to use the word. 'But not this damned silly running off to war again! He might not be so lucky this time.'

Her voice quavered, almost broke, and Iris leaned down and put her mouth close to the neat, grey-flecked head. Now both hands held the thin shoulders, hugged her protectively. 'All

161

right, old girl. Don't get upset.' She straightened up again, her bulky figure facing John. 'You've got to go and talk to him, John. He won't even see us. He was out when we called over there. And Marian. Well, she was in no state to talk to anyone. We didn't stay long. It's not fair. Especially on little Teddie.'

John found time to reflect wryly on the appellation. 'Little' Teddie was now as tall as May, and level with Iris's chin. A gangly thirteen-year-old, who was more at home under this roof, he suspected, than at Low Fell with Teddy and Marian. She stayed at Hexham during term time, visiting her own home at weekends, though more usually it was a Sunday visit only, for she was enthusiastically involved in the games and other activities which took up a large part of her Saturdays. Conveniently, she was out seeing one of her friends in the town this evening.

He sighed, looked at the two figures opposite. His mother, slim, attractive and looking far younger than her fifty-four years, seated in the armchair; the towering bulk of Aunt I, in the thick-ribbed sweater that emphasized her flowing girth, leaning over the back, one hand still placed protectively on May's shoulder. 'Look, I'll try to get over on Sunday. I'll try and talk to him.' He pulled a rueful face. 'But I haven't seen him for ages. And you know he's not likely to take much notice of what I say. Far from it.'

It was nearly ten o' clock when he got back to school. Pausing only to admonish the late night whisperers in Red Dorm, he made his way up to the flat. Jenny was sitting up in bed, reading, a dark woollen cardigan round her shoulders, her head covered with an old scarf, hiding the jag-toothed metal crimps secured in her hair to accentuate the wave in the fall of her dark honey locks, which she was growing long again. She marked her place and snapped her book shut. 'Thank goodness. Hurry up and come to bed. I want to warm my feet on you. They're like ice.'

'Thanks for the warning.' He began to undress quickly.

'How did it go? Did ma ask where I was?'

He hopped about, hauling off his trousers and his underpants. 'She did. You'll have to go and see them, love. They were asking if they'd done anything to upset you.'

'I know. I just feel so embarrassed after – you know. I'm sure they really blame *me* for all this mess.' She raised her knees under the bedclothes, laid her folded hands on them. 'They're right, too,' she went on bleakly. 'If I'd kept my mouth shut, none of this would have happened. Would it?'

'That's nonsense. It would all have come out somehow. Probably far more disastrously.' He slipped his dressing gown on over his pyjamas, picked up his soap bag and towel, prepared to face the chill trek along the corridor. 'That's what caused Marian's breakdown. It *had* to come out. Remember? You were convinced you'd done the right thing. Don't start doubting yourself now.'

When he returned a few minutes later, she was sitting in the same position, staring ahead, the book discarded on the bedside table. He switched off the ceiling light and now only the bed was bathed in the softer glow of the lamp, the rest of the room in dimness. He climbed in beside her, and, as she had threatened, she threaded her legs over his, and he hissed at the coldness of the soles of her feet seeking out his warmth. 'Blimey! You weren't kidding! You should put a pair of bed socks on.'

'It's only October, Johnny. What'll I be like by the time the baby's due? I wish' – she hesitated, then went on – 'I hadn't booked in at the cottage hospital. I wish I was staying here.'

'Well, it's still probably not too late.'

But she said nothing further, instead brought the subject back to Teddy's latest bombshell. 'Is it true then? Is he really going off to Palestine?'

She snuggled down into him, and with his free arm he reached out and switched off the lamp, then held her carefully, avoiding

163

the metal crescents under the thin stuff of the scarf. She took his hand and placed it comfortingly over the bulge of her abdomen, pressing it into the yielding flesh, and he tried to relax, waiting, half squeamishly afraid and half delighted, to feel the strange thrusts of the new life forming inside her. 'Yes, he's going off to fight for the Jews. Not that I think he gives a fig one way or the other what happens to Palestine. At least last time he had some sort of excuse when he enlisted for Spain. He's always been a socialist. But this! Why the heck he can't just move to some other town if he feels he has to get away! But, oh no! Not our Teddy! He thinks he's a kind of Beau Geste!' He gave an angry laugh. 'In fact, I'm amazed he didn't come up with that one and rush off to join the Foreign Legion!' He began to rub softly, tracing the curve of Jenny's belly. 'Of course, they want me to talk to him! A fat lot of good that'll do. He's never listened to anything I say, right from when we were kids.'

His hold on her tightened. 'Listen, Jen. Why don't *you* talk to him?' The idea came suddenly to him, his voice quickened with enthusiasm. 'He'll take far more notice of you than he will me. If anyone can make him see sense, you can!'

'What? You know what he thinks of me! You can't have forgotten – how he was when 1 told him about Marian. And me.' She was glad of the darkness. 'He's got no time for me at all. Not that he ever had much!'

'That's not true. He's always thought a lot of you. In fact, I think he's always fancied you, whatever he might say.'

'Don't be daft!' She was shocked at the thrill of vanity his words gave her. 'Anyway, he'd soon change his mind if he saw me looking like a house end!' A sobering thought struck her, one that she did not voice. It would also be a painfully eloquent reminder, to both Teddy and Marian, of the blighted state of their own physical as well as emotional relationship.

*

'I see you've brought reinforcements with you this time.' Jenny was annoyed with herself at her hot-faced response to Teddy's needling greeting and his scornfully challenging smile.

John shrugged, returned his grin. 'Well, I know it's a waste of breath me talking to you. I imagine you know the state mam's got herself into? Why the heck Palestine, of all places? Since when have you been a Zionist?'

'What? Surely you have some sympathy with their cause? It's your spiritual HQ, after all. Or are you happy to sit back and let the wogs finish off the job Hitler started, and wipe them out altogether?' His gaze took in Jenny again as he added, 'I'm surprised you're not keen to sign on with me, wor kid. We could ride off to battle side by side. Defenders of the noble cause and all that!'

Jenny did her best to indicate how preposterous she thought his ramblings by ignoring them. 'Where's Marian?' she asked pointedly, glancing about her, aware that Teddy had led them straight into the small kitchen, where the cups and saucers had already been arranged on the wooden table, which took up most of the limited space. They sat on the hard chairs placed around it.

'Kitchen's always the best place for councils of war.' Teddy lit the gas under the kettle. 'Just like the old days, eh, Johnny? Remember nana and grandad's? Sidney Terrace?'

Jenny was certain he was deliberately trying to make her feel excluded. 'Marian not part of the council, then? Oh no! Of course not! I forgot. In that good old solid working man's world of yours, the little woman doesn't have a say, does she?'

'Never do for *you*, that, eh Jenny?' His smile was wider and sharper than ever. 'Well, as you can see, I haven't got her chained to the sink or the mangle. As a matter of fact, she cleared off as soon as she got wind that you were coming. She's off to Aunt Julia's. She's made peace with that lot again.' He made no effort to disguise his contempt. 'Fair enough. As long as they don't set foot in here again. I'm still the big bad bugger as far as they're concerned, and it suits me down to the ground. Ah! There's the old kettle. Let's have that cuppa, and you can get it off your chests, the pair of you. But you were right first time, John, lad. You're wasting your breath, 'cos it's all fixed up. Just one thing, before you start chucking in your ha'p'orth! I've talked it over with Marian. She's accepted it, and is quite amenable. I'm not running out on her. I've handed over all the money Grandma Wright left us, we've paid a hefty lump sum off the house, which is hers if anything happens to me, so she's quite secure. Apart from that, the Jewish brigade will pay me pretty well as much as I was getting at Swan's, and most of that will go directly to her. So neither she nor Teddie will be a burden on anybody.'

'And that makes everything fine, does it? You'll be quite happy to swan off and leave your sick wife and your little girl on their own? Because they've got a roof over their heads and money to put food on the table!' Jenny struggled to appear detached, in spite of the emotion churning within her.

'Nobody's *happy*, Jenny!' She almost flinched at the force with which he flung the word at her. 'You should know that! Or maybe we're just not so lucky as you! Maybe having a baby gives you the chance to wipe the slate clean. Start all over again.' He nodded at her thickened waist, evident now that she had taken off her winter coat, despite the loose smock she wore.

She recoiled from his words, stung, yet deeply conscious of the pain behind his bitterness.

'I reckon it does,' John said quietly. 'And I only wish there was something you could find to make you feel the same.'

The compassion evident in his voice held them all powerfully for an instant. Then Teddy gave his harsh laugh. 'Never mind! I could be in Bethlehem for Christmas. Or maybe I could look up *your* lot. Perhaps they'll do a Road to Damascus job on *me* and all!

That'd be a turn-up for the books!'

Jenny sat hunched and silent during the ride back to Corbridge in the cold night. 'Thanks for coming, anyway,' John said, as she crouched in front of the paraffin heater when they were back in the flat. When she still made no real effort to respond to his attempts at conversation, or to rise from her kneeling stance in front of the heater, he said, 'Look, we did our best, Jen. We knew what he'd be like. Why don't you get undressed and hop into bed? I'll make the cocoa. We'll have an early night.'

'What for? It can't be much fun going to bed with me these days!' She felt close to tears, hating her bitching mood, yet unable to stop. 'Why don't you go round to the Angel? I'm sure Mike will be in there. Probably Maurice as well. Have a night with the boys, for a change.'

'No thanks. I'd rather stay here with you.'

She could see the worry, the tension in his face as he watched her, and it made her feel worse. 'Perhaps Teddy was right. You should go off with him. Back to Palestine. You were happy there.'

'It was the most miserable time of my life.'

She remembered vividly the evening she spent writing to tell him of her infidelity with Martin Castleton, the tears she had to keep dashing from her cheeks as she wrote. She had known how much she would hurt him, knew exactly how deeply wounded he would be. Now, she scarcely knew herself why she had done it. She recalled the day she had gone to Hexham to confess to May, and instead had listened appalled to Marian's own wretched confession, and her plea for silence. She should have continued to heed her sister-in-law, and kept her guilt locked inside. Certainly kept it from John; this good man whom she loved, deeply, but nowadays seemed sometimes farther away from her than ever.

'You found your God there.' She knew she was hurting him

again, by her use of the word 'your', but it was true. His faith merely served to illustrate how far apart they were. All at once, she was newly aware of the heavy lump of the baby inside her. She could feel its intrusive solidity, weighting her down as she knelt there, in the glowing warmth. Its future, their future as a family unit, seemed insecure, precarious. 'Nobody's *happy*, Jenny.' Teddy's words rang again in her brain.

'You don't begrudge me that, do you?' As always, John's voice was gentle, more apologetic than reproachful.

'No.' She shook her head, blinked back the tears hovering behind her eyes. 'Sometimes, though, I wish you weren't so good, Johnny. I wish you'd give me a damned good hiding and tell me what a bitch I am.' The tears spilt over, in spite of her efforts to prevent them. She shook her head again, angrily. 'It's bloody hard, sometimes! It's as hard to be forgiven as it is to forgive!' She heaved herself upright and blundered through to the bedroom, thrusting the door closed behind her and leaving him standing alone in the living-room.

CHAPTER FIFTEEN

'Come on. Let's go through to the room for coffee. No, Jenny. You and John go through. Teddie will give us a hand stacking the dishes. Ruby will do them in the morning, bless her.'

'Tell her she's certainly done us proud.' Jenny put her hand on the now prominent bulge of her stomach and blew out her cheeks appreciatively. 'I'm not sure how much of this is baby and how much that delicious dinner.'

'Well, we *did* all chip in and lend a hand, didn't we, girls?' May smiled at Teddie and Iris, while Jenny detected that underlying hint of defensiveness so often there in her mother-in-law's tone whenever the domestic help was referred to. Even after all these years, May's working-class roots did not sit easily with the notion of having hired help in the house. Or was that reflection, Jenny wondered honestly, more an indication of her own edginess and the tension she was feeling right now?

In the large but cosy room, its double windows snugly curtained against the wet December night, the fire was blazing, its cheeriness at odds with Jenny's mood. But she was quite convinced of the reality of the atmosphere she sensed between her and May; a reserve, and a smothered disapproval of the way Jenny's revelation of Marian's guilty secret had changed life so

169

drastically, not only for Teddy and his wife, but for all of them. Not least, his daughter, who came in pulling on her school raincoat and winding the striped scarf about her neck. She was in her uniform, the winter grey felt hat perched jauntily on the back of her dark head. There was a carol service in the abbey, in which the local youth choir was taking part.

'It's not fair, Beaconsfield packing up so early! We don't finish till Wednesday.'

John grinned. 'I know. It's heaven at school now, with all those horrors safely out of the way.' He was standing with his back to the fire, and now he moved. 'I'll get my coat.' He had already insisted on taking her by car and attending the service himself. Now Teddie protested yet again, but he waved her polite objections aside. 'It's not every day I get the chance of being seen with a young lady on my arm.'

'Instead of his fat frump of a wife!' Jenny put in jovially, from the depths of the armchair into which she had carefully lowered herself.

'But you don't even celebrate Christmas!' Teddie returned.

'Hey! Listen you! I've written more notes to Santa than you've had hot dinners. And we've been singing carols and eating Chrissy pud for the past week, so shut up! We shouldn't be *that* long, love.' He bent and kissed Jenny's head. His hand touched her shoulder, gave a brief squeeze.

He *does* know something of what I'm going through, Jenny acknowledged. She forced a smile on to her face as May and Iris came through. As always, Iris busied herself pouring the coffee, while May took up her favourite seat on one side of the fire.

'I feel so sorry for little Teddie,' May began, without preamble, when all three were settled with their cups. 'She's asked if she can stay here for Christmas. Marian's having her mum and stepdad up to Low Fell. And a whole lot more besides, if I know anything of Nelly!' Her lips compressed thinly.

170

Jenny was well aware of the history of Teddie's maternal grand-mother, and how Marian was the product of her illicit relationship with a married man at the munitions factory where she and May had both worked during the Great War.

'That family!' May shook her head. 'There's a fatal flaw there, somewhere.'

Like mother like daughter, you mean, Jenny thought. 'You're not saying little Teddie's tainted, are you?' The question, couched in a tone of ringing criticism, was out before Jenny could prevent it, almost.

May's cheeks reddened. 'Of course not! Poor Teddie's the victim. Robbed of her father, her mother half-mental with her guilt.'

Teddy had left for Palestine over two weeks ago. May had already told John how bitterly the young girl had wept, and how she had riled against her father for what she saw as his desertion of both wife and daughter. Jenny cleared her throat and asked awkwardly, 'Does Teddie know? I mean – what happened . . . between Marian and Teddy. Why they're . . . separating?' May's dark eyes stared at her, and Jenny felt herself colouring. 'The details. . . ?' She felt even more wretched during the distinct pause that followed her trailing question.

May, too, seemed to have difficulty in speaking. 'To be honest, I'm not sure if she knows all of it. About the abortion. She was only six or seven, after all. But I'm sure she knows there was something going on between Marian and that fellow. Jim Moody.' Another pause, the contempt with which May had pronounced the name hung in the air. 'We've never talked directly about it. I don't want to hurt her any more. I just hope she knows it isn't all Teddy's fault. This time, bless him, however foolish he might be going off like this, he has some cause.' Again she shook her head, impatiently, at her own emotion. 'That stupid, stupid, weak girl!'

171

Jenny knew she was referring to Marian. Iris intervened, in her effort to comfort. 'There, there! It's done with, it all happened a long time ago. Teddy will come back soon—'

All at once, Jenny felt her own sadness and her anger choking her. She tried to struggle up, felt the restricting bulk she was carrying pinning her down, her knees scissoring ridiculously, bringing the tears stinging to her eyes as she levered herself up, pushing herself to her feet. 'Look! I can't keep quiet any longer. There's something you should know—'

May waved away her interruption. Her voice, still unsteady, was quiet now, weary. 'Oh, I know! You did what you thought was best. John told me.' May grunted. 'Even Teddy stuck up for you before he left.' She shrugged expressively. 'I don't know what to think any more. You're lucky, I suppose.' Her look was hard as she stared at the standing figure before her. 'I used to be like you. Seeing things in black and white. I—'

'No! No! You don't understand!' Now Jenny returned her stare, her eyes glittering. 'Not at all! I'm not talking about Marian! I'm talking about me. I'm no better than she is! Worse, in fact. And I can't keep quiet about it any longer. We've both kept our secret far too long. You don't know about me – what I'm like.'

Iris had risen, too. Now she stepped forward, reached out as though to restrain Jenny, whose voice was catching with her sobs. 'Look. We're all upset. Let's wait—'

'No! No more waiting, no more keeping quiet. I can't bear to hear you slating Marian when *I'm* just as bad. I've let John down. Twice!' She spoke quickly, the tears streaming down her face, while Iris and May, one standing, the other still seated, were like statues.

May's face was paper-white, she was gasping as though breathless. 'So you see,' Jenny finished, weeping, but with a weary kind of triumph at last, 'anything you say about Marian, you can say

172

twice over for me. Because I betrayed him twice.'

Jenny was aware of a huge relief. But then May amazed her. The slim form rose, came close to her, those brown eyes still holding her, full of pain, of shock – and then the world exploded in a blinding red pain, as May drew back her right arm and smacked her across the left side of her face, with all the force she could muster. It knocked Jenny's head round, almost knocked her off her feet. Vision gone, her hearing buzzed, the pain flared again and she tasted blood inside her mouth. She stumbled, dizzily felt Iris's sturdy arms supporting her, guiding her as she almost fell back into the chair. The tears came, her body was seized with violent trembling, and she was glad of the focus required for the burning discomfort of her branded cheek.

'Put your head between your knees.' Iris's voice seemed to come from a distance. The giddiness was going, but Jenny felt herself obeying, felt Iris's large hand warm on the back of her neck, thrusting her down against the ballooning constriction of her stomach and belly. 'I'll get you a cold flannel to hold against your face.' There was a great comfort in being taken charge of. Jenny felt like a naughty little girl dealt with by firm but loving parents.

She started to weep again. 'I'm sorry. I didn't mean – I couldn't help – I had to say something. Keeping quiet all this time.'

'Hang on.' Iris was brusque. She left Jenny alone. The ringing in her ears had stopped, but the left side of her face felt swollen and throbbed painfully. She could still feel the heat of the blow. In spite of her tears, she felt a bubbling urge to giggle hysterically. She did, when she visualized the serene, beautiful figure of May transformed, letting loose and sloshing her like that. She realized her mother-in-law had left the room. Probably May was as shocked at her own aggression as Jenny was to be on the receiving end. Iris hurried in with a cool face cloth, which she pressed to Jenny's cheek, urging her to hold it there. 'Just hang on.' She hurried out again, no doubt to tend to the one she was most concerned about, and always would be.

When her limbs felt steadier, Jenny rose and went across to the oval mirror hanging on the wall, over the sideboard. Oh God! She took the cloth away and saw the red imprint of the palm running down one side, the top of the cheekbone beneath her left eye slightly swollen. The fleshy inside of her mouth was sore. She winced as she ran her tongue gently over it. At least May hadn't formed a fist. If she had punched her with that force, she might have knocked half her teeth out!

She turned as Iris came back, again on her own. 'May's still upset. You can understand that, I hope. It's been such a shock to her. To both of us.' She looked embarrassed, and Jenny had to admit she had no idea whether Iris was angry with her. It suddenly occurred to her how skilful the large figure was at hiding her emotions. She recalled the time of Dan's death, and the scandal associated with it, and how dignified Iris had always appeared. May was probably the only person in the world who truly knew Iris, the only one before whom she would lower entirely that well-bred guard.

'I'm sorry. I didn't do it to hurt you. I just – I couldn't take it any more. The feeling of – deceiving you. When ma talked about Marian—'

Again, Iris's interruption was brusque. 'I take it you've told John?'

Jenny nodded, shocked. 'He knew all along. I told him about the German boy when we got engaged again. Before we married.' She felt ridiculously youthful again. 'And with Martin Castleton. I wrote as soon as it happened. I offered to divorce him. When he came back from Palestine . . .'

'Look. John and Teddie will be back soon. We've thought of a plan. A white lie. You can stay here tonight. The guest bed's made up. You go up, get into bed. We'll say you had a tummy upset, the rich food, something like that. See how things look in the morning.' She paused, added in quick embarrassment, 'You could always pretend to be asleep, when he comes in.'

Jenny smiled shakily. 'And let's just hope I don't have a shiner when I wake up.' But she was weakly grateful to accept Iris's ploy. 'Tell May I'm sorry,' she murmured, before she did as she was bidden. She even followed Iris's advice and lay still in the darkness when John put his head round the door and whispered her name, before reclosing it and tiptoeing away.

But within minutes there was a soft tapping, and the door opened and closed once more. Jenny knew it was May. 'I have to talk to you.' The voice was a whisper.

Jenny struggled up, groped for the bedside lamp. 'I'm supposed to be asleep.' She moved her legs as May perched on the edge of the bed. 'You're not going to beat me again, are you?'

The look of shame on May's face brought them close for an instant. 'I can't tell you how ashamed I am! It was awful.' She gestured helplessly.

'No more than I deserved.' Jenny hesitated, then said, 'How often I've wished that John would do something similar.'

May's eyes, luminous in the dim light, still showed the hurt she felt. 'You truly shocked me. I can't understand – how you could do something like that. You *and* Marian. But especially you.'

'That's why it was important to tell you. I've wanted to for years. John didn't want you being hurt. But I had to let you know the truth. I'm no different to Marian. Worse in a way.' She held up her hand so that May would let her finish. 'There was – I never had any excuse. Not even of loving them. At least Marian, with this Jim chap – she was really fond of him. And he cared for her. She never told him that she was pregnant. She sent him away, before . . .' May's eyes were on her, strangely pleading, as though she did not want to hear any more. 'The German boy. Horst. I was a virgin. John and I – we'd never – we were tempted.

175

Both of us. But we didn't. We loved each other. But then Horst –
he talked. He was so different from John. So knowing, so
worldly—' She shook her head, swallowed hard. 'It only
happened once. And it was the same with Martin. Oh, I knew
him, worked with him for months. Knew what he was like. He
tried it on. But it was just one night. I was lonely. I loved John
more than ever—'

'No.' May's voice, for all its quietness, cut through her. 'It's no
good trying to tell me. Explain. I'll never understand. How you –
either of you, you and Marian – could betray your husbands like
that. And you say you loved him. How could you do that? With
another man?' Her voice was so full of revulsion that it struck
Jenny far harder than any blow to her face. 'I lost my Jack – when
I was – was only young. I missed him, so much! With my body,
too! Yes, he was the only man I ever loved with. I missed him! But
I could no more think of going with another man – not even
when I knew he would never come back.'

She sniffed, stood so suddenly that Jenny felt the bed shake. 'I
can't face saying anything to John. Not now. At this time. He's so
happy, with the baby coming and everything. It's up to you if you
tell him you've told me. But I won't say anything. I wish with all
my heart *you* hadn't.'

The door closed quietly on her, and Jenny turned clumsily,
pressing her aching face into the pillow to muffle her sobs.

The whole of the holiday period, spent at Keswick with her
parents, was one of tension and increasing moodiness for Jenny.
She sensed that her bouts of irritableness and sullen silences
were spoiling the festivities for everyone, but she was helpless to
prevent them. On the day after Boxing Day, she let John
persuade her to wrap up and go for a short drive with him. The
winter sun shone from a cloudless sky, etching everything with its
sharp winter brightness, and the high fells were dusted with a

picture postcard setting of light snow. Though the sun's power was enough to shift the bite of early frost, he drove carefully as he took their favourite route around the northern edge of Derwent Water and up towards Cat Bells. There was very little traffic on the road, though several parked, empty vehicles on the grassy verges indicated the number of people who were taking advantage of the splendid day to do some serious hiking.

Jenny's lips thinned when she saw where he drew in, high above the gleaming stretch of water. The hurt and anger welled up once again. He was being unfair bringing her here. 'Remember this?' he asked needlessly.

Nearly nine years ago, he had brought her here, when she thought she had lost him for good, and asked her to marry him. She had told him then she was unworthy of him. Now, more than ever, the same thought pierced her. She fought against his nostalgic tenderness. 'Look. Why don't you go back to Hexham? Spend the rest of the holiday with your mum and Aunt I? I'll be all right here, honestly. I'm not fit to be with at the moment. Nerves, I guess.' As she anticipated, his brown eyes gazed at her with that mixture of hurt and gentle reproach.

'I want to be with you.' He made another effort. 'This place will always be special. You made me very happy here.'

'Did I? Did I really? Be honest with me. Are you still happy? Be honest with yourself.'

'I want things to be right for us. For both of us. The baby coming is the greatest thing that could ever happen, for me. I want it to be like that for you. I—'

She cut brutally across his loving tone. 'John. I told your mother. About Horst Zettel and Martin Castleton.' She saw the look of shock and dismay flood his features. 'I couldn't stand it any longer. She started to go on about Marian. How she'd let Teddy down. It wasn't fair.' When he didn't say anything, she continued, 'I ought to tell my folks, too. Don't you think? *That's* not fair, either. Keeping it from them.' She smiled bitterly. 'They'll be horrified. Their little girl! Nothing more than a slut!'

'Can't it wait? I mean, you've waited long enough now. Why Christmas of all times? Or are you looking for maximum fallout?'

The use of the new expression, associated with all the horrors of the new weapons of destruction, struck her. 'Is that what you think this is all about? Me wanting to lash out and hurt as many people as possible?'

He shook his head unhappily. 'I suppose not. You did what you felt you had to do.'

She smiled again, more genuinely this time. 'Speaking of lashing out, your mum clocked me one. That bruising under my eye? Remember? That's where she hit me.' Now she really had succeeded in shocking him. Despite her nearness to tears, she almost laughed at his astonished gape. 'It's all right. I deserved it, after all. I've told you – I don't know why you didn't do it to me years ago.'

He stared ahead through the spotted windscreen to the sunshine dazzling painfully off the long bonnet. His face was a dull red, and she knew from the quiet of his tone how wounded he was. 'Is that the way you'd rather have me? Drag you by the hair, beat you with my club, haul you back to our cave? Zettel's probably dead by now, but I suppose I could still find Castleton. Put a bullet through his head, or offer him pistols at dawn or something. Is that what you want? The two of us – or the three of us – fighting over you?'

She felt withered and small with self-contempt at his passion. 'I'm no good!' she cried rawly, letting her own emotion erupt. 'I'm not good enough for you! I can't ever forget it—'

He caught her by her right shoulder, twisting her round to face him, his eyes burning into her now. 'I'm not perfect! I'm not some holy Joe, or any better than anybody else.' She felt the pressure of his fingers digging in to her, his power kept her tear-filled

178

gaze on his. 'I'm flesh and blood, I fancy you, I want to have sex with you, I miss making love to you. But that's not *all* I want you for. I love you. Yes, I love your body; yes, I feel sick with jealousy sometimes at the thought of you making love with someone else. But you're not just a sexual object to me. I love you for all that you are – for the person you are. I want to be with you. Not just to possess your lovely body. Sex is part of it, an important part. Of course it is! But that's not the whole you! The way you think, you talk, you laugh. All the things that make up you as a person. I want to share my life with you. All of it. I don't want to share it with anyone else. I don't want to beat you when you go wrong, or when you do something I don't agree with, or can't understand.'

His breath caught, he sighed, shook his head as though defeated, the passion ebbed from his voice. 'I love you, Jenny,' he said, with simple weariness. 'I don't know how to tell you – or even to show you. But I do. And will, always.'

She began to cry in earnest, the tears streaming down her cheeks. She slumped, put her head towards him, trying to get close to him, trapped by her bulk in the narrow space. 'Oh, Johnny! I love you so much! I do so want your baby!'

CHAPTER SIXTEEN

Teddy swore with relief when his feet finally touched the gritty dust of the airstrip in the Negev Desert. His body ached from the bumpy ride in the Flying Fortress, his head throbbed from the continuous clattering roar as he and his companions sat in icy discomfort on the floor amidst the crates of arms and ammunition, and the jumbled heaps of miscellaneous supplies the juddering craft was loaded with. Airsickness added to his troubles, but was forgotten when the ex-American bomber began to fling about even more wildly, and the racket of the engines was interspersed with the dull thump of anti-aircraft fire. 'We're over the Egyptian lines now,' a grinning member of the crew needlessly informed them. 'Sorry we don't have enough 'chutes to go round, but don't worry. They wouldn't be able to hit us even if we stopped moving.' Despite his reassuring words, his passengers were all glad when, forty-five minutes later, the plane descended rapidly and made bouncing contact with the crude runway.

For months now, this southern area of the Negev had been virtually cut off by land because of the well-established Egyptian army. Now, the *Mahal*, or overseas volunteer unit, to which Teddy had been assigned, had been moved down to the Beersheba area as part of the reinforcements which would soon launch an all-out

attack to drive the Egyptian invaders back across their own
borders.

Now that the bone-shaking, hair-raising flight was over, most of
the newcomers were happy to feel part of the real scheme of
things. They had had a brief period of training and indoctrina-
tion at a converted settlement on the coast at Bat Yam, just
outside Tel Aviv. With his experience in the regular army and his
REME background, Teddy was quickly drafted to an engineering
unit based in the Jewish sector of Jerusalem. Yet another ceasefire had been arranged just days before he arrived, so his first
operational duties saw him working around the chaotic no-
man's-land, repairing defences and access routes to the front line
– a mess of barbed wire emplacements, heaps of rubble, and,
over all, the stench of putrefying animal corpses. The news that
the unit was to be transferred to the southern front was very
welcome, in spite of the promise of 'seeing some real action'.

They were put into a large tented encampment close to the
airstrip. The Mahal volunteers were kept together, and Teddy
quickly formed a friendship with a tall but corpulent South
African, 'Manny' Grunwald, an ex-regular who had fought in the
desert campaign. 'Last chance to kick over the traces,' was how
he described his motive for joining the present conflict, 'before
I go back home and start breeding.'

The next morning, they formed up as part of the large force
assembled to be addressed by the Operations Officer. Yitzhak
Rabin was youthful looking, yet the thrust of his prominent jaw,
and the shock of dark hair standing up from his brow and blow-
ing back and forth in the strong, cool desert wind, gave him a
no-nonsense, authoritative air. His speech was a mix of Hebrew
and English, his penetrating voice inspiring confidence in all
who heard him. The plan was to follow the Roman road that led
south through the Negev, using this unlikely route to move their
armoured columns to attack the Egyptians head-on. And Teddy's

unit would play a key role in making this ancient track passable for the heavy tanks and artillery. 'Difficult, but not impossible,' was Rabin's forthright assessment.

The road became known as the Ruheiba Trail. The engineers moved out into the desert south of Beersheba and began round-the-clock efforts to make the path through the rocky landscape fit for the heavy vehicles which were to follow. The operation was scheduled to begin on 20 December. On the nineteeth, the weather changed ominously. There was a heavy build-up of cloud on the horizon, visibility closed in. The rain began just before sunset. Within two hours, Teddy and his colleagues, their uniforms darkened and sodden with rain, were struggling to save their own equipment from bogging down in the swirling eddies that grew momentarily about their feet. The sandy pockets between the pale, scoured outcrops of rock turned to liquid mud. Water came roaring down the narrow defiles either side of the roadway, the wadis filled, and the exhausted men watched helplessly as their frantic efforts were washed away. 'It's no good. The tanks will just bog down in this!' The troops sat, drenched and shivering under their makeshift shelters, or tried to sleep, until a grey, miserable dawn filtered through, and the rain continued to fall.

It stopped after two days, and once more they struggled, shoring up, creating hasty diversions, piling up dusty rubble and pounding it to make a surface which would withstand the onslaught of the churning vehicle tracks. Behind them, the armoured columns crept forward once more. On Christmas Eve there was another downpour, when they were within striking distance of the enemy front line. The caked-on mud and dust covering their clothing, and every visible inch of their skin, made them weirdly one with the harsh landscape.

Late that night, with the rain finally easing, they flopped wearily by the side of the track, and watched the tanks rumbling past, managing to raise dust in spite of the dampness in the air. Soon afterwards, the guns of the bombardment boomed out, and they felt the ground quiver, and flashes lit the cloudy night sky. It was well after midnight. Suddenly, Teddy felt a boot prod his thigh, and he saw Manny's teeth startlingly white against the deep grime of his face as he grinned broadly. 'Happy Christmas, you bleddy Christian!'

When they moved forward in support of the advance, they became part of the front line and were caught up in the fighting. They came under shellfire from the stubbornly resisting Egyptians, who were withstanding the assault with unexpected determination. The Israeli tanks used in the attack were old American surplus stock, which had been acquired in Europe via the Czech government. There had been some hasty repairing and redesigning of the weaponry, which had been rendered useless before the Americans abandoned them. Now there were frequent armament failures. Teddy's unit moved about like wayside mechanics, desperately trying to fix the faulty guns while the battle raged around them. At one point, a squadron of Egyptian half-tracks suddenly appeared at the summit of a low, rocky swell and sent them scattering for cover in the dangerously open landscape as shell bursts mushroomed all around them. The enemy sent up dust plumes as they started to roll down the slope towards them, until the haze of the sky reverberated to a new roar, and three fighters, Messerschmitts bearing the Israeli Star of David, skimmed low over them and sent arcs of devastating fire into the Egyptian vehicles, leaving two in flames, while the rest turned tail and fled.

The burst of cheering was short-lived, however, for the planes angled round, wing tips pointing to the sun, and came swooping back, to let loose another deadly spray of machine gun fire at their own troops. Everyone dived to earth again. The shells clattered all about them, and with a whooshing explosion and a brief tongue of flame, one of the trucks went up, showering glowing bits of metal over the prone figures, and leaving a black column of smoke from the burning wreck. A young man, bare to the waist and frantically waving his shirt, leapt up and danced about, until another burst caught him and tossed him aside in a lifeless bundle.

Another scrambled on to the turret of a disabled tank, tore its pennant free and held it high over his head, standing fearlessly in the path of the plane making its second attacking run. The earth furrowed in a series of brown eruptions, homing in on him, but he never flinched, and all at once the nose of the plane jerked violently upward, and the thunder of cannon fire died away. The three fighters came together in close formation, and as they flew overhead for the last time, the leader waggled his wings in acknowledgement before they vanished over the low brow to the east, in pursuit of the enemy column.

The comparative silence was uncanny, until ears registered the distant sounds of battle again, and the curses and cries of comrades as the squad slowly stood, or crawled from their various bits of shelter. Two were dead, and three more wounded, one so badly that it seemed unlikely he would survive. 'What were they doing, the bastards? Surely they could see the Gyppos were shooting at us?'

Manny Grunwald looked shaken, his big face grey beneath its coating of grime. Teddy tried to grin. His voice was hoarse, his throat parched. 'Who needs enemies, eh?' He recalled the night in Hamburg, the flaming hell of destruction which had rained down on the city, when he and his fellow POWs had been caught in the middle of it. 'Friendly fire'. He reckoned that in all his military career it had been the side he was fighting for who had come closest to killing him.

There were three more days of fierce fighting before the opposing force finally crumbled. The Egyptian border was crossed, and by 30 December, the Israeli force was twenty miles inside Egyptian territory. Then came shocking news. Britain issued an ultimatum to the new state, threatening force if it did not withdraw immediately from Egypt. 'We can take El Arish and cut through to the coast!' the Israeli officer in charge of the unit raged. 'We'll have the whole of Gaza cut off. The Egyptians will have to surrender.' The British members of the Mahal felt extremely uncomfortable, but a day later President Truman added his more weighty condemnation of the Israeli 'invasion', and on New Year's Day the withdrawal from Sinai began.

'At least we've cleared the bastards out of the Negev,' the Israelis consoled themselves.

'Feck the bleddy Yanks!' Manny Grunwald grumbled. 'And the Brits! We should have chased the bastards all the way back to Cairo! They'll try it again one day, mark my words!'

'How is he, love? I bet he was pleased to hear from you, wasn't he?'

Teddie nodded vigorously in answer to May's question. Her dark eyes shone a little too brightly, May thought, the young face momentarily flushed with more than just excitement. A painful wave of love and compassion flowed through May as she watched her granddaughter come in and resume her seat on the sofa, smoothing down the skirts of her new dress as she did so. Though the lines of the dress were childish still, and her small breasts scarcely detectable beneath the high bodice, the white ankle socks over the shining patent shoes added to the impression of girlishness, Teddie was already beginning the transition from childhood to adolescence.

May could recall her own fears, and shame, and uncertainties, at that age, and once more felt that helpless regret at the reflection that Teddie had no one to help her. May could not envisage Marian being much good as adviser and confidante. Her mouth twisted in distaste at the thought that such a role was far more likely to be played by one of Julia's girls. She could imagine all too well how indelicate their performance would be. More than ever, she was thankful that Teddie was far different from them and their background, thanks to her schooling, and, May conceded, a little uncomfortably at what she surmised would be swiftly condemned as snobbery by Julia and her brood, her own and Iris's influence over the young girl.

Even this friendship with Michael Porter was nothing to worry about, as Iris was repeatedly reminding her. She wondered if she really *was* as prudish as she feared she was, and as Iris constantly teased her about. Besides, Teddie hadn't seen the boy for almost six months now, and, on her own admission, his letters had tailed off considerably. She had been excited for him at the return of his father in time for Christmas. 'First time Michael will have seen him for five years!' she had told her grandma. Then May had seen the flicker of pain on the transparent features, and felt again that helpless anger at the events which had taken Teddy away yet again.

May had tried to ease the girl's pain, but the youngster had been deeply hurt, and would not discuss it, changing the subject with untypical rudeness, for which May hadn't the heart to reprimand her. Things were such a mess. She made a great effort and pushed them from her thoughts now, on this last night of the old year.

'I expect we'll get a few first-footers. Tommy Hedley and his wife are bound to call round. And Ann and Bob will look in, if they don't get stuck at some party. But we're determined you're going to be our first-foot this year!'

Teddie's face pinked again. 'But I'm a girl!'

'And a very pretty one tonight!' Iris put in forcefully. In honour of the occasion, she, too, had for once got out of her old sweaters and baggy slacks, and, corseted and silk-stockinged under her dark dress, looked imposingly matronly in her triple-rowed pearls, her iron grey hair crimped into severely disciplined waves. She turned from the trolley and brought Teddie a glass of red wine. 'And grown-up enough for this, I think, eh, grandma?'

'You can't have a girl for first—'

'Don't be daft!' Iris laughed. 'Dark-haired, dark-eyed! Just what we need! And with a name like Teddie! Well!'

They all joined in the laughter. May was thankful that Marian had not objected to Teddie's coming over to Hexham for New Year. Though Teddie had loyally said little about the Christmas festivities at Low Fell, May guessed that her granddaughter had not derived much enjoyment, with the house crowded out with Marian's mother and husband, and other boozy relatives. No doubt Julia and her three trollops had been conspicuously present for a large part of the time. It seemed that Nelly Dunn, or Graham, to give her her married name, and Julia were thick as thieves, and doubtless ruling the roost at Low Fell since Teddy's departure.

As always, May experienced that swell of bitterness and anger, underlaid with sympathy, for the hapless figure of Marian, who had been so lamentably foolish as well as wicked. She had paid right enough for her sins. She seemed to spend most of her time in a state of dope-induced tranquillity, sleeping half the day, punctuated by weeping fits of depression when she was unable to face anybody. May felt guilty at the fact that she had seen Marian only once in the two months that Teddy had been gone. But the thought of having to face Nelly, and maybe even Julia, whom she had not communicated with for over a year now, deterred her. That, and the fact that, deep down, she felt herself incapable of forgiving Marian for what she had done while Teddy had been a prisoner in Germany.

Once again, with great effort she pushed away the thoughts

that led on from this, determined not to spoil the night for the young girl sipping at her glass and trying not to screw up her face or shudder at the unfamiliar taste of the wine. 'Perhaps Michael can come through to spend a weekend up here next term.' May saw the colour sweep up the thin neck and face.

'Oh, I don't know.' Teddie stared at the glass she held. 'His dad's home for about four months, I think. Until after Easter. He'll want to spend as much time with him as he can, I expect. And he's got lots of school chums at St Peter's now.'

Iris leaned over and lightly punched her bare arm. 'Anyway, you'll soon be fighting off hordes of young swains! You'll be spoilt for choice!'

Teddie's gaze turned to Iris with such transparent misery in those dark eyes that May's heart went out to her.

In her heavy winter coat, and with a woollen scarf swathed about her head, Teddie was sent out to the front porch at five minutes to midnight, clutching her piece of bread, and a twist of salt, and a lump of coal wrapped in tissue paper. Standing in the hall, waiting for the clock to chime, May was reminded power-fully of other year ends, both here at the cottage and those more distant ones, in the crowded childhood home at Sidney Terrace. Its narrow lobby, packed with vociferous family and friends, mostly well into their cups, contrasted sharply with the restrained tastefulness and the quiet comfort surrounding her now. Too quiet, she thought, with the only family member present her granddaughter. And Iris, she amended hastily, who was as dear to her as any of her family could be. She slipped her arm around the rigidly encased waist and felt the reassuring pressure of a similar embrace from her partner.

Teddie was excited to be the first to cross the threshold in 1949. The whole idea that she should be allowed to stay up to see in the New Year, and even to have a taste of wine, delighted her. And when, almost an hour later, the Hedleys, elderly neighbours, turned up, closely followed by Bob and Ann Swainsby, and Bob addressed her as 'young lady', she did not feel patronized, but took him at least half seriously. However, she was soon nodding, and struggling to stop her jaws stretching in an aching yawn. She was happy to escape when May suggested tactfully she might like to go up to bed, and she was lost in deep sleep when the visitors left at 2.30.

'One for the road – or the blankets?' Iris suggested, when she and May returned to the lamp-lit cosiness and the flickering fire. May nodded gratefully. 'Brandy?'

May nodded again. 'Drown it in soda, please.' She slipped off her shoes and sank wearily into her favourite chair, stretching out her legs and crossing her slim ankles.

Iris brought the drinks across and plonked down in the chair opposite. 'God! This corset's killing me! Like an iron maiden!' She gathered up the skirt of her long gown and hauled it inelegantly up over her solid legs. She unsnapped the suspenders, and rolled the stockings down her white limbs, curling the toes of her bare feet in the thickness of the rug. She left the dress hawked up across her thighs, and splayed her knees apart with luxurious abandon.

'The Honourable Mrs Iris Wright, née Bloomfield, at home!' May giggled. 'That's a fine shot for *Tatler*!' But her light-hearted mood could not last. 'I wonder where Teddy is right now?' She sipped at her drink. She had heard nothing from him since his departure. Teddie had told her that Marian had received one letter a few weeks ago, and shortly afterwards an early Christmas card. 'No news,' his daughter had said. 'Just all his love!' she added bitterly.

John had rung well in advance of midnight, from Keswick, to wish them all the best. He had spent Christmas, and his thirty-fourth birthday on Christmas Day, with his wife's family. May had hoped he might have come across to see the old year out with his mother. 'How many New Year's Eves have we all had together since the boys grew up?' she mused now. 'You'd hardly need two hands to count them on, I bet. It's all such a mess, isn't it? Who'd have thought? Both their marriages—'

Iris heaved herself up, and flopped down on her knees at May's feet, leaned her weight against May's limbs. 'Come on, old girl. They'll come through—'

'It's Jenny I really can't understand.' May sat up, took hold of Iris's wrists, their brows almost touching. 'Why did she have to tell us now, after all this time keeping it all a secret? With Christmas, and the baby due and everything? Why wait till now? I still can't believe it! It's so – horrible!' She shuddered with revulsion. 'All those years ago! That German boy!' Her fingers dug into Iris's skin, her gaze held hers with pleading intensity. 'And John – going ahead and marrying her. Do you think she's telling the truth? Do you think she really *did* tell him – before they got married?'

'Yes. I think so.'

'And he still went ahead?' May sounded genuinely shocked. 'Why? I wish I could— And for her to go and do it again, with John away, risking his life. That was so wicked! I'll never be able to forget it, every time I look at her! And now, with the baby coming . . .' She shook her head, swallowed hard against the choking tears. 'How could she? You can see it's done something to John. He's not the same. Ever since he came back from the war—'

'No!' The interjection came strongly from Iris. Now she raised her hands and took hold of May's shoulders, pressing tightly. 'He's different, but he's all right. They'll both be all right. This faith of his. I don't know much about it, but it's given him something. He's quieter, I grant you. But he was always a thinker, wasn't he?' Close to tears herself, Iris shook May gently and smiled at her. 'Wasn't he? A serious little thing, even as a child.

Remember? Now he's strong. He doesn't say much, I know, but I'm sure he knows what he believes in. And what he wants. And he loves Jenny. The baby – it will hold them together.' Iris paused, and said hesitantly, 'And I think, in spite of everything, she *does* love John.'

'But how? How can she? How could she do that to him – and still claim to love him?'

Iris released her, groped in her pocket for a hankie, and blew her nose loudly. She pushed down, lumbered with a grunt to her feet. 'God knows! I'm no expert in these matters. My record was pretty dismal.' She smiled down lovingly, held out both her hands. May clasped them and let herself be pulled upright. 'At least as far as men were concerned! You go up. I'll lock up. I'll come and say goodnight.'

Iris carried the glasses out to the kitchen, ran water into the bowl and left them standing in it. She wheeled the trolley through from the living-room, checked front and back doors, then put out the lights and climbed slowly up the stairs. May was already in bed, propped up on the pillows on which her still-dark hair was spread. The thin straps of her nightgown against the delicate, pale shoulders, and her breasts under the lace-trimmed silk, made her look desirably youthful.

Iris's own heart thudded beneath her encased bosom. She cleared her throat, wanted so desperately to say, 'Let me sleep with you tonight, my darling.' But she didn't. May lifted up her mouth trustingly, their lips touched softly. 'Night-night, my love.'

Tears stinging her eyes, Iris turned away, the familiar tender ache of love and unfulfilment like a faithful ally as she left the room.

CHAPTER SEVENTEEN

John stared at the letter, headed *HM Prisons*, and the smaller visitors' pass. He felt again a brief sense of anger with Teddy for involving him in this, then shame at his distaste for the meeting that lay ahead. John had been the first to hear from his brother. In fact, Teddy's letter had been posted immediately before the departure for Israel – or Palestine. Many people were still not sure what to call the mandated territory.

He's got absolutely nobody to visit or look out for him, or even to care about whether he's alive or dead. And it'll be a good test of that religion of yours, treating everybody as equals. It's only once every three months or so, and maybe you can drop him the odd line now and then, like I used to. Not that I'm going to stop or anything, but you never know what might happen. He'd appreciate it, I know. I've already told him quite a lot about you, and about all the family, including my own mess. I know it always meant a lot to him, even when we were POWs, with him not having anyone of his own. He doesn't deserve to be shut away for years – he was just a kid, trying to survive as best he could.

Oh, and by the way, don't forget he's as queer as a nine bob note, and don't let that put you off!

John could just imagine the smile on Teddy's face as he penned those last words. They made John even more reluctant to take up Teddy's challenge, which was what his appeal had sounded like. But he had gone ahead and applied to visit Tony Ellis. Now permission had been granted, far sooner than he had anticipated.

He phoned Jenny that evening. 'How are you feeling?' he asked first, as always.

'Fine. The odd niggle. And the backache as usual. Apart from that, it's just this feeling of a barrage balloon stuffed up my jumper!' She sighed. 'This seems to have gone on forever. I'm still petrified, but I wish to God it would happen!'

'You'll be all right, love. Don't you worry. Listen to me!' he added quickly. 'I'm as nervous as a kitten.' They were still more than two weeks away from the predicted date, but he knew how uncertain these things could be. 'Listen. I've had word about the prison visit. A pass has come through for next Saturday. I'm going to go down overnight on Friday. On the train.'

He had half expected her to protest, to ask him not to go, and was filled with love for her when she did not do so. 'I don't envy you. Six hours or more! You'll freeze to death. Wrap up warm, won't you?'

'I'll be coming back on Saturday night. Be up north again early Sunday morning. Don't do anything daft, like having the baby while I'm down in London!'

'I won't. I'll sit with my legs crossed all weekend, I promise!'

She was right about the discomfort of the long journey from Newcastle. He felt that the expense of a first class ticket wasn't justified, so he roughed it in third class. There was no heating on, and the night temperature had dropped to near freezing, so that soon he was glad when the train was crowded. He had managed to get a corner seat, by the window furthest away from the sliding door which led into the corridor. They were wedged five-a-side on both upholstered bench-seats of the compartment, and the jammed conditions ensured a certain amount of warmth, at least for the upper body.

Studiously avoiding eye contact, except for the initial, tentative half-smile of acknowledgement, he stared over the five heads opposite at the garishly bright seaside scenes depicted in the two framed pictures. The one nearest to him proclaimed the pleasures of Whitley Bay, with a beach of a yellow far more vivid than anything he could recall, under a blazing sun more likely to be encountered in San Tropez. Children in white sunhats dug with buckets and spades, clean-cut dads stood about athletically in hooped bathing costumes while young mums lounged in deckchairs and displayed shapely legs of an attractiveness which had more to do with artistic licence than a realistic portrayal of the resort.

He was caught by a wave of powerful nostalgia when the train crossed the high viaduct and he stared down at the twinkling winter lights of Durham city – desolate enough, but stirring profoundly happy memories of what seemed now an idyllic existence he had shared with Jenny when they were students there fifteen years ago. At the next stop, Darlington, the train filled up even more, until the corridor itself became crowded with leaning figures or passengers squatting on their luggage. Some of his fellow male passengers suddenly assumed positions of deep slumber, but John eased himself reluctantly to his feet and trod on several others as he stepped to the door, letting in a fresh blast of colder air and offering his vacated seat to a middle-aged woman shrouded in a winter coat and unbecoming hat. Nodding her perfunctory thanks, she squeezed past and thrust herself backwards into the space he had left.

It was difficult to read in the dimness of the bulbs, so, instead, he leaned his arms on the brass rail running along the inside of the long window. He could see the shadowy outline of his own reflection, and the silver flash of rails speeding by in the blackness, broken by the odd blur of lights as they passed a building. He brought his mind to bear on the meeting that lay ahead. He had to strive hard to overcome his natural prejudice against the young man he was going to see. A traitor to his country. In spite of what Teddy had told him about Ellis, John could not condone the boy's actions, even as a means of survival. John was well aware of the dangers that extreme nationalistic pride could pose. The Germany that Hitler had led had proved that. And the Baha'i Writings confirmed it. *The earth is but one country, and mankind its citizens.* But to align oneself with the evil Nazi regime, to support it actively, as Ellis had done, even if it was to save his own skin, surely was unforgivable? The British authorities clearly regarded it as a heinous crime. He had even been sentenced to death for it. All right, the death sentence had been swiftly commuted, but they had shut him away, were going to keep him locked up for a very long time, it seemed.

There was another, equally grave, barrier against John's open-minded acceptance of the young convict – Tony's sexual deviancy. Teddy had talked to John occasionally about young Ellis. He had explained how being confined in the POW camp had brought to the fore the boy's latent homosexuality. How the constant barrage of references, the attitude of his fellow prisoners, had played upon Ellis's effeminate tendencies until the situation had gone beyond a joke. Privately, John had disagreed with Teddy's casually dismissive, almost flippant tone in referring to his young friend's perversion. 'Queer as a nine bob note.' And once, his brother had told John about a Christmas concert at the prison camp. He had shaken his head, laughing. 'I tell you. He dressed up as a showgirl. Fishnets, the lot! He looked bloody gorgeous!' Then the smile had faded. 'That's what started all this bloody nonsense off. With the Jerries, I mean. The camp commandant fell for him straight away, the dirty old sod!'

In the army, John had heard all the derogatory terms, the endless jokes, about being queer, though in all his almost-six years of service, he had never come across any serious examples of homosexual behaviour. In their discussion, Teddy had reminded him of a legendary character who had lived somewhere near the home of their mother's parents, in Sidney Terrace. 'Ducky' Fairbrother had worn strange silken shirts with long pointed collars, patterned with flowers and looking suspiciously like women's blouses. He 'minced about', according to Grandad Rayner. His mother was a widow, and he was often seen doing housework, even pegging out the washing in the back lane. All this had been a long time ago, when they were little. John could not recall ever seeing Ducky, but Teddy claimed he had once seen him down on his hands and knees, wearing a 'pinny' and whitening the front doorstep.

'Why 'Ducky'?' John wondered, years later.

'Well, he *was*, wasn't he?' Teddy grinned, adopting the exaggerated 'nancy boy' pose, with hip turned out and right arm raised, hand flapping limply from the wrist. 'A right little ducky!'

Even more recently, only days before they had parted at the end of the Christmas holiday, John had expressed his reservations to Jenny about his proposed visit. She had surprised him. He had felt a little embarrassed, even with her, at discussing such a subject as homosexuality, but she had asked him outright, 'Haven't you ever wondered about it? I mean, what it would be like? What they do with each other?'

He tried to smother his shock, the disgust and repugnance he felt at the contemplation of the mechanics of such things.

'*I* have!' she went on, pinking, and with a breathless giggle, in spite of her frankness. 'I mean – you know – not about men. I mean with girls. When I was younger, I – you know – I suppose it's different, with girls. They talk about things – and show a lot more – touching, kissing – that sort of thing.' The colour

196

mounted now, she faltered, giggling nervously again. 'Not that I ever did anything . . .'

All at once, John experienced a rush of deep embarrassment. The thought of his mother and Aunt I sprang into his mind, and all his aunt Julia's wicked innuendos. *The Lovebirds.* 'We can't help our thoughts sometimes. We all have those. And urges. But we don't give way. We don't give in—' He heard himself and stopped, appalled. He saw the flinch, the wide-eyed dismay flood Jenny's features as plainly as the colour that was already there.

'*I* did!'

'I wasn't talking about us! You!' He crossed over to her and persisted, against her moving away, on capturing and holding her. He put his hand on her head, pulled it in close to his chest, felt the swell of her belly between them.

She was glad that her face was hidden. 'You should!' she whispered. 'It's true, isn't it? It's just as big a sin, what I did. You of all people know that.'

'You're sorry for it. You've more than made up for it.' He hugged her tighter, letting her feel the solidity of the child she was carrying pressing between their bodies. 'God's compassionate. And forgiving. We're all imperfect. We can't help ourselves—'

'Maybe that poor boy in gaol can't help it, either. The way he is.'

John hadn't known what else to say, or think. Except, as he thought now, while the train roared and rattled its way down the country to the capital, sin was sin, whether one could help it or not, and we could only pray. *Enable us to conquer self and overcome desire.*

'It's very good of you to come all this way to see me, sir. I really appreciate it—'

'Please! Cut out the "sir", all right? The name's John. And I'll call you Tony, if I may.'

197

John tried to block out the voices all around them, and to concentrate on the thin figure sitting opposite him, through the thick diamond patterns of the wire mesh. In spite of the ugliness of the prison haircut, with its severe crop, shaved at the sides to the temples, leaving the pink ears exposed, so that it made the face look even narrower, and the coarse blue uniform shirt, with the prison number stamped prominently over the left breast pocket, and the reddened knuckles and savagely bitten finger-nails, John could still discern the slim grace, the delicacy of form and feature, which made Tony Ellis physically attractive – that fineness of structure, the soft texture of skin, which strayed a little too closely towards prettiness.

But, equally clearly, there was another quality in the face that marred that youthfulness, which had been stamped there by the traumatic circumstances of the blows life had dealt. A caution – an anticipation of pain, and fear, in the vulnerable eyes, the fine tracery of crinkles around their edges, which somehow made the smooth sweep of facial skin seem tautened. It added to the impression of wariness, and gave a curious tone of age, of world-weary, bitter knowledge overlaid upon the young features.

The opening conversation limped along quite painfully, as John had expected. The young man could not drop his defer-ence of manner, was uncomfortably obsequious in his gratitude. 'I can't believe you've bothered to travel all this way just to see me. You being so busy, with school and everything. Teddy's told me quite a bit about you. In his letters and that. He used to talk a lot about you, too, in the camp. He was very proud of you. Of all the family.'

There was another awkward pause. 'Yes. Well – I think you know. Things haven't worked out exactly as he hoped. That's why he's gone tearing off to Palestine and got himself involved in this Jewish-Arab fight.'

Once they had stumbled through the generalities and had got

down to more personal levels, it was, paradoxically, easier to talk more meaningfully. 'I reckon he took to being a POW pretty bad,' Tony offered. 'I mean, it wasn't a doddle for any of us, but Teddy took it harder than most. Felt he'd been left out – of doing his bit. That's probably why he's headed off again. You were out in the desert, weren't you, sir – I mean, John?'

John nodded, kept the talk focused on his brother. 'He did it before. I expect he told you about Spain, didn't he? He seems to have a weakness for getting himself in dangerous scrapes.'

'He'll be all right, don't you worry!' Tony's robust assurance was so patently meant to cheer and please that John smiled.

'Let's hope so. Now. What about you? How are you managing? Anything I can do for you? You must let me know if there's anything I can help with. I've left a parcel – some cigarettes, a couple of books. They said it would be all right.' He glanced across at the warder standing against one wall.

Tony blushed. 'That's great! Thanks ever so much! I don't want to be a trouble—'

'Nonsense! No bother at all. I'll write to you. Don't suppose Teddy will have much time where he is. We haven't heard from him at all since he got over there. Marian's had a letter, I believe.'

'It's all such a rotten shame!' The words were spoken with such evident feeling that John was surprised. His heart warmed towards the young man. 'If you knew just how much he was looking forward to getting home again. To his wife. And his little girl. That's all he wanted . . .'

'He's had four years at home now,' John gently reminded him. He saw the wounded reproach in the eyes opposite, more eloquent than any words. The look told him that this lad didn't need reminding. That he had spent four long years in this harsh place, and that he had nothing more to look forward to, perhaps for many more years. 'Look,' John went on quickly, 'I really mean it. I want to help all I can. I don't know much about – things here. But I'm going to find out. Maybe there's some way we can get them to look at your sentence again. Give you some idea of when you can be released. Now that the war's been over a while—'

Tony leaned back a little, as though consciously distancing himself from his visitor. That careworn, ugly look was back again. The red scrub of hair shook. 'I shouldn't bother yourself. I been told I'm looking at a twenty stretch.' He gave a low laugh that was more like a gasp of pain. 'I'll be bleeding forty-something when I get out of here!'

'No! I don't believe that. Attitudes will change, I know it. We'll get support for you. Organize things. Petitions—'

'It's not so bad in here – now.' The face looked pinched, the expression bleak, glazed over. 'It was rough at first. But now – well, like I said. It's not so bad.'

'What do you do? Do they make you work?'

'Oh, yeah. In fact, I've got a right cushy number now. That's one thing about the lifers and long-term blokes like me. Once you're settled in, you get the odd perk. Like now, I work in the laundry. It's a good number. One of the best.'

John saw the grey eyes flicker away, just for an instant, and a sudden heightening of colour sweep up the thin features, and wondered at the brief flash of embarrassment, or shyness. It brought back again that air of youthfulness. He was reminded of the boyish guilt he saw at school, when some pupil was caught in a petty misdemeanour. He wondered why mention of his work should cause such a reaction from Tony, then dismissed it from his mind.

The buzz of the electric bell took them by surprise. 'Time's up!' the prison officer bawled. John all at once felt helpless and inadequate. He wanted to help Tony, give him some hope and strength. He couldn't even shake his hand.

'Listen,' he said urgently. 'Don't give up hope. Remember,

whatever it's like in here, however bad, nobody can really get to you, if you don't let them. They can't get at the real you. The son of the Founder of our Faith – a Persian – visited England when he was an old man. Back in the year I was born. He came to Wandsworth Prison. He said, "There is no greater prison than the prison of self." It's up to you what you are inside yourself. God's the real judge.'

Tony smiled sadly as they stood. 'I'd like to know a bit more about that faith of yours. I can't even remember what it's called. Teddy did tell me.'

'Baha'i. I'll send you some literature, if you like. But everyone has to search out the truth for himself. You can think about it. I'll apply to come and see you again. And I'll write.'

On a sudden impulse, he dug into his jacket pocket and pulled out the small cloth-bound copy of the book of prayers he carried on journeys. 'You might like to look at this.'

'Oy! *I'll* take that!' The warder was there, at their side, and he snatched up the little book from the table.

John felt himself blushing hotly. 'It's just a prayer book. You can see—'

'I'll pass it on.'

'Goodbye.' John tried to put as much warmth as he could into the smile, dismayed at the sudden barrier of reserve which gripped them, almost as solid as the wire partition between them. Tony nodded, and quickly turned away, to join the line of prisoners.

'Just hold on a minute. Where do you think you're off to, my son?' Charlie Lewis's thick arm stretched across the front of Tony's chest, barring his way. In the split-second before he lowered his gaze, Tony saw the sadistic grin, the gleaming lips curving in a smile, and for an equally brief instant his slim frame stiffened with an elemental desire to resist, to scream and hurl himself at the burly uniformed figure who held such power over him. Then his muscles relaxed, the resistance drained away, and he murmured a respectful reply.

'Your new boyfriend better learn the ropes, Alice. Slipping you little love notes like that. Not allowed, is it?' That was another taunt of Lewis's that had stuck now, this play on his surname. Alice, or, often, Slack Alice. No worse than Antonia, which was another of his mocking epithets. 'Body search. In there.' Lewis pushed him roughly to one side, out of the file of prisoners.

A few minutes later, Tony stood naked in the centre of the room, arms held out horizontally. Lewis chuckled, nodded to his fellow warder. 'Found another Mr Wright, has our little Alice. Brother of the first one. Keeping it in the family, eh?' He nodded towards Tony's loins. 'Look at him. You can see how excited he is, can't you? Over that table, sonny! Christ knows what he's been slipping you! Those holy Joes are the worst of the lot. Don't you know that, Tony, me old fruit?'

Tony laid his cheek against the cool wood of the table top and tried not to respond physically to the lingering, invasive exploration he was subjected to. He thought ahead to the other, gentler hands, and the embraces he would share a few hours from now, in the dim privacy of the laundry room. Harold Skinner was paunchy and middle-aged, old enough, probably, to be his father. His fearsome reputation around the East End caused many of the cons, and even some of the more bent screws, to refer to him as 'Mr Skinner'. He was in for a long stretch, though undoubtedly lucky to have escaped the charge of at least one murder, and was considered to be one of the hardest of a hard fraternity inside the prison.

But to Tony, he was as clumsily gentle as a lamb, and with him as protector even sadists like Charlie Lewis would not go too far over the top. Even if Lewis himself were on duty on the landing this evening, he would condone Tony's quiet disappearance for an hour. When he had put his clothes back on, Tony was handed the parcel and the prayer book. He smiled wryly when he reached the cell he shared with three others, gazing round at the scratched paint over the rough brick walls, the narrow two-tier bunks, the row of lidded chamberpots, with the toilet rolls lined precisely on the wooden shelf above. What was it John Wright had said? Something about looking after yourself? Nice bloke that he was, he would be horrified if he knew what you had to do in here to do that! But that's just what I'm doing, Tony told himself as he hid the prayer book away under his pillow. And God helps those that help themselves, everyone knows that. He felt a tremor of excitement stir him at the thought of what lay ahead, and slipped the bottle of heavily perfumed cologne into his trouser pocket.

CHAPTER EIGHTEEN

The waiting ended at last, or almost, just after 6 a.m. on 12 February. Shivering, in pyjamas and dressing gown and slippers, John stood blearily in the lamplit dimness of the Head's study and heard his mother-in-law's voice, taut with tinny asperity caused, he decided charitably, by her worry, crackle in his ear. 'Good Heavens! It's been ringing for ages! Doesn't *anyone* listen for the phone in that place?'

He ignored her complaints, and asked frantically, 'What is it? What's happened?'

'I thought you ought to know,' Mrs Alsop answered tartly, 'though Jenny said we shouldn't ring until we had definite news.' There was a brief pause, during which John had the urge to shout an obscenity down the mouthpiece. 'Jenny's gone into labour. Soon after we'd gone to bed. Sandy's taken her in. He's coming back later to get me.'

'Didn't you go with her? Surely she'll want you there with her—'

Now she was really indignant. 'Of course I'll be there. She won't be having it for a good while yet. They don't just pop out, you know, like – like . . .' She stopped, mortified at her indelicate lapse. She clicked her teeth in disapproval instead.

'Sorry, er – mother,' he managed. 'Just a bit tense. I'm still not properly awake. Look, thanks. I appreciate your ringing, letting me know. I'll stay close to the telephone. You'll let me know, as soon—'

She cut him short with an abruptness that indicated she was not mollified. 'Of course! We'll ring from the hospital as soon as there's any news.'

'Tell Jenny' – the receiver clicked in his ear – 'that I love her,' he finished softly, to the crackling emptiness.

James Challoner was waiting outside eagerly in the chill of the corridor. He was also clad in a dressing-gown, his winged hair standing up in disarray. 'Well? What news?'

'Jenny's mum's rather jumped the gun, I'm afraid. Jenny's just been taken to the hospital. Her pains have started. They'll ring back later – when there's something definite.'

'Look, John, why don't you organize things and head off today? We can manage – where are we? – Thursday. At least until Monday. You could be there for the happy event—'

'No, really, that's very good of you, but I promised Maurice – I'll make sure my classes have work set, then perhaps tomorrow—'

'You leave Maurice to me!' the Head answered severely. 'You're going by car, aren't you? You've got the petrol? Just scribble something for your forms to do and dump it on my desk. Then get yourself off, and don't break your neck getting there!'

Just over two hours later, in the mild but murky morning, whose low cloud held the threat of a steady downpour, John skidded to a halt in the drive of Tea Cosy Cottage. He made his way round to the back where the lights were still on in the kitchen. Ruby's bellow of pleasure turned in mid-roar to a scream of frantic enquiry, and brought Iris thundering downstairs, pulling on her dressing gown as she came. 'What is it? What's happened? The baby—'

Hastily, he stilled their queries, only to be interrupted by May's arrival, straight from her bed and agog with anxiety and excitement. 'No!' he pleaded. 'I can't stop. James has given me time off, I'm on my way now. I just wanted you to know – in case anyone rings you while I'm on the way. Tell them I should be there just after lunch. I'll go straight to the hospital. No, Ruby! Honestly, I—'

But Ruby was already pouring tea and thrusting slices of bread under the toasting grill. 'Come on, man! You've time to sup some tea and eat a slice of toast. Then you won't need to stop on the way. Little Teddie'll be hopping mad. You just missed her. She went off for the train five minutes before you came.'

It was twenty minutes before he could extract himself. 'Be careful, John.' His mother held him by the arms. Her face was alive with love, and with worry. 'Don't go speeding. You know it'll be hours yet. Especially a first baby. And don't worry!' Her expression belied her words. 'I wish one of us could go with you.'

He laughed, hugged her tightly. 'Mum! I'm all right. Now look! I'm off! I've eaten my toast and drunk my tea, like a good lad.' All three women clung to him. 'I'll ring straight away. Let you know. You're going to be a grandma again!'

'God bless!' They watched him drive off, then quickly shut the door against the damp morning. May felt Iris's eyes on her as she led the way back to the long kitchen table, where Ruby had set things out for breakfast in a more orderly fashion. 'Sorry for disturbing you last night. I tried to be as quiet as a mouse—'

'I've told you! Wake me if you can't sleep. We can always catch up and lie in for a bit.'

Ruby pounced at once. 'You bad again?' she said accusingly.

May coloured, avoided the sharp gaze. 'Just heartburn. Same old trouble. I'll really have to start dieting. I'll be floating away with all that bicarb!'

'You want to get her to the doctor,' Ruby declared, and Iris grimaced.

'Tell me! Now listen, madam! You get back into bed, and stay there for an hour or two. Looks like we'll be having enough excitement later on today. Take it easy while you can.'

Jenny's labour was a protracted one. John reached the cottage hospital by mid-afternoon. 'I think it will be a few more hours yet,' a Sister told him. Like all the nursing staff, she seemed to think fathers-to-be were very unnecessary appendages once the process of fertilization had been performed. 'You'll have to wait in there. But please don't wander about. You'd be better off at home, you know. We're all rather busy at the moment, as you might have guessed.'

He spent a wretched half-hour sitting on a hard chair, glancing at the Spartan surroundings and tensing at every swishing, uniformed figure. Until his mother-in-law appeared, looking decidedly agitated. 'Not even Rosemary took this long!' she admonished him, while John wondered distractedly what she meant. Was she referring to her eldest daughter's giving birth? – Moira was a grandmother three times over – or was she referring to Rosemary's own arrival in the world? 'You know, you left it far too long to start a family!' she continued, even more aggressively. 'Thirty-two's far too old to be having your first baby!'

'What's the matter? Is Jenny all right? There's nothing wrong, is there?' His anger was lost in his apprehension.

'Oh, nothing wrong!' Moira repeated, in heavy sarcasm. 'She's only been in agony for over twelve hours! You men! Honestly! You've no idea—'

'Can't they give her something? To help . . . I mean . . .' he floundered helplessly, half convinced himself of his guilty uselessness. 'I don't suppose they'd let me see her?'

Moira's expression was eloquent in its withering scorn. 'She's giving birth, for goodness' sake! It's not something one would relish doing in public! Why don't you go for a walk or something? Find a café – have a cup of tea.'

Stung by her dismissiveness, he wanted to yell at her, 'It's *our* baby she's having. Mine as well. Something we made together. A miracle.' But he hoped his silence would speak volumes as he left without a word.

The baby was born just before seven in the evening. John had been back, endured a further two hours of discomfort and frustration in the waiting room, with Moira returning every now and then for more sniping and cutting. By now, her remarks scarcely registered, he was so alarmed for Jenny's welfare. Other visitors began to appear, but they offered little distraction. He was desperately close to breaking the decorum of this closed female sanctum, especially when he thought he heard, faintly, some shrill agonized yelps or screams, which his horrified mind told him could be Jenny. But then a junior nurse appeared, red-faced and breathless as though she herself had played an active role in this reproduction. Behind her glasses, her blue eyes shone, her face was wreathed in a beaming smile. It transformed John's opinion of her profession, of his surroundings, and of the whole world. 'Congratulations, Mr Wright. You're a daddy. A fine boy. Seven pounds three ounces. Mother and baby doing well!' Speechless, he grabbed her by the arms and whirled her round, just preventing himself from kissing her, and she turned beet red, giggling with delight, before she gave him a swift, grabbing hug and hurried off again.

He had to wait another endless two hours before he could see Jenny and his son. He strove not to feel cheated when Moira was admitted first, and came back tearful with relief and much more kindly disposed towards John, whom she squeezed and kissed tearfully. 'She's very tired. And sore,' she added, still with a hint of reproach. 'They're having to stitch her,' she could not prevent herself from telling him, though she blushed at her own indelicacy.

John himself was tearful, almost shamingly unmanned, when

at last he saw Jenny, and beside her the tightly bound bundle, only the brown, wrinkled head showing, with its startlingly abundant tuft of dark, glossy hair. The closed eyelids were a darkly delicate shade John could not find a colour for, the dark lashes curled perfectly against the pouch of cheeks, the lips and chin miniature perfection. 'Hello, old chap,' he whispered unsteadily. 'You're beautiful.'

Jenny looked wasted. Her hair looked darker than its natural, dark honey colour, and clung in damp ringlets against her brow and the pillow. Her complexion was pale against the white linen, her lips pale, too, bloodless and cracked. Her eyes were turned on him with love, but also with great weariness, and were clouded with the sedative they had given her. But then he watched them fill and sparkle with tear drops. 'It was awful, John,' she whispered hoarsely, as he bent and kissed her gently on the brow. 'I don't think I could bear it again. I'm sorry, love.'

He had been told this was a common reaction. He refused to be hurt by it. 'Never mind you, mum! I don't think *I* could, either!'

Jenny stayed in the cottage hospital for nine days. At first, John was seriously worried, for the birth had indeed sapped her strength, though the doctor who looked after her assured John in a confidential 'chat' on the Sunday, before he prepared for the long cross-country drive through the winter night back to Corbridge, that everything had been, and was continuing to be, perfectly normal. 'Well, she's a little on the narrow side, hips-wise, and yes, there was a bit of tearing of the tissue, but that happens more often than not. She's stiff, of course. Let's face it, she's used muscles she didn't even know she had!' John tried not to feel annoyed at the doctor's hearty laugh. 'But no reason why you shouldn't make other baby Wrights for – have you picked out a name yet?'

They hadn't. Diffidently, John had put forward 'Jack', both on his own account, and knowing how much it would please his mother. He knew at once from Jenny's hesitation that she was not happy with it, even before Moira chipped in with, 'Oh. Can you actually have someone christened Jack? I thought it was another form of John.'

He half hoped that her mother's dismissive tone might push Jenny towards accepting his suggestion. However, he had noticed in the two short days since the birth, Jenny's self-assertive attitude towards Moira seemed to have been put in abeyance. With an appeasing smile aimed at him, Jenny said, 'Certainly for one of his names. After your father.'

'Come to that, there's always been an Alexander on your father's side.' Moira didn't quite bring off the light-hearted tone she tried to attain. 'You'll have to make up your mind soon. We can't keep calling him 'baby'. And we'll have to fix a date for the christening soon. The vicar needs quite a bit of notice.'

For a wicked second or two, John was tempted to throw a huge spanner in Moira's planning. Actually, I'm no longer bothered about a Christian ceremony, he felt an urge to say. But he knew what a seismic upheaval that would cause. Besides, he was well aware that Jenny would still class herself as Christian, by birth and tradition, even though it was years since she had been to a church service, and the last thing he wanted was to upset his wife at this emotional time. But he could not resist saying now, 'Do you mind if I say goodbye to Jenny?'

The colour swept up Moira's face. For an instant she pretended to be nonplussed. 'Oh? Secrets, eh?' Her laugh was forced. She stood, looked down at Jenny. 'I'll come back when your hubby's finished with you, if that's all right?'

When they were alone, the tears sparkled on Jenny's lashes, then spilled over. She clung tightly to him, and he trembled with love for her. 'I don't want you to go!' she wept. 'I don't want you to leave me.'

'I'll peep in at the laddo before I go.' The regime in the hospital was strict. The babies were brought to the mothers for feeding, and for a brief period afterwards, then they were bedded down in the rows of cots in a room down the corridor. 'You do what the doctors and nurses tell you. You'll be out of here in no time. Perhaps when you're allowed up I can telephone. In any case, Dr Shields says you should be out before the end of the week.'

They managed only one phone call during the remainder of Jenny's stay in the maternity hospital. To John's dismay, she sounded dispirited, and she was soon sniffling back the tears. At the end of their talk, he felt helpless, a world away from her, and his son. The next time they spoke, she was installed back in her parents' home. 'We've got to decide on a name!' She sounded desperate. Her voice lowered. 'Mum's started calling him Sandy, for God's sake! Listen. Thomas has come top of *my* list. What about you?'

'Sure. Tom sounds a good honest name to me. That's it, then, yes? Decision taken.'

'Thomas Jack Wright.' Her voice cracked, scratchy with emotion. 'I want the three of us to be together. In case you've forgotten, I love you.'

Into a conventionally blustery March, and Jenny was much more her old self. She took the chance to call him when she had the house to herself. 'Mum's driving me mad. And Rosemary's even worse! The world's authority on babies! I need you, Johnny. Please! Get me out of here!'

'I will, love. Soon as I can. It's just – James is talking about the Easter hols. To get the flat fixed. Give us the extra room, where Fallon is. I reckon by the end of next month—'

'John.' Her voice sounded hesitant, pleading. 'What about your ma and Aunt I? Could they – do you think they'd have me and the baby at the Tea Cosy, just for a while? I'd keep out of their way – I know what your mother thinks of me – but, oh,

John! I just want us to be together!'

'They'll be absolutely delighted!' he answered strongly. 'Start packing! I'll be across on Saturday evening. We'll leave Sunday morning! And stop that weeping. You're supposed to be happy!'

'Well, I'll tell you one thing, kidder! *Her* conception wouldn't be immaculate, that's for sure!' Dora Dale's remark about the birth of John and Jenny's son, which was greeted with such a storm of laughter by her sister and most of those within earshot, caught Teddie on the raw.

'What do you mean?' The nudges and winks following her query only served to make her angrier. There was a houseful, as Marian and her mother were playing host to a gathering in cele-bration of Julia Dale's fiftieth birthday. As usual, the assembly was all female, for the few men, including Julia's husband, Alf, and Marian's stepfather, together with the young men squiring Julia's three daughters, had all made their early escape to one of the pubs along Durham Road. Teddie sometimes felt ashamed of her contemptuous attitude towards these boozy parties, which had become more and more frequent in the months since her father's departure. She accused herself of being a snob, but the coarseness of her relatives, their raucousness and drunken senti-mentality, as well as the character-shredding nature of much of their talk, filled her with anger. That, and their insistence on treating her like a little child all the time. As now, with the snig-gering innuendo, making her feel more and more outside the grown-ups' circle. I bet I know a darned sight more than most of you! she thought rebelliously. But not about this kind of thing, it piqued her to admit.

She was determined to question her mother about it, but when Marian came upstairs, waking her as she fumbled into bed, Teddie could smell the sweetness of the drink, which, combined with the effect of the pills Marian took each night, soon had her mother snoring in open-mouthed unconsciousness. Teddie eased herself from the clinging embrace and lay on her back on the edge of the mattress. Once again, she was ashamed of her reluctance at having to share her mother's bed because of the extra company in the house. But Nana Nelly was up here so often now, not to mention Julia or one or more of her daughters, that Teddie scarcely felt she had a room here any more. She thought with longing of the comfort of her room at the Tea Cosy, all her things laid out in the fragrant drawers, her possessions on the dressing table, her pictures on the walls. Even with Jenny and Baby Thomas staying there, she still had her own sanctum – in fact, it was a joyful bonus having a new mother and baby with them. And then she felt even more ashamed and upset.

But when Marian was still lying abed in mid-morning the next day, Teddie took her up a cup of tea, and perched determinedly on the edge of the double bed. 'Mum. Why is everybody so bitchy about Aunty Jenny? And why don't Grandma and Aunt Julia see each other any more? What's it to do with you and dad? His going off and leaving us?'

Marian shifted, drew up her knees, moved away from Teddie as though she was trying to escape. 'Oh, don't bother me now, love.' Her voice took on the plaintive whine Teddie had grown to hate. 'I'm not well this morning. I have to take me pills—'

'I'm not a kid, mum! I want to know! It matters to me! It's important! You and dad – splitting up. He could get himself killed out there! Why? Why can't you live together any more? What happened – while he was away – in the war? What went on? It was that man, wasn't it? Jim Moody. I can remember him. How he used to come. Sit me on his knee. It was him, wasn't it? That's why dad went off. Did you and him . . . Were you in love with him?'

Teddie was shocked, and frightened, at the transformation. Marian gave a cry of pain. She knelt up, the teacup went flying, spilling the dregs over the counterpane. Her red face was twisted with grief, the tears spilled profusely over her shining cheeks, the fair hair a tangled, lank mess. 'For God's sake, leave me alone! Your dad didn't even want me when I fell preganant with you! He married me and then ran off till long after you were born. And I loved him, so much! Yes – I did wrong, when he was away, a prisoner of war. I did wrong! And so did your precious Aunt Jenny! Ask her! Ask her all about it! She'll tell you, like she told everybody else!'

She fell back, twisting her shoulders, burying her face in the pillows. Her body shook with her weeping. Teddie saw the meaty pale bareness of her upper arms, the torso heaving, heard the muffled anguish. She started to cry herself, lost and desolate. 'Mum! Mum! Don't – please! I'm sorry.' Her own tears came faster and she lay down, put her arm round those quivering shoulders, fitted herself closely to the soft body and tried to share the pain she had caused to erupt to the surface.

CHAPTER NINETEEN

Jenny laid Thomas in his crib, keeping her back towards Teddie as she adjusted her clothing and rebuttoned her blouse. She was very conscious of the tension in the atmosphere, the preoccupied manner of the young girl since she had returned to Hexham two days ago. 'We have to supplement his feeds with the Cow and Gate now. My milk's not enough for him. He's a greedy little beggar.'

'Does it hurt?' Teddie nodded towards Jenny's bosom. Jenny had felt unaccountably shy when the youngster had asked if she could accompany her up to the bedroom and watch her breast-feed the baby. Now she blushed again, this time at the waywardness of her thoughts. She let out an embarrassed little laugh. 'Well, sometimes – I'm a bit tender. But no. It sort of tickles.' She gave a little shiver. She could not tell the girl the truth, that sometimes the action of suckling Thomas made her feel deeply sensual, roused her to a state of physical excitement. Now she waited, apprehensively, wondering what it was that Teddie was wanting to talk to her about. Clearly, there was something bothering her. She had sat down on the edge of the double bed, nervously picking at the hem of her dress, plucking up the courage to speak.

'Aunty Jen. Can I talk to you? About something very private – and personal?'

Jenny smiled, pretending to an ease she was far from feeling. 'Yes, love. Shoot away.' She smiled, and moved to sit by Teddie's side. The baby had snuffled back to a contented sleep. 'What is it? Just between us, of course. I'll help if I can.'

'It'll help if you'll tell me the truth. No one else will.' The young face turned towards her, red with embarrassment, but also stamped with a deep sadness. 'Tell me what's wrong between mum and dad. I know it's about what happened during the war – while dad was away.' There was a fractional pause. 'And I know it was to do with mum and Jim Moody. The chap she knew from where Dora worked. But why now, after all that time? The war's been over – dad's been home – four years. Why did it all happen this last year – mum's breakdown, everything? I asked her. Tried to talk to her in the holidays. She got into one of her states. Sobbing and screaming. Told me to ask you.'

Jenny felt the accusation in the last sentence. She had impulsively made to reach out an arm to the young figure. Now she withdrew, folded her hands in her lap, and stared at her knotted fingers. She struggled to find the words, which came with painful slowness. 'I knew, right from the beginning. Well, no – I mean I knew at the time – when your mum finished with Jim Moody. I was still in the Wrens – we met up here, one weekend.' Her voice broke, she swallowed hard. 'She told me all about it – and – and I told her, too. You see, *I* had gone off the rails, too. I was involved with another man – while John was out in North Africa.'

'You were both unfaithful?' Teddie could not keep the shocked condemnation from her voice, and Jenny flinched.

'Yes. We kept each other's secret for five years.'

'Was it you that told my dad?'

Jenny nodded. She could feel the tears gathering, wet upon her eyelids. 'After your mum took ill. When she was in Winyard

House. It was keeping it all from your dad that *made* her ill. I thought I was acting for the best. I thought if they could both face it, put it behind them—'

'Like you've done, with Uncle John?' Teddie nodded towards the crib. 'Everything's worked out fine for you, hasn't it? I guess Uncle John's not like my dad, is he?'

'I'm sorry, Teddie,' she whispered miserably. 'I—'

'But that's not all, is it?' Teddie pressed on, the accusation in her tone stronger than ever. 'The miscarriage mum had three years ago! Her not being able to have any more children! Is that something to do – because of her being with Jim Moody?'

'Look, love – I can't – really, your mum should be the one—'

'I'm sick of all the whispers! The secrets!' Jenny was startled at the desperate ferocity of the girl's cry. 'Dora! Aunt Julia! I'm not stupid! I think I know – mum was ill, wasn't she? When I was little – I can remember, she was in bed for weeks – after Jim Moody had left. Did she – was there a baby? Tell me!'

Jenny was even more shocked at the force with which Teddie turned and clutched at her, sobbing. 'Shush! Be quiet! You'll wake the baby! The whole house will hear you!' She spoke more forcefully than she intended, but it had the effect of making Teddie exert some control over her emotions. She got up, rummaged in a drawer for a clean handkerchief, handed it to the weeping girl, who wiped her face then blew her nose. She knelt down in front of Teddie, leaning in to the bony knees, and reached up to take her hands in hers. 'Your mum got pregnant. Just before Moody left. He didn't know – he never knew. She got rid of it. As soon as she found out. Julia and Dora helped her, arranged things. It nearly killed Marian.' Jenny squeezed the thin hands she held. She spoke with quiet emphasis. 'Your mum took a great risk trying to have another baby with your dad. She could have died. She did it because she loved him.'

The tears made glistening channels down Teddie's cheeks.

Her dark eyes were wide as they met Jenny's gaze, and did not look away. 'Because she was guilty.' Now her gaze *did* move, to the cot where Thomas slept, and the look stabbed through Jenny's conscience, for, more eloquently than any words, it placed her in an identical position with Marian. 'I guess you've been a lot luckier than mum.' She slipped her hands from Jenny's hold, and moved round her. She went out, leaving the figure kneeling by the bed, on which her clasped hands rested as though she were saying her prayers.

Teddy saw no more action after the strike into Sinai and the subsequent withdrawal in January. Apart from a few skirmishes, the UN negotiated armistice, which was officially recognized on 24 February, held good, and by April peace had been agreed between the new state and all its Arab invaders. 'You see,' Teddy told Manny Grunwald, 'Just send a few Brits out and the whole show's over in no time.'

'It's the bleddy Brits caused it in the first place!'

Their *Mahal* unit was being held close to the border of the Gaza Strip, but its future seemed uncertain. Many were ready to head off home again. Teddy received a letter from John late in May, with snapshots of Thomas, now three months old and thriving. It came soon after two items of more cheerful news on the international scene. The Berlin Airlift finally came to an end with the lifting of the blockade, and, only a day later, Britain established full diplomatic relations with Israel. John gave him the address of the kibbutz where Sara and Berni Lightman stayed and, partly out of boredom and partly from an interest in meeting the girl with whom John had been involved, Teddy wrote to try and arrange a meet-up. Like most young Israelis at the time, they were still part of the military machine, so it was not easy to fix a time when they could all be free, but eventually they agreed on a weekend when they would meet in Tel Aviv.

Teddy recognized the smiling girl straight away from the photographs he remembered, except that she was much prettier than he had thought. Dark horse John! He grinned to himself, then reassessed his evaluation of 'pretty'. She was more than that, he acknowledged, taking in the voluptuous figure shown to effect even in the khaki drill shirt and skirt. Her legs were bare and very brown, her narrow feet and toes displayed in the simple brown leather, non-regulation sandals. Berni was no taller than Teddy, with a lively, usually smiling face, dark eyes, and black hair whose tight curls soared to a miniature peak over his forehead. He was in uniform, too, but his almost portly shape did not contribute to a warrior-like look. 'It's married life!' he chuckled contentedly, patting the straining waistline above the belt. 'I've put on a stone at least!'

He enjoyed their company, and their obvious efforts to entertain him and to make him feel at home. 'I'll always be grateful to your brother. And your Uncle David,' she told him. For a moment, the seriousness that came over her expression indicated the sadness and loss she felt. He was even more glad for her that she had so obviously found a love to replace that loss, and that the love was clearly mutual. As the shops and cafés began to close for *Shabat*, they made their way to the military hostel where they were staying, and sat on the veranda, drinking and talking well into the warm night.

Next day, when Teddy told them of his uncertainty as to the future, they sensed his reluctance to go back to England. 'Look,' Berni suggested, 'we're both posted to a *Nahal*. That's a unit for personnel who are going to be settlers when their service is over. We're going to be working down south. At the Dead Sea. One of the jobs is to build a road along the western shore. That's your line of work, isn't it? You'd be ideal! Probably make you an NCO at least! Why don't you apply? I can give you the name of the commandant. I'm sure they'd jump at you!'

219

The task of road building was far more appealing than the unit's present job of clearing the mostly deserted Arab villages in the area. Besides, the attraction of seeing the dramatic desert setting of the fabled Dead Sea was strong, too. And lastly, the thought of being around the Lightmans, especially Sara, weighed heavily with him. His admiration of her was, he assured himself, discreet and wholly honourable, except in his most private thoughts, which he would never act upon. He liked them both. He was touched by their infectious warmth, the friendliness with which they had accepted him. It was even more welcome after the months he had spent in the harsh, masculine environment of the *Mahal*, and the desert campaign.

His transfer was arranged without problem, as Berni had forecast. Teddy's experience made him a welcome asset to the new unit. Its relaxed, almost democratic atmosphere was a pleasant change from the strict discipline of the more regular units. The work was demanding, and often physically exhausting, as the burning heat of summer rose, but Teddy embraced it, glad to be so totally committed and occupied. The landscape was every bit as exciting and grand as he had imagined. The strange, towering rock formations, standing darkly like weird sculptures against the fierce, cloudless blue, or pale and scoured in the blazing sunlight; the steep canyons plunged into long fingers of deep shadows, breaking out into the open, lunar rockiness of the Negev. They slept in tented camps alongside the heavy equipment, forging their route northward, towards the gleaming waterway they could see, dazzlingly promising ahead of them. They began from the potash works already situated in the desert. The road ran parallel to the Jordanian border, and not many miles distant from it, so they were armed and stood guard, and there was a detachment of fighting soldiers with their light armoured vehicles always on hand. But the work progressed quickly, with no incursions from across the border.

Teddy saw little of Sara and Berni, who were stationed to the north, somewhere near the proposed destination of the new route, at Ein Gedi, where there was already a settlement, and some precious freshwater springs, at the head of a narrow valley. They met up only once in the first two months, and then briefly, for no more than a couple of hours, when the couple came overland as part of the convoy bringing fresh materials. Sara was, like all her companions, covered in dust, her brow and eyes palely and comically ringed where they had been covered by her beret and goggles. She was wearing baggy overalls and scuffed desert boots, and laughed as she hurried to him and flung her arms about him. Her teeth flashed white, her lips were warm and full as they touched his cheek, and beneath the unprepossessing garb, he could feel the softness of her body as they hugged.

He sat with them at the long wooden trestle table of the field kitchen, savouring almost greedily her laughing conversation, her liveliness of looks and gestures, and unaffected openness, realizing how much he had missed such things. He remembered the Irish girl, Rosie, in Spain, and the uncomplicated loving they had shared. He felt an intense sadness and longing. 'Look. You must come up to us. Ein Gedi's lovely. We'll have a picnic. We go up there nearly every Shabat. I'm sure you can fix up some transport. See if you can get off early. Hitch a lift with a supply truck, or put in for a jeep. Spend the weekend. You'll love it.' For the first time in weeks, he felt moody and restlessly discontented after they had left.

The feeling eased as he became caught up in the work once more, and as they gradually edged near the southern margins of the inland sea. Soon, the humidity had them sweating, their body fluid soaking and staining the thin clothing they wore. They were as brown as the nomadic tribesmen who, passing in clusters with their scrawny goats and overladen little donkeys, stopped to stare in brief curiosity, or stared pointedly away from them as they moved on. He bathed in the strangely buoyant, pungent water, which rolled him about on its surface, making it impossible for him to swim. He floated, knees drawn up out of the water, posing for the obligatory photograph, with newspaper open in his extended arms. I'll send the snap to Teddie, he thought. It might amuse her. Not that she had ever replied to any of his letters. Marian's short, neutral and infrequent notes always ended, *Teddie sends her love*, one more pathetic lie to sit between them. It pained him to think of the parting with his daughter; her white-faced, clenched silence, her abrupt leaving of the room, without even a kiss. He had wanted to rush after her, to explain to her all the deceit and hurt that had gone to drive him away, but he couldn't burden her with all that. Besides, it wouldn't have helped to take away his own sense of guilt and weakness, which no amount of self-justification could dispel.

When he sat under the brilliant spread of stars, his aching body cool and refreshed by the sluicing-down from the jerry cans of precious fresh water, he could not help dwelling on his loneliness, and the aridity of his personal life. At these times, his thoughts drifted helplessly towards Sara Lightman, and his body stirred with a desire he could not repress. He was able to mock himself wryly. What would she see in you anyway, you dirty old man? She probably thinks of you as a silly old uncle. She's got everything she could want out of life, with lucky old Berni. And good luck to both of them.

It was late August before he saw either of them again, and this time it was Berni, on his own, who was once more part of a team bringing in supplies. 'Listen, you're just down the road from us now. There's a party planned at camp next weekend. You've got to come. And no excuses! Half the boys here will be coming, so there's no need to worry about transport. And on Saturday, Sara's planning a picnic along at the springs. We'll set off early in the morning before it warms up, and hike along to the falls. It's great.' As the truck ground off on its return journey, Berni leaned out, still grinning, and bawled, 'We might have some good news for you!'

As the day approached, Teddy found he was looking forward to the break more and more. The road had made good progress along the side of the lake; they could see the massive plateau of the ancient fort of Masada rearing over them to the west now. The journey northward still had to be made in a convoy of reinforced jeeps, and though only twenty miles took them the best part of two hours, it was worth it. The settlement at the southern end of the valley that led up to the springs was well established. The wooden huts, the ablutions area, the large dining hall, seemed luxurious to the visitors. Teddy bounced on the squeaking upper bunk in the dormitory he had been assigned to, and grinned down at Berni. 'My God! Sleeping off the floor! Luxury!' He glanced around in a parody of secrecy. 'Hey! You and Sara. Do you – have they got married quarters here?'

Berni tapped the side of his nose. 'We manage!'

The Lightmans made sure they sat with Teddy for the special *Shabat* meal on the Friday evening. A petite blonde girl, Sonja, joined them, and soon it became obvious that Sara and Berni were making sure he had a partner for the concert and the dancing which were to follow. Sonja was pleasant enough, though Teddy was glad that her imperfect English limited their conversation, both in depth and quantity. He would much rather have stayed close by Sara the whole time. As it was, he did not manage more than one far too lively dance with her.

It was late when he escorted his new partner back to her sleeping hut. In the shadows, a number of other couples were closely entwined, and soon Sonja was clinging to him, her mouth open and wet seeking his, her thin body jerking against his in blatant invitation. 'You want stay?' she whispered.

He felt her hand brush swiftly across his loins. 'I'd better – I'm

223

a bit tired,' he answered, feeling foolish, as well as embarrassed. He saw the sharp features close, knew that she had felt the harsh abruptness of his rejection of her. She pulled free at once. 'OK. I see you tomorrow.' She left quickly, and he turned back, cursing himself for his stupidity. What a prat you are! How long is it since you had anything? Any longer and you'll have forgotten what to do! These girls are like that. It doesn't matter to them; if they like you, that's it. They don't muck about. He thought of Sara, and immediately felt ashamed of his lust. *She* isn't like that. Never would be.

Once Berni had woken him, in the earliest light of a mist-layered dawn, he felt a great surge of happiness. They had procured a light back-pack for him, like the ones they each carried. Sara was wearing one of her khaki shirts, but it hung loosely outside a pair of pale drill shorts of a brevity which drew Teddy's appreciative eyes to her muscular brown legs, and then to the fine curves of her behind filling the material to a tautened smoothness.

They picked their way, mostly in single file, along the narrow, stony track at the bottom of the defile. The vegetation was surprisingly abundant, and they frequently passed through thickets of thorn trees, with pale, twisted limbs under which they ducked, and between low scrub. Sara yelped at the scratches to her bare legs. 'I told her to wear pants.' Berni shook his head unsympathetically. 'But no! She has to show off her legs to all the guys, as usual!'

'Shut up, pig!'

'You won't catch me complaining!' Teddy called, from the rear, and Sara's laugh rang out.

'You English are always so polite! And such good liars. That's why 1 fell for Lightman's sweet talk!'

They kept stopping for a few minutes' rest and to drink from their water bottles. Teddy noticed that, despite his banter, Berni was very solicitous of his wife, continually enquiring if she was all right. By the time they were approaching the falls themselves, it was midday, and the heat felt trapped beneath the vertical walls of the canyon, with its narrow rock ledges. All three were dripping with perspiration when, up ahead, Teddy heard the unbelievably sweet plash of falling water. He watched Sara's alluring bottom as she broke into a run, her boots stumbling over the rocky floor, which suddenly broadened out, and there, its force thinned by the summer but still exquisitely tempting, a wide stream of water cascaded down to a shallow pool and then flowed in miniature falls over natural steps of rock to a series of smaller pools.

'We're the first here! Let's make the most of it.' Sara was already sitting, tugging off her boots and the thick grey ankle socks. She hastily slipped off her shirt, and thrust down her shorts, kicking them free of her flying feet with impatience. Teddy realized that the brief garments she wore underneath comprised a two-piece bathing suit of a dark brown colour, then she was half hidden, standing under the curtain of water, squealing breathlessly at its cold.

'Just wear your underpants!' Berni laughed at Teddy. 'I am!' Then he, too, was standing beside his wife, and Teddy scrambled out of his clothes to join them.

They spread the picnic on a flat rock, where they could sit with their feet in the cold water flowing by. Berni produced two bottles of wine. 'For a special occasion!' When he had poured generously into the three tin mugs, he glanced across at Sara, who suddenly looked away, with uncharacteristic shyness.

'Go on! Tell him!' she murmured.

'All right.' Berni beamed at him, raised his mug. 'That news I mentioned. We have it. We're going to have a baby.'

Teddy felt awkward. He had to struggle to compose his face into a suitably congratulatory expression. 'Well done, you two. Congratulations.'

Sara was still unaccustomedly serious while they sat and sipped at the wine. 'I wasn't sure if I – if we should really have a baby, yet. It's not the most stable of situations here, is it? I didn't know if it was right to bring a baby into it all—'

'Rubbish!' Berni interjected strongly. 'The more the merrier! We need new blood, here of all places!'

Sara gave a wry laugh. 'Anyway, nature intervened. In spite of . . .' She blushed a little, and shrugged. 'I found I was pregnant. The doctor's just confirmed it.'

An hour later, the two bottles of wine emptied and the meal eaten, Berni was snoring in the shade, and Teddy joined Sara, under the tingling chill of the falls once more. The wine stirred his senses, he could feel his excitement at being so close to her. He could see her full breasts straining against the thin cups. There was a fine edging of white skin showing, between her natural tan and the seam of her bathing top. Her brown belly curved entrancingly, above the tiny wet patch of material hugging her sex. Teddy saw the narrow, shallow eye of her navel, tried to force his thoughts away from his hunger for her. 'All the rage, these babies. I showed you the pictures of John's son and heir, didn't I?'

She laughed. Hidden under the curving roof of the small cave, the curtain of water screening them, she suddenly reached out and put her hand on Teddy's shoulder, kept it there. His whole body seemed to blaze at her touch. 'You know, when I was young – younger, I mean – I used to think I was half in love with your brother.' She lowered her gaze, genuinely shy, yet sharing these hidden, intimate moments. 'After I met him that first time, in Haifa. He was so handsome, so dashing. I even used to dream about him.'

'Not like me, eh?' His voice was tense. Her arm was still stretched out to him, her hand still resting on him. 'I'm a bit of a rough-cut. Johnny was always the bright one—'

'You're just fine, Teddy. I want you to be happy.' She leaned in towards him and kissed him on the cheek, letting her lips linger there. All at once, he grabbed her, his arms pulled her against him, his mouth sought hers fiercely. He felt her lips, full, soft, parted; felt her almost naked body cold, agleam with the water coursing down over it, pressing into him. His right hand moved, fitted to the contour of her buttock, his fingers dug in the resilient flesh, and he thrust his loins against hers, the sexual excitement pulsing through him.

He expected her to pull away, to claw and fight him, or to scream out in horror. Instead, the lips remained pressed against his, he felt her tongue returning his intimate searching, her loins still against his beating flesh. He broke the kiss, both of them gasping, and released his hold on her. Both her hands came up now, lay on his shoulders, holding him close to her, her brown eyes wide, searching his. 'I'm – how do I say it? – very physical, a very sexual person. I didn't know it, how much, at first. I found it out with my first lover.' She smiled, her eyes holding his. 'Not Berni. But another Britisher. I want you to know, I love Berni. Very much. He is so good. I could not do anything to hurt him.' She glanced down at their bodies, still so close. 'I could not betray him. If I was free, I would want to make love with you. You understand? I hope you can be happy again one day. With your wife. Or with someone else.' She leaned in, and kissed him again, her lips on his, but gently this time, and he responded in kind, a gentle, loving embrace, and a parting one, too, in recognition of what could not be.

CHAPTER TWENTY

'Have you heard from young Porter lately?' John's glance took in the colour which touched Teddie's cheek briefly as she shook her head.

'We don't write any more. Anyway, he's busy with his school cert this year. He reckons he's got loads to do.'

Michael had paid a swift visit to his old school in July, in the last week of Beaconsfield's term, and John had invited him out to Hexham for tea, making sure that he would meet Teddie there. The youngsters had had an hour together, gone for a walk along the river bank, but Teddie had not been very forthcoming about the rendezvous. But now John had more important matters on his mind. His niece had not been very forthcoming about most things, at least not to him, and certainly not to Jenny. He knew why. Jenny had told him about her confidential talk with Teddie not long after the event, and John had seen for himself its results. Teddie's untypical coolness with Jenny, and embarrassment in his presence, was too obvious to miss. His mother had noticed it, too, and, without anyone referring directly to it, he suspected she had some idea of the reason for it.

It was made more complicated by their being all under the one roof during the spring. Though both May and Iris were at pains not to show any change in their attitude towards Jenny since her revelation before Christmas of her infidelity, there was a difference. Perhaps it was the fact that they tried too hard not to let it show. Things were easier once John, Jenny and Thomas had been able to move into the converted flat at school, at the beginning of May. They still visited Tea Cosy Cottage every weekend, and Aunt I frequently drove over to Corbridge and picked up Jenny and the baby during the week, for days out or simply to spend the day over at Hexham.

But the change in Teddie was too pointed to ignore. He had many a time told himself he must try to talk it out with the young girl, but kept postponing the difficult task, until, now that they had come back from a stay over in the Lakes with Jenny's folks, his mother had confronted him. 'I wish you'd talk to Little Teddie. She's always been close to you – and Jenny. She's been so moody lately. Not like her old self at all. I thought it was to do with her being over at Low Fell in the holidays. Being with Marian, and that lot.' May could not keep the note of condemnation from marking the last phrase. 'But it's more than that, poor child. Have a word with her – before you get wrapped up in school again.' There was more than a hint of admonition in these last words, too.

Knowing that his mother and Aunt I were away, in fact visiting at Low Fell, and that Teddie was not accompanying them, he had driven over to Hexham on his own. The early September day was beautifully sunny, and John carried the tray of tea and biscuits out on to the paved area of the garden, just outside the living-room windows. Ruby had joined them for a 'cuppa', then retreated back inside, with her typical, 'Well, we can't all sit here sunning ourselves. Some of us have work to do.' The strains of 'Music while you work' drifted faintly out to them.

'You all set for school? Another year, eh? You'll be into school cert yourself next year, won't you? Fourteen in a couple of months! You're growing up so fast!'

'Not according to some people!'

Her plaintive remark encouraged him to strive against his reticence. 'Teddie – is everything all right for you? I mean – I know – I can tell – you're not very happy about things just now. Especially with your Aunt Jenny and me.'

'It's not *you!*' she blurted, and her face flamed.

He smiled. The closed-down surliness of her expression made her look very childlike all at once. 'I know, Teddie,' he said gently, and saw her head lower, the colour still deep in her face. 'I've known about your chat with Aunt Jenny for ages. I've been wanting to talk with you. I've been putting it off far too long. Too embarrassed, I guess. But we shouldn't be. Should we?'

Now her eyes were lifted, they met his. He could see how troubled she was, saw the shine of tears in her gaze. 'I'm sorry.' He wondered what she was apologizing for. 'But I can't stop thinking about it. My mum. *And* Aunt Jenny. What they did. I can't believe it. Except – it's true. It was so wrong!'

He was moved with compassion for her, at the anguish, and the uncertainty in her. He was deeply aware of the transitional confusion she was suffering from, this awful clash of the safe, ordered world of childhood, and the terrible, grey reality of the adult world waiting out there. 'Yes, it was.' The quiet simplicity of his agreement shook her, he could tell. Her eyes widened a little in surprise. 'No good trying to wrap it up, to beat about the bush. You're right. It was bad. Awful. Grown-ups do awful things to each other. I don't have to tell you that, though, do I? You've seen them for yourself. The war. The bombings. Millions of people killed. Those terrible death camps. And now we're busy making bombs so huge it's possible we'll all blow ourselves up – destroy the world – it could happen any time. A lot of people think it will, soon. Do you?'

She stared at him, her own sadness in abeyance. She shrugged. 'It could. Easily. One day, someone might want to use one –

might be desperate. Then someone fights back.' She nodded solemnly. 'Now that we've got them, I suppose, one day, it's going to be inevitable, isn't it? They'll use them.'

'What can we do about it?' She gazed at him, didn't answer, and, after a pause, he went on. 'It's easy to say, "Well, there's nothing *I* can do. Poor old me. I'm just one individual. What difference can *I* make?" But we're all just individuals, aren't we? The whole human race, we're all made up of individuals.' He smiled suddenly, lightening his tone, and the atmosphere. 'I just say my prayers, and have faith in God. And love. *Love ye one another.* Sounds simple enough, but by heck! It's hard to do, isn't it? And we keep getting it wrong. We've made an awful mess, in some respects. But we've got to keep on trying, over and over. And forgiving. Look at Germany. Should we punish them all? Wipe out the whole race for what they've done? Why are we trying to help them sort out the mess, get back on their feet again?'

She was still staring at him intently. He sat back deliberately in the striped canvas deckchair, screwed his face against the morning sunlight. 'There's a lot to forgive all right.' Again he smiled. 'I reckon on the scale of the wrongdoing that's gone on in our world lately, Jenny's sin, and your mum's, is pretty small.'

She looked chastened. She looked away from him again, he saw the top of her dark head, could sense that she was close to tears. 'I'm not saying it wasn't wrong. Like I said, I agree with you. And I'm not saying it didn't hurt. You of all people know how much it's hurt – quite a few people, when you tot it up. Not just me.' He paused. 'And your dad. Still hurts, for some of us. Not least your mum. And Jenny. They've been hurt more than anyone, I reckon.'

In the silence, he saw the quiver of her shoulders, then there was a loud, long sniff. 'Have a good blow.' He held out his handkerchief, and she reached out, took it, still without meeting his gaze, and did as he had bidden.

231

She cleared her throat. 'I'll keep it, and wash it. I'll give it back.'

He struggled up out of the low chair. 'I'd better be getting back. There's heaps to do before the monsters return.'

'Thanks, Uncle John—'

'We love you, you know. Jenny feels so bad. And your mum – well, you know what it's done to her. She needs your love more than ever. *And* your dad. Whatever you think of him, he's always loved you. And he's as proud as punch of you, doing so well at school, and everything. We'll probably see you on Sunday. Good luck with school.' He grinned. 'We'll both need it, eh?'

As he turned to go back inside and say his goodbyes to Ruby, Teddie suddenly lunged at him, flung her arms round his waist and laid her head against his chest, clinging to him for a long second before she released him.

The car pulled up outside the row of terraced cottages. Several lace curtains twitched. May knocked on the door, and Iris came to stand by her side. Julia's face assumed a pantomime expression of amazement when she opened in response to the knock. 'Why, ye bugs! I wondered who the hell it was, banging on the front door.' She stood there, staring challengingly, and did not move aside, or invite them in. She was wearing a grubby green headscarf, from which the odd dark twist of hair escaped on to her brow. A floral pinafore was fastened over a dark jumper and shapeless skirt, the pattern of the pinafore was faded, the edging frayed. She had a pair of old sand shoes with no laces in on her feet. Her legs were bare and pale, despite the fine weeks of summer that had passed.

'We've been to see Marian,' May said. 'I thought it was time we came to see you. Have a talk.'

'You've got summat to say, have you?' She nodded carelessly at Iris. 'Mind, it's not everyone has a real live lady to chauffeur them around.'

'Aren't you going to ask us in?' May said, meeting the insolent look head on.

At last, Julia stepped back and made way for them to enter. 'You'll have to excuse the mess. Not quite what you're used to. But you just can't get the staff nowadays, you know. Least ways, not round here!'

'Knock it off, our Julia.' May spoke calmly and moved to sit down by the dining table placed squarely in the middle of the small front room. 'Whatever you think of me, we're family, and it's ridiculous to go on like this. It's nigh on two years now since we've spoken. What's done is done. We're none of us getting any younger—'

'Speak for yourself, missus! You've got five years on me, don't forget!'

May smiled, held up one hand. There was a hint of weariness in her gesture.

'You don't have to tell me. That's why I'm here. It isn't right we should never see each other.'

'I said my piece in that letter!' Julia glared, not willing to give an inch.

Still May's tone was quiet, almost reflective. 'You certainly did. You're a hard one, Julia. Even when—'

'Aye! Well, some of us have had to be! We haven't all had the advantages you've had—'

'Oh, for God's sake! Not that old claptrap again! Change the record, can't you?' Iris had not said a word until then. Her outburst was full of passion, stopping Julia in her tracks. 'May's come to make it up with you. She didn't have to. She's not well—'

May crimsoned. Again, a hand was held up in protest. 'Iris! There's no need – that's not why I came—'

'What's wrong with you?' Julia asked aggressively.

Iris swept aside May's diffidence, her voice trembling with

233

emotion. 'She's got a bad heart, that's what's wrong with her! She should be taking things easily, not getting herself all upset.'

'It's just a touch of angina. Nothing that can't be dealt with. They've got new tablets now . . .'

But Julia was staring at her, her aggression transformed. 'Like me mam. And Nana Bell. What's the doctor say? Is there nowt they can do?'

May gave an amused grimace. 'Yes. Seems to run in our family, doesn't it? That's one thing the doctor *did* manage to work out. But like I said, they have all kinds of new pills these days. In fact, it's a wonder I don't rattle like a pillbox, the amount I take.'

Iris's deep voice was still unsteady. 'I've told her she should start taking notice of what the doctor said. About taking things quietly, resting up. She's still on the go far too much. And the worry. You're not supposed to get yourself agitated. She won't take any notice of me!' The appeal, and the anxiety Iris felt, was very evident.

Julia looked almost comically taken aback, the glowering set of her turned-down mouth even more exaggerated. She cleared her throat. There was a note of hushed apology as she said, 'I'll pop the kettle back on.' But there was still just a hint of her old cockiness as she turned back on her way to the tiny kitchen, and her head came up as she announced to Iris, 'We've got a gas oven now, you know. Fire's only on for the back boiler!'

Only a few miles north of Ein Gedi lay the Jordanian border, making the northern half of the Dead Sea part of the territory of the Arab state. Berni was driving one of the trucks in a three-lorry convoy, bringing supplies back from Beersheba. They had been escorted by a light military vehicle, but as darkness fell, it turned and headed back westward, leaving only the guards in the trucks themselves. They were close to the camp. Another hour at the most and they would be there. Besides, there had been no sign of trouble in this eastern sector of the Judaean Desert since the signing of the armistice eight months ago. But, after one of the trucks became badly bogged down, it took them nearly an hour to dig and haul it out, during which time the weather deteriorated rapidly. The sand was whipped up in the fierce wind until visibility was reduced to a matter of yards, and they had no alternative but to sit inside the vehicles and wait for the desert storm to blow itself out.

Berni knew Sara would begin to worry. She had been assigned lighter duties so that she remained within the camp. Soon she would have to be transferred back to the kibbutz, where there were proper medical facilities, and a nearby hospital to monitor her progress. He would be relieved when that happened, even though it would mean that they would see far less of each other until he came to the end of his active service.

Dawn was indicated only by a vague lightening of the darkness. Once again they had to turn out in the searing sand storm and dig out the lorries. 'We can't spend the day here,' the young officer ruminated, as they crouched in the canvas-sided rear of the lead vehicle and held a fairly democratic discussion.

'I think we should try to push on,' Berni advocated strongly, thinking of Sara back at camp. 'I know it's hard following the trail, but even if we're a few miles out, we're bound to hit the water sooner or later, if we keep heading north-east.'

'But we might cross the border!' someone objected. 'We could end up in their territory.'

Berni shrugged. 'So what? They don't even have patrols out most of the time. Especially in this weather. We'll be back in camp before anyone knows it.'

'One more day and we're going to be running short of water. I say let's go on.'

They were grinding slowly along, enjoying the shelter of a towering cliff on one side of a wadi when there was a flash, and the stunning crack of a grenade as it burst on the bonnet of the lead truck. Machine gun bullets tore into the sides, the petrol caught alight, and then the whole lot erupted in a flame-filled explosion. Screaming figures tumbled out, to be cut down by a hail of fire. There was no opportunity for the other two trucks, following closely behind, to turn round or to bypass the burning wreck. Grenades rained down on them and burst with devastating effect.

Berni was not driving on this stretch, and he was able to grab his rifle and leap through the passenger door before the packed rear of the lorry caught fire. The bullet smacked into his upper thigh as soon as he began a crouching run to escape. Its force jarred his whole body and spun him round and up into the air. His head was filled with roaring, and for a minute or so, he was not fully conscious. When he recovered, he knew he was badly, perhaps mortally, wounded. The pain in his lower body receded swiftly, but he could feel the flowing wetness of blood loss, then a cold clamminess on his skin, and a dreadful nausea. The sounds of the fight were faint over the roaring in his head.

Someone grabbed his shirt collar, trying to drag him away from the vicinity of the burning lorries, but then collapsed over him, struck dead or unconscious by a bullet. The firing died down. Pain, and full consciousness, was returning. He found himself staring up at long, ragged gowns all around him. Bedouin? Their heads and lower faces were hidden by dark cloths draped round them, like cowls. Perhaps they would help? But then he felt their hands roughly pulling the body from him, and pain flared agonizingly as they dragged him roughly along the ground. They had weapons with them, and he realized with despair that these men were their attackers.

He heard other frightened cries, of pain and fear, some thuds, and a shrill scream. The brutal hands tore at his clothing, stripping it from him, and probed cruelly at the mess of his wound.

'*La! La!*' He heard the Arabic word for no, then a figure knelt over him, filling his vision, and he looked up into a pair of black eyes, implacable, expressionless. He saw the long knife, its blade dull, held high above him. He wanted to speak, to plead for his life, but he couldn't. His mouth seemed to be filled with thick liquid.

Sara! Her name rang in his head, he wanted to say it, to cry out to her. He heard a soft, guttural sound, it might have been him, and felt a deep, tender sadness as the knife came down for him.

CHAPTER TWENTY-ONE

It was never satisfactorily proven who the ambushers of the convoy were. Only three survivors eventually managed to make it back to the camp at Ein Gedi. The Israeli commander on the spot led an incursion across the border into Jordan, shots were exchanged briefly with a Jordanian patrol. But the Jordanian authorities denied responsibility for the attack on the convoy, the UN intermediaries swiftly intervened, and this minor blip to the uneasy peace was smoothed out. The mutilated bodies of Berni and his companions were brought back from the desert.

Sara was persuaded not to see Berni's corpse. She had little spirit for resistance. For a long time, she was in an almost somnambulistic state of numbed shock, and made no protest when, before the quickly arranged military funeral service could take place, a message came that Berni should not be interred with his comrades, and that his father would be arriving as soon as possible. Sara's consent was needed for the body to be shipped back to England. She gave it without demur.

In his grief, Mr Lightman did not try to hide his feeling, and clearly that of his absent wife as well, that Sara was mainly to blame for his son's death, that, but for his love for her, Berni would not have been caught up in the conflict or had any lasting stake in the new country. His antagonism, and the injustice of it, scarcely registered with Sara. Nor, in spite of that antagonism, his strange offer that she should return as soon as possible to England, to have the baby there. 'It will be our grandchild. We want to take care of it.'

She was indefinite, her abstracted air adding to her vagueness. 'There are things to be settled here. I'll have to go back to our kibbutz.'

'Let us know as soon as you finalize things. We'll send the money for your ticket.'

Teddy attended the funeral ceremony. He had little chance to talk with her, though he could see at once by her glazed expression, even by the way she moved, how dazed and lost she was feeling. 'I'll come up to see you, once you're back at the kibbutz,' he promised her helplessly. 'I can get some leave. The road's nearly finished now, anyway.'

It was another three weeks before he could keep his promise and travel north, to the settlement where Sara and Berni had met and lived. The numbness had worn off. There was only the pain of her despair. She cried frequently, her eyes and face ravaged by her grief. 'I'm not going to have the baby,' she stated bleakly. 'I can have an abortion. They will terminate it.'

He thought of Marian, of the guilty secret she had borne for years. Of the miscarriage, and her sinking into that black misery which had almost destroyed her, which might still be doing so. 'You can't! You can't do that! It's Berni's. Yours and his. All he's left you. You can't kill the baby!'

'Why not? He's gone! He's dead! Somebody took *his* life. What good is his baby to me now? I want *him*!' She smote with the flat of her hand at the still indiscernible swell of her belly. 'I'd give this up without a thought if I could have him back!' The sound of her crying was ugly, wrenching sobs that tore from her and took her strength, and he gathered her to his arms and held her

239

while the storm of it buffeted through her shaking body.

Later, wearily calm, she sat surrounded by the few personal touches she and Berni had imposed on the tiny living-room of their quarters, while Teddy faced her across the low coffee table. 'I don't want to have the child on my own.' Her voice was low and hoarse. 'I've lost Berni. I loved him deeply. I've lost everyone I've ever loved. Mama, Papa, my brother. All my family. There's no one left.' She shook her head, leaned back against the white lace cloth draped over the back of the uncomfortable little sofa. She had removed her glasses, her eyes were deep circles of shadow. 'I don't want to love anyone else, Teddy.' Her eyes opened, gazed at him pitifully. 'You can understand, can't you? You know what I'm saying.'

He nodded. 'I know a bit. Even when you haven't lost it, love can still hurt.' He told her about Marian's unfaithfulness, about the miscarriage and her inability to have any more children. 'I didn't want Little Teddie. I ran away before she was born, even. Now, goodness knows, she'll probably grow up hating me. But how glad I am now that we didn't get rid of *her*!' He stood up, edged round the table, fitted himself into the narrow space beside her. Their legs touched, he put his arm round her shoulders and drew her into him. He let his other hand rest on her midriff, above the waistband of her skirt. 'This is part you and part Berni. I dunno. Maybe it's the only way we all live on. John would shout me down all right if he was here. He really believes in God and His heaven. But Berni wouldn't want you to harm this, would he? You know how happy he was when he found out. You owe it to him, Sara. And to yourself.'

She sniffed loudly, reached for a handkerchief. 'I can't think any more tonight. I'm exhausted. Just hold me, Teddy. Stay with me, will you?'

'Of course.' He smiled, his face half-hidden in the thick, aromatic cloud of her black hair. 'Give them all something to talk about at breakfast in the morning!'

'Do you care?'

'What? With the chance to spend the night with a lovely girl like you? You must be joking!'

She slept in the dim lamplight. His arm became numb, but he didn't move. He dozed, too. He awoke when she stirred, moved from his embracing arm. 'God! I must have dropped off. What time is it? After eleven? You get off to bed, love. I can kip down here, with these cushions. I'll be fine.'

But she stood, pulled him by the hand, leading him across to the bedroom. 'Sleep with me,' she said simply.

She went into the bathroom. He heard the toilet flushing, the tap running. When she came out, she had taken off her shirt. He could see the white brassière standing out against the duskiness of her skin. 'You want the bathroom?'

The bedroom was in darkness when he returned, but there was enough light from the window for him to see her lying naked on top of the covers. He was shocked, deeply, and, just for a moment, panicked. 'The baby?' he murmured.

She patted the bed beside her. 'It's all right. It won't be harmed. I want you, Teddy. I told you at Ein Gedi. I am very sexual. Who knows? I might even become a harlot. Maybe I'd be good at it, eh?' Her effort at light-heartedness failed her, her voice caught. 'Right now I don't want to be alone. You're my friend. Come and be with me.'

She did not get rid of the baby, nor did she go to England, in spite of the urgent pleas from Berni's parents. 'There's a new settlement starting quite close to here,' she told Teddy. '*Kfar Mordechai.* Mostly British. They want to start a dairy farm, and grow citrus fruits. Why don't you apply to work there for a while? I might join you. I don't think I can stay here on my own.' Her smile carried a trace of her former liveliness. 'Broad-minded as they are, I think we've shocked a few people!'

He tried to avoid debating with himself whether he was in love with her or not. It was all so outlandish, her carrying Berni's child – the pregnancy was making her bloom even more, her body round and inviting. She took such obvious and deep pleasure in the sex they shared, and showed no sign of guilt or shame, so he pushed his own secret, disturbing thoughts firmly aside. They made love unselfconsciously, with awareness of mutual need, ensuring that those needs were satisfied fully, for both of them. They felt as though they were somehow insulated from all those around them, in spite of the demanding work of establishing the new settlement. Teddy also felt in a curious way that time itself was suspended, except that the evidence of its passing became more and more clear in Sara's changing body, which he grew to know so well and to cherish. He would spend a long time, on the bed, smoothing the scented oil into her naked flesh – her limbs, and the wonderful, gradually increasing rotundity of her belly. He would lie with his ear pressed to the smooth curve, and delight in making her laugh at his wonder at the rippling gurgles he swore he could detect.

He was proud of his ability to make her smile so often, and desolate when he awoke to feel the tremors of her weeping in the dark, and feel the wetness on her cheeks as he gently held her close. 'I'm going to miss you when you go,' she said, and he was startled at how her words hurt.

'I'm not going anywhere.'

Her eyes were full of warmth and sadness as they held his. 'You have to go home. You must. I've been very selfish, I know I have.'

'I don't want to leave you. Or the baby.' He nodded at the bulge.

'I'm all right now. I swear it. Even if I am thought of as a fallen woman round here.' She smiled tenderly at him. 'We'll meet again some day. I shall come to England. The child must know his only grandparents. Or hers. I have the feeling it's a girl in here.' She rubbed her hand over her belly. 'I want her to meet your family. And I want to meet your daughter. Fourteen now. A young lady!'

The letter from Teddie came a few days into the new year. He was shocked. She had never written, in all the year and more he had been away. Teddy was equally startled at the greeting. '*Dearest Dad*'! She had never called him that before, either.

Dearest Dad,

I've been meaning to write to you for so long now, and kept putting it off and putting it off, largely because I didn't know just what to say. You'll see what I mean in a minute. Before that, let me get some other things out of the way. First, thanks, belatedly, for the lovely birthday presents you sent. The silk scarves were just beautiful, and that lovely Arab jewellery had all the girls at school green with envy. It seems a long time since November. And thanks for the cheque for Christmas. It was far too generous, but I can't pretend it wasn't appreciated, and was put to good use!

I haven't told anyone I'm writing to you, not yet at least, but I know they would all send their love – mum, and grandma and Aunt I, and Uncle John and Aunty Jenny – oh, and not forgetting Ruby. I wouldn't dare leave her out. Baby Thomas is gorgeous by the way – he's shuffling round at lightning speed on his btm now, and pulls himself up by the furniture, or any person who's near enough for him to grab.

But here I go, putting off again from saying the important things I want to tell you. I know now about the trouble between you and mum – about her and Jim Moody, and the abortion – and about how much you wanted another baby and that mum can't have any more. And before you start getting mad at anybody, it was me that found out. I was so sick of all the hints and the mysteries, with Dora and that lot, that I tackled mum about it last year. She got herself very upset, I'm afraid, and told me to ask Aunty Jen. I did – and more or less made her tell me. Not that I needed much telling. I'd already put most of it together, and made four out of two and two.

I was pretty mad with Aunty Jen at first for telling you, and all the bother that was caused, but then I had to admit she was probably right when she said she did it for the best, whatever disasters have followed. Mum couldn't have gone on living with it, could she? She's still seeing that Dr Hennessy, and taking those pills, and still having her bad days, but in between she's OK, as they say. I think she'd be a lot better if Nana Nelly and Aunt Julia weren't around so much – and I know you'll agree with me on that one!!

I'm just sorry that I behaved so badly towards you, dad. I never got to know you properly when you came back from Germany. And then I used to listen to Dora and Alice and Rose going on about it – how you went off even before I was born. I used to think you never wanted me, even though you never did anything to make me feel that way. That one time you gave me a good slap, I was a right little brat and thoroughly deserved it!

I've been thinking about you a lot. We were all worried for you, especially Grandma. I pray every night for you, and hope that you'll come home to us soon. Mum's a bit of a mess, but I know she loves you very much, and I don't think she ever stopped, even when you were a prisoner in Germany and Jim Moody was around. Please don't think I'm just being cheeky, or a know-it-all kid. I just feel I've learnt a lot lately. Aunty Jen also told me about her trouble in the war, how she did just the same as mum. She said she loves Uncle John, and always has. I can't understand why she or mum got messed up with another man, but I have to believe her about the loving bit. I guess I can't be grown-up yet, eh?

But I know I love you, and want you to come back, soon. I want us to be a family again. Take care,
  Your loving daughter,
  Edwina xxx

PS I'm trying to persuade everyone to call me by my proper name. I'm grown-up enough to be absolutely sick of being Little Teddie!

'Bad news?' When he looked up at her, Sara could see the struggle to hide his distress, and his failure to do so. She experienced a deep wave of sympathy and love for him. For an instant, she was shaken by the depth of her feeling, and wondered bemusedly how it could be so, when she was still so deeply wounded from Berni's loss that it was like something physical she carried inside her, along with the growing baby. And then another sadness came, as she realized that in her need and her weakness she could so easily settle for this good man, would be glad to lean on him, depend on him, and keep him by her side.

'It's just – a letter from Teddie.' His smile smote at her sensitivity. 'Whoops! Edwina, I should say. She doesn't want to be called Teddie any more.'

'She's growing up.'

'Yeah.' He smiled again, held up the thin sheets of paper. 'Fourteen. This is the first proper letter I've had from her. She used to send funny little drawings when I was in the POW camp.'

'She needs you.'

He looked at her desperately, gave a little shake of his head. 'I've never been much good – as a father,' he said thickly. 'She'll be all right—'

'No, Teddy!' Her words were firm, almost harsh in their denial. 'Why has she written?' He didn't answer, glanced away from her, gave an unconvincing little shrug of his shoulders. 'She has a father. You should be with her. And your wife.' She cupped her hands round her belly's protuberance in an unconsciously eloquent gesture, which Teddy noticed.

'I don't want to leave you now. I want to stay till the baby comes.' And after! part of his mind added, and he felt the weight of the inner conflict tearing at him.

Sara, too, felt all the magnitude of this critical moment, felt the intense tug of a desire to be selfish and keep him with her; acknowledged, without pride, that perhaps she could, if she spoke now. She resisted bravely. 'Listen, Teddy. It wouldn't work out. You and I. You've been wonderful. I'll never forget what you've done for me. And I'll never regret it. Our being lovers, everything. You have got me through such a bad time. I couldn't have done it by myself. But I have, honestly, been meaning to talk seriously to you for some time.' She nodded at the letter, still in his hand. 'Now, the time has come. I feel bad, as though I've just used you, but it was never meant to be like that.'

She came over to him, stood over him, her hand on his shoulder. The curve of her belly was almost touching his face. 'This baby is Berni's. Berni's and mine. As you told me, remember? I don't think I can share it with anyone else. I don't want to find another father. Lately, I can feel myself becoming more and more self-absorbed. I want to have this child on my own. I want to be alone with it. At least for a long time.' She hesitated, then said softly, 'Now I feel that by turning to you, becoming lovers, I've let Berni down after all.'

It was the biggest lie of all, and the tears that rolled down her face were for the pain it caused, both to her and to the still figure sitting in front of her.

CHAPTER TWENTY-TWO

John sat in the room, savouring its quiet, after the effervescence of the delegates, their overflowing excitement, with which it had so recently been filled. Over the muted roar of the traffic, the sonorous notes of Big Ben could be heard, and the chime of bells from the adjacent abbey. The buoyant mood of his fellow Baha'is, which he had shared during the convention, contrasted now with his more sombre private reflections. Around the walls of this modest meeting place, and on its shelves, lay evidence of the vigorous efforts on behalf of the Faith that had taken place over the past six years to promote it in Britain, and in which over the past three he himself had played an active part.

But, as always, he questioned whether he had been active enough. There was a score or more of letters and cables, from the Guardian himself, Shoghi Effendi, in Haifa, the unassuming figure whom John had been privileged to meet, in the sanctified surroundings of the Master's house at the foot of Mount Carmel. A meeting which had had such a permanent and beneficient influence on his life, confirming the spiritual belief he had first found when he had been guided to that peaceful, welcoming shrine halfway up the slopes, at the end of the winding track.

Phrases from the letter the Guardian had written nearly a year ago, to all the British Baha'is, came to his mind now. *The newly enrolled believers, on whom . . . the mantle has now fallen . . . from among such a vast multitude of their slumbering countrymen, to serve and glorify His Faith.* And only a few months ago he had urged them to *exhibit the rarest evidences of courage and heroism, and choose to subordinate their personal interests to the immediate needs and the future glory of the community to which they belong.*

John had helped, it was true. In the short time during which he had been a believer, he had seen the number of Baha'is swell from what was virtually a handful of scarcely more than a hundred to treble that figure, which was the cause for their present ebullience. They had more than achieved their target, set out in their plan formulated in 1944, six years ago, with the encouragement and prayers of the Guardian himself.

But still, John felt, there was more he could do. Work was worship, the Holy Writings stated, but often he accused himself of being too preoccupied with his own career, too wrapped up in the enclosed world of Beaconsfield. And of Jenny, and Thomas, and the rest of his family. His own joy in the fellowship he had shared these past few days in London had been tempered by his visit to the prison that morning, and his meeting with Tony Ellis. His prayers, and his efforts, had not been very successful, judging by the despondency he had met with in the hour he had spent with the young prisoner.

He had visited Tony at least seven or eight times during the fifteen months of their acquaintance, and John's faith had become the staple topic of conversation between them. Not wholly at John's instigation. He had been careful to encourage Tony to study the literature he supplied him with, and to approach its content with an open mind, pointing out that he must make his judgements independently. And Tony had displayed a lively spirit of enquiry, had been willing, even eager, to talk about religion in general and the Baha'i Faith in particular. He seemed to look forward to the visits, and wrote regularly in the intervals.

It was clear at once that day that things were very wrong: visibly clear, from the bruising about his face, the stiffness of his movements, the wincing of pain. 'What happened?' John asked immediately, suspecting brutality on the part of the staff.

Tony would not meet his gaze. He shrugged dismissively. 'Private. A bit of a ruckus, that's all. There's some vicious bastards in here.' He was usually much more careful of the language he used with John. Now he brushed aside John's efforts to find out more about the beating. The hands, folded on the table, twisted and jumped nervously, another indication of the tension he was under.

'Teddy's back home now.' John injected brightness into his tone, striving to lighten the atmosphere. 'Been back over a week. He'll be getting in touch soon, I expect. You'll be getting a visit from him one of these days.'

'Probably won't want no more to do with an old lag like me. Anyway, he'll have enough on his plate, sorting out his own affairs. What's he going to do? Will he stay with that wife of his, or will he ditch her?'

The harshness of his words surprised John. 'I hope they'll stay together. It was a long time ago. We all do wrong things, don't we? And live to regret them. And want forgiveness. We expect forgiveness from God. The least we can do is forgive one another.'

'Huh! Not much forgiveness in here, I can tell you!' His fingers moved up to trace gingerly the swollen, dark bruising of the upper cheekbone, below his left eye. His gaze met John's squarely now, alive with pain and anger. 'You wanted to know how I got this? Right, I'll tell you! In here, blokes like me – queers!' – he spat the word at John, who struggled not to react, not to show the revulsion he instinctively felt at the ugly word – 'we have to have a daddy, see? Someone to look after us, in return for our – favours.' His thin smile was as ugly as his

249

language. 'I've got one. A right hard case. Old enough to be me real dad, but he takes good care of me. Trouble is, there's a young bloke come in who fancies me – and he did something about it. My daddy found out – he had two of his goons work me over.' He gave a low, bitter laugh. 'What you can see is nothing. You should see the rest of me! They kicked shit out of me! I won't be doing no favours for no one for a while!'

John stared in horrified compassion. 'You should tell someone! Complain – the governor? One of the warders?'

Tony's laugh was louder now. 'Who the hell do you think kept watch while they did it? Made sure they weren't disturbed, like!' His thin face, marked by the beating, was stamped with the ugliness which had enveloped them, and was reflected in their bleak surroundings. John could see that Tony wanted to hit out, to wound him. 'Oh! And before you go getting too upset for me, it was me own fault, see? 1 brought it on meself, in a manner of speaking.' Even the syntax was deliberately coarsened.

The sensitive features were marred by the twisted smile. 'He's so gorgeous, this new bloke. A real hunk! Know what I mean? And when he came on so strong, with his chatting me up, well! I couldn't resist him, could I?'

John stared, sickened, at the sudden, lowering flutter of those long eyelashes, the downward glance and smirk of the lips, the glimpse of deviant sexuality they revealed. He sat dumbly now, while the soft voice probed on tormentingly. 'So! What do you reckon your lot would make of that? I been doing a lot of reading, all them things you sent me. No room for poufters in there, is there? Lost cause, I reckon. Can't help it, can I? That's the way I am.'

John had tried to argue, to give some light of hope. 'We have to try, to keep fighting against self, against our passions.' A sudden vision came to him of Jenny, her clenched body under him, rutting furiously, her thighs clamping him, eyes tightly shut, mouth gaping, lost in the frenzy of crisis, oblivious of him except as an instrument of hard pleasure. His own guilt, afterwards, at being plunged into that maelstrom of flesh with her. His words now felt leaden and useless as he dragged them forth.

Hurt himself, he had weakened, said at the end of the visit, abruptly, 'Do you want me to come again?' and Tony had shrugged, both of them helpless. 'I'm sorry,' John added.

'It's always nice to have a visitor,' Tony conceded gruffly. 'Something to look forward to.' He turned quickly away, joined the line without saying goodbye.

Sitting in the basement room in Westminster, John admitted to himself that somehow he had let the young man down. He thought of the comfort and happiness of his own life, compared with the unimaginable horror of Tony's existence in prison. Thought of the love waiting for him, only a few hours away. Of Jenny and his little son, of his mother and Aunt I, and Teddy, a very different, more contained and reflective figure, marked by more than the deep bronzed, almost scoured quality of his skin from that land of searching sun.

Iris put her hand firmly on Teddy's shoulder, her fingers pressed into the hardness of bone she could feel there. 'I'm so glad you've come home, Teddy.' She was gruff with emotion.

He smiled. He drove out of his mind the pregnant figure of Sara, standing by the gate of the settlement, smiling beautifully, and waving, while the tears rolled down her cheeks. 'So am I. And hey! No more blubbing, right? There was enough of that last week! I'm here to stay, this time. I know you've heard those words before, but I mean it. All right?'

She nodded, turned away. 'I do hope so. What about work? Will you go back to the yards?'

'I don't think so. Not if I can get into something different. You know, in the army, and then this last year over in Israel, I've been working in engineering. Road building, mostly, and civil engineering. Uncle David's got a lot of contacts. There's some big contracts, more coming, up in the north. Big firms are going to be crying out for staff. I haven't got the paper qualifications, but I've had some experience. Uncle David seems to think I could get taken on with one of them. I'd really like to give it a go.'

'That's good.' Iris glanced towards the door. He saw the anxiety on her florid face. 'May's so happy that you're back safe and sound. She's been worried. Talk to her. Try and make her start taking things more easily. She won't do what the doctor tells her. I have the devil of a job getting her to take a lie-down in the afternoon.'

'How bad is she?'

'She gets pain. A lot more than she'll acknowledge. I have to watch her like a hawk. She tries to hide it—'

He went over to her, patted her arm. 'You of all people know what ma's like. She never could sit still, could she? But we'll do our best.' He broke off quickly as May came through into the kitchen.

'Teddie's finished packing her things now. She'll be down in a minute.' May paused a little. 'She's got all she'll need for the holidays. She's not quite sure what to take, really. About next term.'

Teddy nodded. 'We'll have to see. She was thinking we would try the travelling from home. There's a bus nearly every ten minutes now into Newcastle. And there's the Northerns, as well as the town buses. It'll probably be quicker than going from here.'

'She's no bother,' May said quickly. 'In fact, we'll miss her, won't we, Iris? We've got so used to her being here—'

'Well, we're not far away, are we?' Teddy said heartily. 'Who knows? If I get a half-decent job, we might be able to afford a car. 'Specially now they're going to end petrol rationing. Besides, it's time you old fogies started putting your feet up a bit more!'

'I'll have you know I'm not even fifty-six yet! You'll be thirty-four yourself next week, in case you've forgotten, so less of the old fogy, please!'

Teddie came in on the end of the remark. 'What's he been saying, Grandma? Take no notice of him!'

'A houseful of women!' Teddy grumbled. 'What chance does a poor bloke have? All set, Edwina?'

Teddie glanced sharply at him, her cheeks tinged with pink, but saw no sign of mischief. 'Yes, thank you, father,' she answered, with theatrical primness. 'Ready when you are.'

'Let's go, before Ruby insists on another pot of tea,' Teddy whispered comically, and his daughter giggled. 'I'll put your cases in the boot.' Aunt I was giving them a lift back to Low Fell.

'Why don't you stay here?' Iris tried casually, as she pulled on her old workaday coat against the April chill.

May was wrapping a scarf around her shoulders, crossing it over her bosom. 'No fear! You'll forget to get home once you start gossiping.' She chuckled, slipped her arms into the coat Iris, gracefully accepting defeat, was already holding out for her. 'Anyway, you know you like to keep me under your eye, you old bully! I might pick up a cup and saucer, or do something equally rash, if you're not keeping tabs on me.'

'Don't take one of your pills yet, mum,' Teddie whispered that night, as they washed up the supper things together in the small kitchen. They could hear the wireless, and the soft crackle of the newspaper that Teddy was reading, stretched in slippered ease before the blazing fire, through in the living-room. Marian stared at her uncertainly, and Teddie grinned back. 'It's lovely being home again. All of us together!' She hoped her mother felt that way, too. She had an idea how difficult it must be for her, after all this time separated from her husband. Sometimes,

Teddie felt that her dad tried too hard to make things seem heartily normal. Every meal, every cup of tea, even, was 'absolutely splendid', and her mum hovered around both of them with the expression of an anxious domestic eager to please. The tension was there, in spite of all their best efforts to ignore it. Her father was sleeping in the little front bedroom, as he had done for so many months before he had gone away.

Still, Teddie felt that surge of hope and thankfulness as she and Marian went back into the cosy warmth of the living-room and settled down once more, Marian in the other armchair, across the hearthrug from her husband, Teddie sprawling along the length of the settee. It was nearly ten o'clock, but no one told her it was time for bed. She was glad she had persuaded her mum not to take one of her sleeping pills yet. When she did, she had to be in bed within minutes, otherwise she would be snoring inelegantly in her seat, and have to be practically carried upstairs and undressed. Teddie wanted to spare her such an indignity, not to mention the embarrassment it would cause her dad.

In an effort to prolong the evening, and to foster the new closeness she wished for with her father, Teddie began to question him about his experiences in Israel. At first, she assumed his seeming reluctance to be drawn was from his natural modesty. He refused to cast himself in any semblance of a heroic light, in spite of the adventurous life he had led, and his daughter's readiness to see him as such. She pressed on. 'It's terrible what happened to that friend of Uncle John's. Sara. They went to her wedding a couple of years ago. You've seen her, haven't you? She's pregnant. Just imagine. Being left on your own like that.'

'Yes. Well, there's a lot of bad things have gone on out there. And it's not over yet, I'm sure of that.'

'How is she really, though? What will she do now?'

He shrugged. 'Dunno. She might come over to England. Her husband's parents wanted her to. Perhaps you'll get to meet her one day.' He pushed his paper to the floor, stood up suddenly, and gave an exaggerated yawn. 'God! I'm whacked! Doing nothing is hard work! I think I'll head off to bed.' At once, Marian began to lever herself from the cushions of her chair. 'You don't have to move,' he said quickly. 'It's just me—'

'No, it's way past my bedtime. And time you were up the wooden hill, young lady!' Marian turned to Teddie. 'Get me a glass of water for my pills, love.'

Teddie pulled a face. She felt disappointed, and a little irritated, then was penitent as she thought that her questions might well have upset him and stirred up some painful memories he would rather forget. 'I think I might stay up a bit. I'm on holiday after all. I don't have to get up early. There's some good music on AFN at this time of night.'

Marian began to admonish her, but Teddy cut in quickly. 'It's all right. She's a big lass now. What's AFN when it's at home?'

'Everybody knows that!' she answered scornfully. 'American Forces' Network. It's great!' She gave her mother a swift peck on the cheek as Marian went off to bed.

'Don't forget to put the lights out,' Teddy said. 'And put the guard up.' He nodded at the glowing fire. 'Don't want to burn the happy home down. Night-night.'

She reached for his arm as he turned to follow Marian out into the hall. 'Dad! I think it will be, now.' Her voice was breathy with embarrassment, and she blushed a little, but she put her arms round his neck and kissed him hard. 'Night! Love you!'

He nodded, feeling his throat closing. He held her to him.

Upstairs, Marian was undressing when he entered the bedroom. Her eyes widened, then she coloured deeply, folded her arms across her breasts, which strained against the pink brassière and the lace-trimmed slip. Her expression of shyness, and shame, pained him. She didn't move, stood there, her fingers hugging her upper arms. 'I know I'm fat,' she muttered. 'I've

255

been trying – I'm going to go on a diet. Sort myself out.'

'You're just fine.' He came close to her, and he saw her eyes fill with tears. 'Listen. I'm moving back in here, with you. If that's all right.'

The tears were spilling over, and he held her, felt her shaking under his embrace, and kissed the top of her fair head. She tilted her head back, looked at him, the tears shining on her cheeks. 'Will it – it's going to be all right again, isn't it, Teddy?'

He closed his eyes, pulled her tightly against him. 'Yes, love. I promise. It's going to be all right.'

CHAPTER TWENTY-THREE

'Oooh, look! The rain's stopped! The sun's coming out!' Ruby levered herself up from the dining chair, where she was sitting between her husband and her niece. 'Now then! Who wants a refill?'

'Sit down, Ruby, for goodness' sake!' May said firmly, from the splendour of her armchair in the front row. 'Watch the procession. We're all capable of finding our way to the kitchen if we need anything.'

'Not *you*, missus! You'll stay right where you are.'

For an instant, May felt a quick stab of irritation at Ruby's fussing, then it gave way to a wave of contrite love for the concern of the plump figure who had been so close to her for all these years. As she turned her eyes back to the screen of the brand new television set, the doors of its handsome walnut veneer cabinet wide open and fastened back, she experienced also a deep sense of wellbeing, and gratitude for the gathering of people, ranged in an arc like a cinema audience, in the living-groom: the Hedleys, elderly neighbours from down the lane; Ruby and her husband, Tom, and their teenaged niece, Pat; Teddy and Marian, and Teddie – whoops, no! Edwina – it was so hard to get used to using her proper name, despite the squawking protest every time anyone made a mistake; and, of course, her beloved Iris, the

257

rock-like figure to whom she had clung, often literally, and with whom she had shared this home, and her life, for so long.

If only John and Jenny, and little Thomas, could have been here, her happiness would have been total, but even there she felt a surge of thankfulness that, within weeks, her prayer would be answered, and she would see them again, after two long, long years. It was all part of this resurgence of hope everyone was feeling, after such gloom. The New Elizabethan Age, they were calling it, though there had been little felt but uncertainty and compassion for the young woman on whose shoulders the burden of sovereignty had fallen in that bleak February sixteen months ago. May had wept – all the women had, and, she suspected, the menfolk had swallowed choking lumps in their throats, at the magnificent spectacle of the coronation they had just watched. The good-looking young husband kneeling to his wife, pledging his loyalty, their young children peeping awestruck from the gallery. It had been another long and hard year leading to this truly crowning moment. But now things augured so well – only yesterday, the news had come of another splendid achievement, the conquest of Everest by Edmund Hillary and Sherpa Tenzing.

Perfect timing for this wonderful event. It seemed magical, as magical as the moving images they were staring at right now, in the comfort of their own home, which were actually happening over two hundred miles away. May pushed aside the uncomfortable feelings she had already endured at the thought of how expensive it had been for them to make it possible, and again was grateful for Iris's blustering determination to have the set installed in time, and hang the cost! 'Come on, old girl! We can damn well afford it! And think of the pleasure we'll get! It's like having your own private picture show, every night!'

Yes, she had a lot to be thankful for, May acknowledged gladly. Teddy, bless him! How proud of him she was for the way he had finally faced his responsibilities, and for the effort he had put into the regeneration of his marriage. Marian, poor girl, was so much better. She still suffered from her 'nerves', was still over-weight and battling constantly against her tendency to over-indulge, particularly in sweet things, with new diets and sporadic bursts of fitness regimes. But then Teddy himself was thickening out. May guessed he still drank a lot, and it worried her – but he worked so hard, and often travelled long distances all over the north. And he was doing well, in a managerial post with a large construction firm – a lot of the drinking seemed to be an inescapable part of his new career.

Most heart-warming of all was the closeness he had forged with his daughter. At sixteen, Edwina was already strikingly pretty. 'She's so like you when you were nobbut a lass!' Iris had affirmed, to May's secret delight. Now, when she observed the familiar ease with each other that father and daughter displayed, May felt another of her prayers had been answered.

Perhaps God, in His wisdom, had decided the perfection of bliss would have been too much for her tired old heart if John and his family had been able to make it back to England for the coronation. She could recall less painfully now the deep shock and the dawning sense of dismay she had felt when he had told her of his decision to go abroad. And not just that, but to take his wife and infant son to a part of the world where, yet again, danger threatened. The press had been full of the atrocities against the whites taking place out there in Kenya by those savages who called themselves by that ridiculous name – Mau-Mau.

'Look, mam! Uganda's miles and miles away from all that. There's no bother there at all.'

His words had failed to convince her. In spite of herself, she could not help the bitterness against this religion of his, which was the motive for his going. 'Surely there's enough you can do here at home, if you want to preach your faith—'

259

'We don't preach—'

But she ignored his interruption. 'You have a responsibility towards Jenny and Thomas. It's no place to take a baby, out there, with those – those natives!'

She tried to align Jenny with her own opposition. 'I can't believe you would agree to take the baby out there. As his mother you've got to put your foot down, Jenny. It's not right. You know it isn't!'

'Thomas is two now,' Jenny reasoned gently. 'There are good health clinics, especially for the Europeans. The climate's ideal.'

'I'm surprised at you! John's got a good job here. The school will really miss him—'

Her words seemed to get through to Jenny at last. She saw the look of regret on her features. 'I know. I'll miss Beaconsfield, too. I've loved it there.'

'Well then! Make him listen to you.' May hesitated, then continued, almost grudgingly. 'He won't listen to any of us. But you – you're the only one who can make him see sense. You've got to tell him!'

Jenny blushed a little, but her solemn grey eyes faced May bravely. Her voice was grave, and quiet. 'It's something he really wants. Something he believes in. There's a small group of Baha'is already out there. It means so much to him. It wasn't an easy decision for him. He loves his work at Beaconsfield. He knows that James was grooming him for Maurice Nicholls's job, and hoping eventually that he might even take a share in ownership, take over as Head one day.'

She paused, and now her gaze was almost shy, and far from the groomed confidence she usually portrayed, as she sought for May's understanding. 'When John first mentioned that he wanted to apply to the colonial office for a teaching post, I was as shocked as you were. I honestly thought he wanted to leave me and Thomas. To go off on his own. I tried not to let him see how shattered I was. I didn't argue, I just said, "OK. If that's what you really want." And then I realized that he was shocked, too. At the fact that I could think that he wanted to go away alone. He said, "There's no way I would leave you and Thomas behind, in anything I do." I just hugged him and cried.'

She paused once more, gazed at May still with that vulnerable look. 'I know I haven't been good for him, but I do love him. I do want to make him happy.'

May stared back, the tears close for both of them. 'I can't understand you,' she said slowly, 'but I believe you. Come here.' And they, too, hugged one another tightly, and cried.

'There she is! Hi! It's good to see you again!' John held the dark-haired figure close. Their arms stayed round one another for several seconds. Sara was smiling, and swiftly wiping the tear away from her cheek as they disengaged.

Jenny stepped forward. 'Hello again, Sara.' They embraced more fleetingly, their cheeks brushing. 'And this must be Master Bernard! Thomas, say hi to your new friend.'

'Berni,' Sara corrected.

Thomas, tall and gangly for his four years, stared uncertainly at the other boy, plumper, darker, a head shorter and a year younger, whose podgy hand reached up for the reassurance of his mother's grip.

'It's lovely to see you both again!' Sara said, as they emerged from the shadow of the customs shed into the full glare of the July sun.

'I wrote as soon as I heard the ship was stopping at Haifa. It's a shame we've only got the one day, but it's great to be able to meet up.'

Sara nodded. 'I was so happy. We've been looking forward to it for ages, haven't we, Berni? You must be dying to get home again. How long is it? Two years?'

John nodded. 'It seems to have gone so quickly for us, though. And now we've got nearly four months' leave!' He squinted up at the glare of sun, the vivid blue sky. 'Bet it won't be as hot as this at home. Ah! I remember this! The light!' He stared around him. 'Isn't it marvellous, Jenny?'

The two women linked arms, their other hands holding on to their children. They were both wearing light summer dresses, flower-patterned; their long hair was arranged simply, to their shoulders. Jenny's was fairer, against the rich thickness of Sara's black. Though Jenny's face and bare arms and legs were tanned, Sara's skin was darker, too. She looked buxom, in contrast to Jenny's slight figure. The fair head bent towards the darker, as Sara laughed. 'He's been like a kid at Christmas for the past couple of days, waiting to meet you.'

'I don't suppose the YWCA's still here?' John asked. He looked towards their left, along the seafront.

Sara grinned. 'The café's still there. Shall we have a drink? The boys can play on the shore afterwards.' They set off along the uneven paving. Sara nodded over towards the right. 'I got my backside kicked by a British Tommy somewhere near here. And whacked with his stick. I could hardly sit for days!' She told them the tale as they made their way to the shoreside restaurant.

When they were seated at a table beside the long windows looking out over the sea, John let his hand touch briefly over Sara's and asked, 'How have things been? How are you now?'

She glanced at him shyly, then looked away, towards the dazzle of the breaking waves. 'OK. Fine now. I still miss him, though. But life goes on.'

'Of course. We were hoping you'd get over to England. If you do, you must come and see us.'

'Oh yes. One of these days. Berni's parents come out a lot now. I'm glad. The little one loves his grandma and grandpa. They've even bought an apartment. Just down the coast.'

'You're still at the settlement? The one you moved to when . . .'

She rescued John from his embarrassment. 'After Berni died, yes. It's well established. Your brother worked there for a while, after the peace treaty.' She paused. 'He was very good. How is he? Have things worked out for him?'

Jenny watched her. She had been struggling against an increasing gooseberry feeling while her husband and Sara were chatting. Now, with the detached eye of the outsider, she picked up something from Sara's words and her manner, some intuitive nuance that made her glance more sharply at the good-looking young woman. She studied her face while she listened to John's enthusiastic reply.

'Things have worked out really well. I don't know how much he told you, but his wife, Marian, was ill. A nervous breakdown. Things were bad for a while. But everything's fine again now. Their daughter, Edwina, is a lovely girl. Really bright. And a real smasher! Isn't she, darling?'

'I'm so glad.' Sara was still smiling. Intrigued, Jenny detected something buried behind the smile. Then she felt ashamed of her prurient speculations. She knew herself how impulsively warm and friendly Teddy could be. And charming. Ashamedly, she dismissed her flights of fancy.

After a midday meal, they took a taxicab up the winding side of the mountain, to the Carmelite monastery at the top. They gazed out over the panorama of the bay. The building perched on the crest, which the British army had used, where John had interrogated the frightened Jewish youths, was still there, now part of the Israeli Defence Forces, bristling with barbed wire, its gate guarded by an armed soldier. 'Remember? We sat over there.' Sara reached out impulsively, took John's arm. 'We said we'd walk here again one day. I'm so glad we have made it.'

There's something very sensual about this girl, Jenny acknowledged, with a kind of wry amusement. She can't help it, it's just the way she is. I wonder if John was as immune to her charms as he made out? Again she was ashamed of her private thoughts, especially when, later, John guided them down, over a busy street and into the amazing, verdant gardens surrounding the Shrine of the Bab. The fruit trees, the exotic plants, the orderliness of the brilliant flowers, the green and shady coolness in the midst of that bustling, fierce heat and pale glare, seemed almost magical.

She was deeply moved, for the first time comprehending something of the strength of John's belief, when she saw how transformed he was at seeing the shrine itself. She could see his emotion as he stared up at it. 'It's beautiful,' he murmured. 'You should have seen – when I saw it . . .' He was struggling for words. 'It was so simple. Now this.'

He knew that the Guardian had been working ceaselessly to enhance the shrine's splendour, and that of the gardens, over the years, but this was truly wonderful. The original building had been encased in a splendidly carved colonnade at ground level, all in the palest Italian marble, and above soared the splendid superstructure, the columned octagon, topped by the marble balustrade, from which rose the drum, crowned by its high dome. Through the laced intersections of the scaffolding that still clothed the top of the edifice gleamed the golden tiles, which the workmen were still fitting into place to complete this momentous undertaking, it was hoped, by the anniversary of the Declaration of the Bab, in October. John had no doubt that it would be finished on time.

'Come into the shrine,' John said. 'It's open to everyone.'

Sara shook her head. She seemed strangely uneasy in this place. 'No. I'll take the children for a walk. You and Jenny go inside. Pray.'

Thomas was looking increasingly anxious. His face crumpled

in what presaged a fit of weeping. John crouched, held him close. 'Mummy and Daddy want to say a prayer in there. Why don't you wait with Aunt Sara and Berni? Let him see what a big boy you are. We won't be long.'

They removed their shoes, felt the cool marble under their feet. Jenny hesitated at the tall, open doorway through which John had passed. He turned, smiled, held out his hand, drew her in. Now she felt the pile of the richly patterned carpet under her. She was stirred by the airy coolness, the fragrance – and the stillness. She saw a plain marble tomb in the inner shrine, through the misty transparency of the curtains. In front, on a low stand, was a shallow bowl of fragrant rose petals. She stood, watched John kneel, then bow his head low, crouching forward, touching his forehead to the ground. Still, she stood, beside the open doorway, as if afraid to pass further in. An old man, Indian-looking, came in, without glancing at her, and prostrated himself on his face, lying full-length on the carpet. John had raised his head. He knelt upright, took his small prayer book from his pocket, began to read.

She felt faint, looked up at the myriad points of light in the large glass chandelier at the centre of the room. She moved away, to the wall, and sat, folded her feet to her side, holding the thin stuff of her dress over her calves. She felt a deep tiredness. *Bring thyself to account each day, ere thou art summoned to a reckoning.* The words popped into her head. She had heard John quote them before. She knew they were from the Baha'i scriptures, yet they sounded so familiar to her. Surely Jesus had said something nearly identical?

She found herself praying. God forgive me for all my sins, my constant imperfections. Help me to do better. Help me to love purely, like John. Help me to share that love. I love him, Lord. Forgive me for not being true to that love.' She scrambled up, hurried out, head down, trying to stem the flow of tears. She slipped her feet into her sandals, stood on the grass, gazing down from the edge of the terrace out across the bay. He called her, and she turned, saw the light shining in his face, held out her hands to him. He embraced her gently, and they turned and walked hand in hand, away from that focal point of peace and beauty.

Late in the evening, they leaned on the rail, along with many other passengers, and watched the receding land as the ship steamed slowly out of the harbour. The range of Carmel was a long hump, lit by the sun, which was rapidly lowering into the sea, over their shoulders. All at once a twinkling flash appeared on the mountain slope, as though someone were signalling with a bright light. The shrine beamed its departing message to the travellers as the sun's rays reflected from the golden dome.

The heavy downpour during the night had refreshed the garden, its colours washed with a new brightness in the morning sun. Raindrops still diamond-sparkled on the leaves and flowers, and in the cropped neatness of the grass. May could feel the warmth on her forearms, and through the thin cardigan she had draped around her shoulders. She was lounging deep in the deckchair, her feet crossed on the low stool Iris had insisted on placing for her. She revelled in the recovery of health and spirits she felt rising within her. It was so good to be up and outside again after the days she had spent in her bed. She smiled, watching Iris lumbering about the flower-bed, cutting the fresh blooms and cursing as the sticky wet soil oozed about her canvas shoes.

She knew that both Iris and Ruby, not to mention the rest of the family, had been deeply worried. And so, she had to admit, had she. The pain had been there all day, niggling at first, catching her with those warning stabs in her chest. Then had come the more steady discomfort, in her arms, and her neck. Her arms felt leaden again, and when that pain didn't ease, she began to be alarmed. She gave in, lay back on the settee, afraid to move, paper-white, and a frantic Iris had phoned for the doctor.

The trouble was, the more frightened May had become, the more erratically her heart had fluttered and thumped. She welcomed the wooziness of the sedative pills, tried to imagine the giddiness was caused through being drunk, as the bed swayed gently and Iris's deep voice disintegrated into dreamless slumber. 'But don't take me yet, God,' she murmured, in her mind, on the rim of her oblivion. 'Just let me see my John first. And Thomas. And Jenny.'

The pain was there when she woke in the early morning, terrifyingly real and constant this time, right across her chest, and up into her neck, and jaw, crushing, squeezing; a weight pressing her down, so that she couldn't move, could scarcely speak through her clenched teeth. They gave her the crushed tablets, under her tongue, and the pain eased. Iris, ravaged by an almost sleepless night herself, sat with her, her craggy face stamped with her fear and her love, and held her hand. The pain kept coming, then receding. The doctor looked in every few hours, May still managing to feel ridiculously embarrassed each time he and Iris hauled her forward from the propped pillows, and Iris slipped the straps of the nightgown down, baring her for the cold investigation of the stethoscope, the doctor's impersonal fingers digging into the base of her neck, then pressing on her thin wrist.

She knew that he was debating whether to accede to Iris's increasingly urgent promptings. 'Shouldn't she be in hospital?' May could not keep her thoughts from centring on her mother's death, that haunting grip on her hand, and the pleading look of pain and fear, the bleakly impersonal Victorian surroundings of the ward. She knew that fear now, could understand its depths.

She struggled to face it. If it was happening, she wanted it to happen here, at home, in *her* world, with her beloved Iris.

Another day, of drugged dozing and dulled pain, and then she had woken miraculously free from all signs of discomfort. The doctor had insisted on two more days of galling immobility in her bed before he allowed her to come slowly downstairs, and sit propped up on the settee. Today was the first time she had been allowed to get anywhere near back to normality, enjoying the bliss of a proper bath again, even though Iris refused to relax her vigil and sat on the bath stool while May soaked luxuriously. She would have washed her like a baby, too, if she'd been given half a chance!

Yesterday, Teddy had come over to see her, taking time off work to do so. In spite of his over-hearty cheeriness, she knew how anxious he had been. 'Don't worry,' she reassured him. 'They've knocked it on the head again with all these pills and potions. Thank goodness we've got it out of the way before John and Jenny and the bairn arrive. Just one more week, eh? They'll be in the Mediterranean somewhere now, I think. Must get fighting fit for them!'

She beamed a smile at Iris now, who was approaching with an armful of cut flowers, wiping her muddy shoes on the grass, with an expression of ludicrous disgust. May rose. 'I'll get a vase for them. We'll do them out here.' She turned, before Iris could admonish her, and headed for the open door to the kitchen.

The pain caught her, cleanly overwhelming her before she could cry out, passing immediately, to leave her breathless, mouth gaping. She fell silently to her knees, then over on to her right side. Iris saw her fall, cried out her name torturedly, bounded over to her as Ruby emerged, and shrieked. Iris scooped her up by her shoulders, held her in her arms, both she and Ruby sobbing and yelling. 'Get her up! Get her inside!'

They bundled her up, Ruby clutching the thin legs, and

carried her through to the living-room, placed her along the cushions of the settee. May's eyes were black, piercing pinpoints of light reflecting in them as she stared intently at Iris, whose arms were still about her. The mouth was open, the chin jutting, Iris could see the tendons standing out, below her jaw on her straining neck. Then she relaxed, her head sank back, and Iris watched the dying of the light in those eyes, the unfathomable distancing of that gaze.

For May, the world spun crazily, a whirling kaleidoscope of light and shade, and a vast roaring. It was as though in a single pace she had stepped off its edge. 'John!' She heard herself clearly, shouting out his name, and felt a deep sadness. She was not going to get back to him. The spinning and the roaring ceased, and a darkness came stealing into the formlessness, creeping like a fog, filling it. She was shocked at the way her sadness had slipped away from her. Now she couldn't remember why she had felt so sad.

The darkness was lightening a little, into dimness, and all at once vision and sensibility returned, and she shivered with cold. She could feel her clothing clinging wetly to her. She found herself gazing down at the hem of her long dress, heavy with the rain, and her dainty, soft, best boots, all bespattered with mud. My da will go mad! she thought. She glanced up, at the dim loftiness of a church nave, the light filtering in beams through its high, narrow, stained glass windows. Ahead of her, a dark grey wall protruded, forming an angled doorway, and in the doorway stood an outlined, shadowy figure. 'Nelly!' she whispered. 'Where are you?'

The figure stepped forward. A thin young man, with a moustache drooping around his upper lip. He was in working clothes, holding a cap in his hand. 'It's all right, May. You're here now.' He stepped forward, she saw the white of his teeth as he smiled.

'Jack?' She couldn't believe it! The joy welled up through her, strong enough to burst her heart, and, as it did so, he stepped towards her again, his smile radiant, into a light so dazzling it was like the sun's rays striking full on a surface of pure gold.